PROVIDENCE

Lisa Colozza Cocca

F+W Media, Inc.

Published by
Merit Press
an imprint of F+W Media, Inc.
10151 Carver Road, Suite 200
Blue Ash, OH 45242. U.S.A.
www.meritpressbooks.com

ISBN 10: 1-4405-6927-4
ISBN 13: 978-1-4405-6927-2
eISBN 10: 1-4405-6928-2
eISBN 13: 978-1-4405-6928-9

Printed in the United States of America.

10 9 8 7 6 5 4 3 2 1

Library of Congress Cataloging-in-Publication Data

Cocca, Lisa Colozza,
Providence / Lisa Colozza Cocca.
pages cm
Summary: Fleeing her father's temper, 16-year-old Becky boards a freight train, finds a newborn child, and decides to bring the baby girl along with her to begin a new life.
ISBN 978-1-4405-6927-2 (hc : alk. paper) -- ISBN 1-4405-6927-4 (hc : alk. paper) -- ISBN 978-1-4405-6928-9 (ebook) -- ISBN 1-4405-6928-2 (ebook)
[1. Runaways--Fiction. 2. Foundlings--Fiction. 3. Babies--Fiction. 4. Family life--Georgia--Fiction.] I. Title.
PZ7.C6375Pro 2014
[Fic]--dc23
2013037661

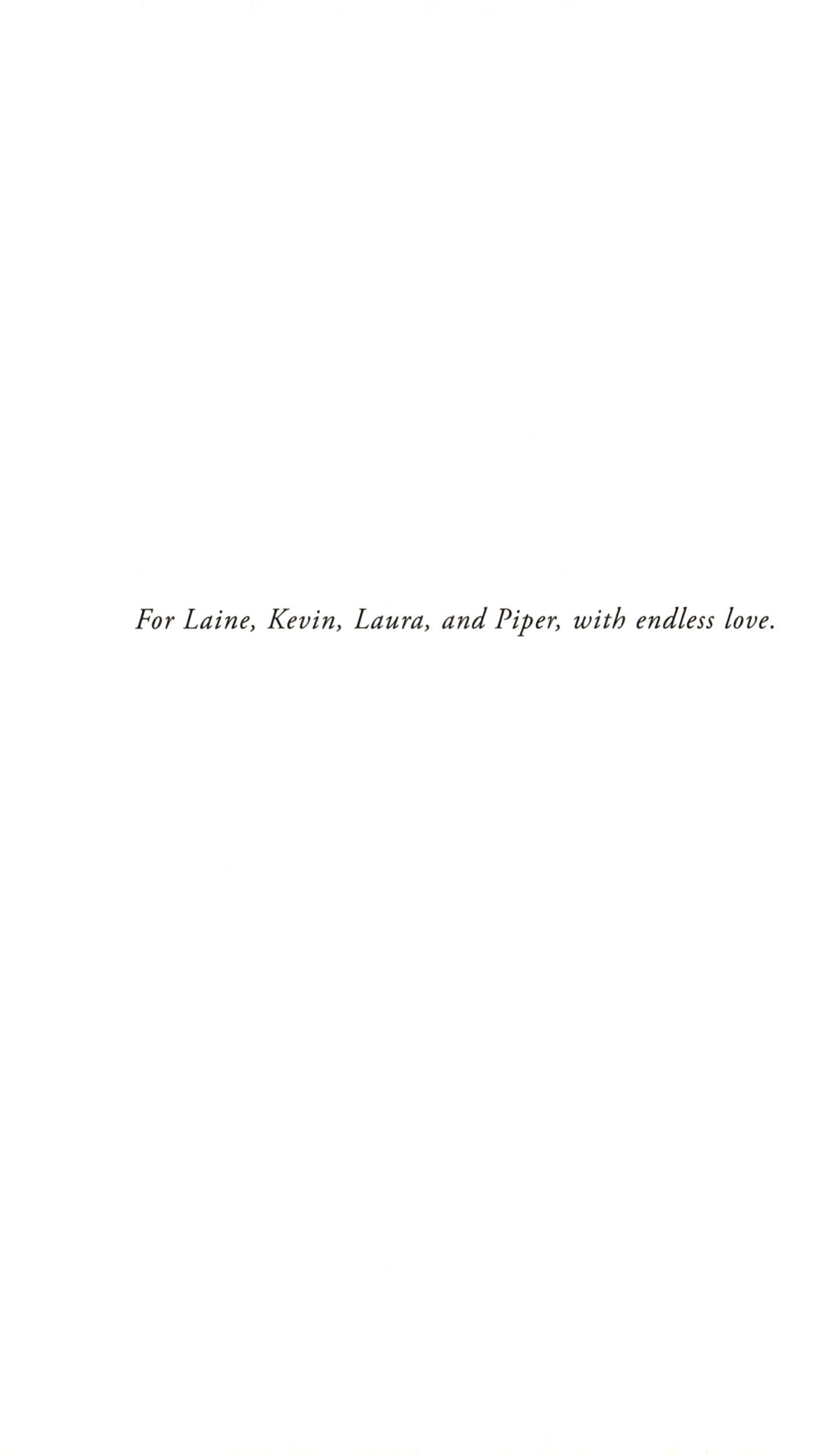

For Laine, Kevin, Laura, and Piper, with endless love.

ACKNOWLEDGMENTS

Thank you to Jackie Mitchard for choosing my manuscript from the slush pile and guiding me through the publishing process. I greatly appreciate the opportunity and your expertise. Thank you, too, to everyone else at Merit Press who helped mold my manuscript into a book and my dream into a reality. My thanks, also, to my first readers: Betsy, Gail, and Wendy. Your critiques helped make the story stronger.

CHAPTER 1

I first met Baby Girl in a freight car.

I was carrying a bag.

She was sleeping in one.

It was as if that old train was just there on the tracks waiting for me. The doors on the last car were flung open as if to say, "Come on in, Becky!" I climbed in and looked around. When I saw that lime green gym bag just sitting there, I worried that someone else had already taken the train up on its kind invitation. I thought it best to move on before its owner returned; but when that bag started moving, I had to take a peek. What I saw set me reeling. Two little legs kicked out at me with feet no bigger than my thumbs. Her little hands were curled into fists and her face was scrunched up tight. What really caught my eye was the bright red cloud of curls that sprang from her head.

Now, Mama always said, "If there's trouble to be found, Becky will find it." Mama was usually wrong. I don't go looking for trouble. It finds me. But in this instance, I guess we found each other.

I knew how I had gotten in that train car, but I was at a loss for how a baby had landed there. For me, it happened when a thick blanket of dark clouds rolled out over the sunshine-soaked sky. Within minutes, the black sky was split by a cluster of lightning flashes that looked like someone had tossed a handful of tinsel in the air. A thunder boom shook my insides, and I had to go searching for cover. The train looked like an okay place to save me from a good soaking if those clouds opened up. Necessity had brought me into the freight car, but the newborn was a real puzzle. She sure didn't get there on her own.

I looked around for some sign that this baby's mama was coming back for her. I squinted into the dark corners of the car. There was nothing but a big old spider hanging from a web in one corner and a broken beer bottle in the other. I crept toward the doors to peek out. The sand on the floor of the car ground into my knees. I thought about that broken bottle, and for a moment I worried that some of that sand might be broken glass. (I tend to lose sight of my real worries when my mind races in all kinds of directions.) The baby let out a sigh and I was reminded of what my genuine problem was. I took a quick look around at what was outside the car, then crawled back to Baby Girl.

I lifted the baby out of the bag and moved us and our belongings into one corner of the freight car. Those welcoming open doors also made us easy to spot, so I was hoping we could hide there in the shadows until I figured out what to do. The rain had quickly grown steady, making it less likely anyone would walk down the tracks checking the cars, but I was still worried about getting caught where I didn't belong. Worse yet, I was afraid of getting caught with a baby to explain away. Who would believe I just happened upon her here?

I pulled my long legs—my too-long legs—as close to my body as I could and pressed my backpack against the rust colored metal walls. The bundle of coins and the wire binding on the notebook in my backpack made it a less than ideal cushion. When the train finally jerked into motion, it banged my head against the wall. Daddy would have said that a jolt like that should have knocked some sense into me.

I'm sure he would have been disappointed by the actual results.

I should have been home helping Mama with the chores. Instead, I was hitching a ride on this train out of Tyson. When I woke up this morning, it had seemed like any other June day on our farm. The air was a little hotter and heavier than usual, even for our neck of South Carolina, but that didn't shorten the list of chores any. Mama and I got an extra early start on the canning. By mid-morning, her feet were swelling; baby number ten was due before school starts up again, so I sent Mama upstairs for a rest. I stacked the jars of strawberry jam on the shelf and called in my brother Joseph. I asked him to take the other boys down to the pond to fish. Then I promised the girls I'd play all afternoon with them if they would take a nap before lunch. Thinking about breaking that promise hurt my stomach some. When the last little one closed her eyes, I snatched a book from my room and headed for the front porch. The bubble of silence burst when Daddy came in the back door looking for an extra hand. I know I should have helped Daddy, but I was tired and in need of some quiet time myself. So, when I heard Daddy call my name, I ran to the far side of the barn to hide.

I had only read five or six pages of my book when Caleb Brown cast his shadow over me. Now, I've heard folks around home say I'm pretty, but they usually say it with a sting. *That poor child, such a shame, and Becky's such a pretty girl, too.* I want to tell them there's no shame in me helping out my mama instead of hanging around town with the other girls talking about clothes and makeup. Most days, I don't even mind helping Daddy. I know the farm is too much work for one man, and Daddy says there's no money to pay help. As for Caleb, you'd never hear anyone adding hurtful words to their approving thoughts of him. Not by a long stretch. He is one of the handsomest boys in town, and he would not deny that fact. He has hair the color of honey and eyes you could drown in. His feeling so sure of himself makes his whole face light up when he talks, which makes everything he says seem more real and important.

I'm not trying to make excuses for myself, but rather trying to explain how once again trouble found me. I wasn't looking for it.

Caleb had a bunch of fireworks with him and wanted to test a few out before the Fourth of July. I know I should have said no, but sometimes reason escapes a girl. Looking at Caleb's long curly lashes and lightning smile just separated me from my common sense.

That boy spent a good deal of time arranging the rockets in a circle, pointing them to a creek that ran through the back fields. It all looked like a science experiment until he lit the fuses. The rockets went up, but instead of heading for the creek they made a loop in the air and crashed through the roof of the barn.

The walls of that barn shook with every bang and the ground rocked beneath my feet. My knees felt like they were about to give out under me when I got my first whiff of smoke. I saw Daddy running up the hill as flames began shooting out of the hole in the roof. By the time Mama made it up there, the whole barn was on fire.

Caleb had run off, leaving me alone with the burning barn. The animals were all out in the fields, but seeing that building disappearing in smoke made my heart ache. My great-grandpa had helped build that barn back in the 1930s when he was only a teenager. It had held up through decades of storms and the passing of the farm from generation to generation. And now in only a few minutes time, there seemed to be no hope for it. There were no words to describe how truly sorry I was, but I had to at least try to explain to Daddy what happened. I should have known better than to tell him I wasn't alone.

Knowing I was behind the barn with a boy made him even angrier than the barn being on fire. "What were you doing back there with a boy? I didn't raise you to be acting like that! How long has this been going on?"

"Daddy, we weren't doing anything. I was just reading my book in the shade back there when Caleb passed by. He just stopped to talk, that's all."

Daddy's eyes showed no mercy. "Don't you be lying to me on top of all this," he said, waving toward the barn. "I know what teenage boys want from girls."

"But it wasn't like that, Daddy. Honest, we were just talking." Daddy took a step forward and I thought he was about to raise his hand to me. Mama must have thought it, too, because she stepped between us.

"Joe, please, we can talk about this after," she said. Just then sirens wailed as fire trucks turned up our road. Someone on one of the neighboring farms must have seen the smoke and called for help. "Help is on the way," she said.

Daddy must have heard the sirens too then, because he stepped back and walked toward the sound. Mama turned to me and took me by my shoulders. "What were you thinking, child, talking back to your daddy like that? If you have a lick of sense you will stay out of his way until he has time to cool down. Go spend the night with your friend Tammy. Maybe by morning, everything will be all right." She looked over her shoulder in Daddy's direction. The volunteer fire fighters were climbing up the hill behind him. "Go on, now. Get away before all these folks leave."

Now Daddy has always had a temper, and I've received more than my share of his whippings, but I'd never seen him that mad before. It only took a minute for me to decide that Mama was right. I would be a whole lot safer away from him for a while. I couldn't go to Tammy's house, though. We hadn't been friends in years, at least not the kind of friends that have sleepovers. Besides, the fire in Daddy wasn't going to die out overnight. Every time he looked at that charred building, it would flicker up again.

I ran back to the house and went straight to the third board in the upstairs closet floor. That little hiding place was my own personal safe. I didn't have much cash in there, but what I had I had come by honestly. At least, mostly honestly. Last year, Mrs. Gordy, my English teacher, had a talk with Mama and Daddy. She told them I had real potential, but that I needed some time every week for reading and thinking. Now Mama and Daddy don't put much stock in that kind of thing, but I think they were a little afraid of Mrs. Gordy. They came home from school and told me to take every Wednesday afternoon off from my chores to go to the library to smarten myself up. Daddy warned me about what would happen if the results didn't get Mrs. Gordy off his back.

Every week, I walked from school to the library where I read books about places around the world. I never faced much competition for the books I wanted. Almost all of the kids there stayed in front of the rows of computers. Most of the kids I knew from school had computers at home and cell phones in their pockets. I wondered if these library kids' families subscribed to the same thinking as Daddy did. He would never allow these things in our home, and let us know in no uncertain terms that we were not to bring the subject up. I never really minded that much, though. I guess you really can't miss what you never had.

So I kept reading my books, and before long I knew I wanted to go to college, then travel around the world and write a book about my own adventures. My teachers all told me if I kept my grades up, I'd be sure to get a scholarship. Even if they didn't have to pay a penny, Mama and Daddy would never go for that though. In their minds, college was a big waste of time—especially for a girl who belonged on the farm, helping her family make ends meet. As far as they were concerned, I would stay on as the unpaid help until I found a husband to tell me what to do. So each week, I took a longer route to the library, stopping along the way to pick up pop bottles and cans, which I then turned in for nickels and dimes. I hid the money in a box under the third board from the right in the floor of the upstairs hall closet.

One day, my route took me behind the Main Street Bookstore. I found a whole box of books with their front covers torn off. Since they were in the trash, I figured I could take some home and it wouldn't be stealing. It didn't take too long to figure out that a new box was put out the third Wednesday of every month.

One afternoon, the owner, Mr. Tyler, caught me back there. He asked me if I wanted to work a couple of hours a month pulling off the covers. That way, I would know which books I was taking. He didn't pay much, but he paid me in cash. So one Wednesday a month, I skipped the library and went straight to the bookstore.

Mama complained about me bringing home trash. Daddy said, "You can't judge a book without a cover." Neither ever asked where the books came from. I kept bringing the books home and putting the money under the board. Now, I know a wiser girl would have turned all of that money over to her daddy for the good of the family. Hiding it away was playing with fire, and I have a knack for getting burned, but that money tied me to other activities that I had no permission for and it fed my dreams for a different future. So with every deposit I made into the Bank of Becky, I added a new place, a new adventure to the list I wrote in my notebook. I tried real hard to not think about the consequences if I got caught.

With the barn in flames and Daddy's temper ablaze, I pulled out my money and went to my room. I grabbed my backpack and stuffed my notebook, some clothes, and a couple of books inside it. I counted my money and put half of it in my bag. I thought it would be enough to last me until Daddy had time to calm down. I left the other half of the money on the kitchen table to help pay for a new barn. I hoped that might make me more welcome when I returned.

The train's shrieking whistle brought me back to the here and now. Had I slipped off into a doze? Was the baby okay? I opened my eyes and concentrated on how the boxcar shook, rattled, and swayed along the tracks. I held the baby tighter. This wasn't the way I had pictured my travels starting out. I had no fancy traveling clothes, no luggage, and no plane tickets in hand. My dry lips reminded me of just how unprepared I was. Even if I could get into my backpack without putting down the baby, I knew there was nothing to eat or drink in there. My lack of supplies made me wonder about my traveling companion's situation. So I opened the gym bag that had doubled as her cradle and looked inside. No food. No diapers. No nothing.

Now, I may be only sixteen years old, but I know a whole lot about taking care of a baby. As the oldest of nine, most of the feeding and changing and rocking fell to me. And although you would never hear Mama say so, I'm darn good at it. Which is why, as I brushed a ringlet from the baby's forehead, I whispered, "I just might be the luckiest thing to happen to you in the few days you've been on this earth."

As soon as the words passed through my lips, I laughed at myself for saying it. Truth be known, I've never been lucky to be around. As hard as I try to do the right thing, something bad always seems to come out of it. "No, Baby Girl, I'm no one's lucky charm," I said. "But I'm afraid for the moment I'm all you've got."

I felt her breath like a whisper on my cheek and wondered what her mama was thinking, leaving her in an old train car. I started thinking about all the 'what ifs.' What if I hadn't been sitting against the barn this very morning, just trying to get a moment's peace? What if Daddy had listened to my side of the story? What if that lightning storm hadn't started up just as I happened upon this rickety old train? And what if—what if I didn't hop into this very car with this little bundle in it?

Now the last thing I needed was a baby to take care of, but what choice did I have? I could just leave this little one on the train, but if no one had seen the two of us in that car, what chance was there of someone else finding her? I couldn't risk her not surviving the wait. I could go to the police to tell them about my discovery, but they were sure to call Mama and Daddy right away. That would not end well.

I could hear Daddy now. "If 'ifs' and 'buts' were candy and nuts, we would all be living in a sweet world. And this ain't a sweet world, Becky. So stop wasting what few brain cells you have on 'what ifs' and start working on what *is*."

In this instance, Daddy may have been right about concentrating on the here and now. This baby was hungry. Her once peaceful body heaved as she tried to catch her breath between cries. I was worried about how long it had been since her last feeding, and about my lack of supplies. I also admit to worrying that her cries would draw attention to the boxcar, and trouble would find me again. I hoped that the rain that was tapping like a drum on the metal walls would drown out the baby demanding to be fed. Maybe the constant bumping and rocking of the car soothed her, or maybe she just wore herself out crying, but the baby finally fell back asleep.

Deciding my best course of action was like answering a multiple-choice question with no right answer. I remembered what they told us in school about taking a test—if you can't see the right answer then pick the one that seems the least wrong. Making sure this baby was safe and keeping me out of Daddy's reach for the time being were at the top of my needs list. This made the least wrong choice easy enough to see.

When the rain stopped, the air hung heavy over us. It wouldn't be long before that old rusty boxcar heated up like an oven, baking us inside. We had been on the train for hours, so this baby was sorely in need of a bottle and a clean diaper. I grabbed hold of her bag and slid toward the door. Keeping a safe distance back so we didn't bounce out of the opening, I waited for a place to hop out. A raindrop hanging from the roof of the train car wiggled back and forth. It broke free and landed on my cheek. I wiped it away and found an eyelash on my finger. I looked at the dark crescent of hair, made a wish, and blew it off my finger. Having no idea where this train was heading, I used my wish in search of a safe place for us to get off.

The train lurched to a stop. I threw my arm out to brace myself and to protect the baby as I was flung onto my side. My aching arm let me know it was definitely time to make a change. Like Daddy always said, "When opportunity knocks, you go running out that open door." I held the baby close to my chest and swung my legs out of the car. My feet didn't meet the ground, so I wriggled my butt toward the edge of the car floor until my toes touched the gravel. It wasn't the most comfortable way to go, but life had already served this baby a few too many jolts.

The first thing I saw was a giant sign by the side of the tracks. I knew right away that this baby and I had just shared a first in our lives: we had crossed the state line. The sign had a picture of two huge peaches on it, just smiling and making eyes at each other. In big, bold letters it said "Welcome to Watson's Grove, Georgia! There are no strangers here—just friends we haven't met!"

"Well," I said to my tiny traveling companion, "this looks like a good enough place to spend a few days."

CHAPTER 2

I walked down the road with the baby curled up against my shoulder. A big part of my money was in nickels and dimes, and it was weighing heavy in the bag on my back. I saw a gas station up the block and headed in that direction. I was hoping for a bathroom, and for once my wish came true. The door was locked, so I asked the old man by the tanks for the key. He started giving me a hard time, saying it was only for customers. I was about to point out that I didn't have a car when I noticed a little convenience store behind the tanks. "Is that your store?" I asked.

"Yup," he grunted.

"Well then, I'm about to become your customer," I said. I marched over to the little store and looked around. I grabbed a baby bottle, water, and formula mix and put them on the counter. I stared at the shelves a little more. Mama never used anything but cloth diapers, and the store sold nothing but disposables. I finally snatched a package from the shelf along with a package of wipes and told the old man I was ready to pay. He took his time ringing up the sale, giving me time to add a bottle of soda and a candy bar for me to the order.

The old man muttered, "You want anything else?"

"No that's all," I said. "And the key to the restroom," I added.

"I told you," the old man said. "The restroom's just for customers."

"I am a customer," I reminded him.

"You're a store customer," he said. "The restrooms are for gas customers."

The baby started to fuss. I looked that man straight in the eye and said, "Fine, then you won't mind me changing my baby right here on your counter." He grunted and handed me the key. He made me so mad that I paid the whole bill in nickels.

After I took care of my needs, I changed the baby's diaper and gave her a little rinse to cool her off. I mixed her a bottle and headed out the door. Now, I pride myself on being honest, so even though that clerk was one of the nastiest people I've ever met, I felt pretty badly about the lie I'd just told. I don't even know why I said she was my baby. That lie surely would lead me into bigger troubles.

A park bench across the street under a big weeping tree looked inviting. I sat in the shade feeding Baby Girl and thinking about what to do next. I didn't need to dig into my backpack again to know there wasn't enough money for the two of us to get by on for long. I was hoping my situation would change faster than the money could disappear, but my gut was reminding me that wishing something doesn't make it true.

Only a few hours had passed since I left home this morning. I wondered what Mama and Daddy were thinking, now that the flames must be gone. Mama didn't even know Tammy and I weren't close anymore. Would she even check to see if I was there? What was going to happen when Mama and Daddy realized I was really gone? Would Daddy call the police to fetch me home, so he could do the punishing?

Baby Girl's fussing drew me back into the here and now. I laid her belly-side down across my arm and rubbed her back, trying to draw a burp from her. As worried as I was about my current situation, I couldn't imagine a mama leaving a baby alone in an empty train car. I thought again about going to the police, but then a whole other batch of 'what ifs' came into my head. What if her mama meant to be on the train with Baby Girl and the train just pulled away without her? What if she was searching all over for her baby right now? What if the police were looking for us both?

I finished burping Baby Girl and looked back toward the gas station. I noticed the nasty old man talking to a police officer and pointing my way. I picked up our bags and hurried down the block. I ducked into a store called Second Hand Rose and hid in the back behind a stack of old blankets and curtains.

"Can I help you, miss?"

I nearly jumped out of my skin. I turned to face the store clerk. She was shaped like a comma with hair as white as milk.

"Boy or girl?" she asked, reaching out to stroke Baby Girl's head.

"A girl," I answered.

The old woman smiled. "I thought so. That baby is too pretty to be a boy. What's her name?"

I was just about to say that Baby Girl's name was Trouble with a capital T when I looked down at her innocent sleepy face. "Her name . . ." I hesitated and looked toward heaven for the answer. What I saw instead was a great big old map of the state of Georgia hanging on the ceiling. "Her name is Georgia," I said, finding it impossible to cross my fingers since my hands were otherwise occupied. And then, because I always talk too much when I'm nervous, I added, "I'm looking for a carriage."

"I just got a beauty in," the clerk said. She put her arm around my middle and shuffled us up front. When she let go, I peeked out the front window. The policeman was gone, so I breathed a little easier.

"Back here," the old woman said, waving us in behind the counter like we were a crop duster looking for a landing.

I came around and let out a whistle. I had never seen such a fancy carriage in my whole life. The clerk looked pleased as punch. "Brand new," she said. "Never been used." Then she opened the cartons next to it and started pulling out baby clothes and bottles, and rattles. "You get first pick," she said.

At first, I got real excited. Then I started to think about my money situation again. "How much is the carriage?" I asked.

The old lady thought for a minute. "Hmm, it's the nicest one I've ever had in here. I think fifty dollars seems fair."

She might has well have said fifty million dollars as far as my funds were concerned. I turned to the cartons and plucked a couple of undershirts and sleepers and an extra bottle from the box. "How about just these?" I asked. I stepped back onto the customer's side of the counter and started twitching and turning, trying to get my money out while holding Baby Girl and all our bags.

The clerk looked at me and said, "I got so many new things in this week that I could really use some help around here. Money being tight and all, I can't pay much but I'd be willing to throw in some merchandise. You wouldn't happen to be looking for a job, would you?"

I took a deep breath and stood there, shuffling my feet. I felt Baby Girl's legs ride up my chest as she started to fuss. Her beet red face could only mean one thing—she was going to need another diaper change. I looked back at the old woman. On one hand, we had walked into this store less than twenty minutes ago and here this woman was offering me a job. I couldn't help but feel a little suspicious. On the other hand, diapers cost money and money was in short supply. Then the old woman came around and started rubbing the baby's head again.

"Having this little princess here every day will draw in the customers," she said. "Do we have a deal?"

The baby squirmed into a new position. I looked down and saw a stain on my shirt where the diaper had leaked. What was it that Daddy always said about desperate times? "Deal," I said.

The clerk grabbed my hand and shook it. "My name is Mary Rose Perkins, but everyone calls me Rosie."

I smiled, and without thinking said, "And my name's Becky Miller." I wished I could grab hold of my words and swallow them back up. Telling a stranger my real name could be dangerous, since I didn't know just how much trouble I was already in.

Rosie wheeled the carriage around and said, "Take this as an advance on your pay. Be here at ten sharp."

I looked at the carriage, unsure of what I should do.

Rosie must have sensed my uneasy feeling because she reached up and patted my shoulder. "Please, take it," she said. "I'm not worried. Mother Nature might not have given me a pretty face like yours, but she did give me a sixth sense about people. I know in an instant if I can trust folks or not, and I've got a good feeling about you."

I walked down that block pushing Baby Girl in her carriage, with all our bags tucked in the deluxe basket on the back. I didn't know where the old woman's kindness was coming from, but I promised myself then and there that somehow I would live up to her trust in me.

CHAPTER 3

I stopped at a laundromat called Super Suds to change Baby Girl's diaper. When I was done, I noticed a pay phone against one wall. A phone book hung below it, chained to the wall. I skimmed the yellow pages, looking for an ad for a motel nearby. I had never stayed in a hotel or motel before, so it was on the top of my adventures list. I'd read enough books to know a motel would be cheaper.

Baby Girl started crying again, so I started pushing the carriage back and forth while I balanced the open phone book on my knee. This first adventure wasn't going to be quite the way I imagined it. There would be no sunbathing by the pool with my little friend, here. But it would give me time to think over my situation and try to figure a way out of it.

It didn't take long to realize I was dipping my pail into an empty well; there were no motels listed in town. I dropped the phone book and looked over the cork board hanging on the wall. A few notices announced rooms to let. I skimmed over them and sorted them in my head. The one with NO KIDS written in big red letters and the one that cost more money than I've ever had at one time were of no use to me. I dug a pen and paper out of my backpack and jotted down the addresses of the other two. Maybe I could talk one of these folks into renting the two of us a room for one night.

I counted what was left of my money, and started thinking about the price of diapers and formula. I told myself to stop wasting my time. Thinking about how little there was wasn't going to make my money grow any. I was going to have to use what I had as wisely as I could.

I could feel the wire binding on my notebook as I stuffed my money back in my bag. I'd made sure to bring it with me when I left. I didn't need to open it to know that the words Super Suds did not appear anywhere on my adventure list. Then again, neither did taking care of a baby. But here I was, surrounded by peeling paint and dented clothes dryers, house hunting in the Super Suds.

The air in there was starting to curl my hair, so I decided to ask the ladies by the washers if they knew about a motel nearby or could point me in the direction of the addresses on the notices. They whispered to each other and turned their backs to me. I felt like I was back in school when the girls would all huddle together to compare their new back-to-school shoes and pretend to not notice when I walked in the room. I guess it was easier for them to ignore me than to have to look at the worn down heels and scuffed toes of my shoes.

Standing there in the Super Suds I did exactly what I'd done back at school—looked for the closest doorway to pass through. In this instance, I was glad to see the door to a ladies' room. Since I was going to have to search out these addresses, Baby Girl and I would likely have a long afternoon ahead of us. That would mean having to stop to feed her again. I rinsed her bottle in the bathroom sink and filled it back up with water. When we came out, the laundromat ladies, who had been staring at the bathroom door, turned away again. I was starting to think that Rosie was the only person in town who had read that welcome sign down by the tracks.

I could feel the heat penetrating the soles of my sneakers as soon as I stepped back onto the sidewalk. I hoped to find someone to help me get my bearings, so I didn't have to push the stroller all over town looking for those two houses. As I searched the dusty storefronts for a friendly face, something up the road a piece caught my eye. I turned my attention to the black and white car heading in my direction. I put my head down and kept walking. I pictured the officer jumping out of the car and chasing after me. I tried to listen to the tires on the pavement, hoping they didn't slow down as they approached us, but all I could hear was my own heart pounding against my chest. I kept my head down and plowed forward. About a half a block later, I felt a jolt and the carriage bounced back at me.

"Whoa!" a voice said. The rest of his words were drowned out by Baby Girl's crying.

I bent over to lift Baby Girl out of the carriage and when I stood up straight I came face to face with my traffic victim. He brushed a mass of dark hair from his eyes. The expression on his face looked like worry, not anger.

"Is she okay?" he asked, in almost a whisper.

I swayed back and forth, rubbing her back until she quieted. "She's fine," I said. "I'm sorry, I should have been looking where I was going."

"I guess we should be happy you are steering a baby carriage and not a car," he said.

I bent down to put the baby back in the carriage and to hide my red cheeks. I fidgeted with her for a while, making sure she was far enough up to be covered by the shade of the carriage top. When I stood back up, the boy was still standing there smiling at me. I guessed he was waiting for some kind of an excuse or explanation for my running him over on the sidewalk.

"My mind was on where I was going instead of where I was. We're new in town and I don't know the streets," I explained, hoping I hadn't said too much.

"I think the problem was more where your eyes were than where your mind was," he laughed. He reached out and pulled the slip of paper from my hand. "I know this area."

He was giving me directions when music started playing from the phone hanging at his hip. He glanced down at the number and said, "I'd take you there myself, but I'm already late getting back to work."

I shook my head. "You've already been enough help," I said. "Sorry again about running into you and making you late for work."

"No problem. Maybe it will teach me not to be rushing around all the time. If I hadn't plowed out of the store and right across the walk, I wouldn't have been such an easy target," he said. "Take care now."

I watched him climb into a truck with a stallion painted on the side of the bed. Almost like a knight in shining armor, I thought. Luckily, my common sense made an appearance and reminded me of one of the contributing factors to my current troubles. I pushed away any more thoughts of this boy and got back on my way.

The good news was that both places were within a few blocks of each other. As I walked along, I decided to visit them both and then make up my mind as to what would be best for us. Since waking with the sun that morning, I had made enough rash decisions to last me a month of Sundays. Plus, letting on I had options might make the owner more inclined to let us have the room for only one night too.

It didn't take long to reach the first place. A red and white sign declaring a room to let hung in a first floor window. I picked up Baby Girl, carriage and all, and carried her up the porch steps. Before I even knocked, a woman wearing a flowered housecoat and bright red lipstick swung open the front door. "Who are you looking for?" she asked.

"I came about the room to let," I said.

"Speak up," she said, in a voice loud enough for the neighbors to hear.

"I came about the room to let," I repeated.

She stepped closer, took a good look at the baby in the carriage, and scowled. "How old is that baby?" she asked.

"She's just a couple of days old," I answered.

"A baby that young shouldn't be out in this heat," she said. She stared at me a moment and said, "There is no room."

"But the sign," I said, nodding toward the window.

She threw her shoulders back and placed her hands on her hips. "I said there is no room to rent," she said. "I was just going to take the sign out of the window."

She turned her back to us and went inside, closing the door tight behind her. I lifted the carriage down the steps, then turned and looked back at the window. The sign was still there.

When I reached the second house, I saw a man aiming a hose at a rabbit that had invaded his garden. He had the poor thing trapped between the stream of water and the fence. The old man seemed to be enjoying the rabbit's dilemma. Taking notice of me standing there staring at him, he turned off the water. Dropping the hose, he walked toward us as the rabbit made its escape. He stuck his cigar between his teeth, wiped his hand on his dirty T-shirt, and grabbed my hand and shook it. "Are you here about the room?" he asked, looking me up and down with a smile.

I crossed my arms and moved so that the carriage separated us. He looked at the carriage as if he was noticing it for the first time. "Does this baby belong to you?" he asked.

I nodded.

"Well, I'm not set up here for babies. Plus, the price is per person not per room. I'll have to charge you at least double the rent, maybe more if she's a noisy one," he said, rolling the cigar between his teeth.

"Thanks anyway," I said. I got us away from that house as quick as I could.

The further away from the center of town I walked, the bigger the houses and yards got. But they weren't the only things getting bigger. I would be fine bunking out under the stars, but Baby Girl was a whole other story. I was running out of options, and my worries about the night expanded with every step.

Baby Girl was waking up again, and I knew from my own brothers and sisters that it would only be a few minutes of time before she would start wailing to be fed. I reached into the carriage basket for the bottle of water and the formula mix. The water felt like it had been boiled for tea. I turned the corner and started searching for a solution to my newest problem. There was a group of children playing in their bathing suits on one of the lawns. The biggest one was holding a hose up in the air, producing a shower for the little ones to run through. I wondered how long it would take for one of them to run and tell their mama about us if I asked to fill Baby Girl's bottle from their hose. I didn't have a chance to weigh the odds. A woman opened the front door and yelled, "This is your last warning! I want you children in the house, changed into dry clothes, and ready to run errands in ten minutes."

The girl dropped the hose and chased the little ones inside. I knew it would be safer to wait until the family had gone off on their errands before touching their hose. Unfortunately, Baby Girl was starting to rumble like a volcano ready to blow and I knew we didn't have the luxury of ten minutes to wait. I hurried up the block, pouring some of the hot water out as we went, and quickly grabbed the hose and started adding fresh water to the bottle. As soon as it was half full, I hightailed it back to the carriage and practically ran down the block.

I turned the next corner, eager to get out of sight, in case someone had spotted me with the hose. I ended up on a street that finished with a circle. There was no way out but the way I'd come in. At the end of the road, three trees sharing one large trunk grew. I decided to hide behind it to feed the baby. This street was quiet, but I walked down the block trying to look like I belonged there. I settled behind the tree and hurried to mix the formula before Baby Girl started to cry. I sat and leaned against the trunk, positioning myself so I could peek between the trees without our being seen. Baby Girl was gulping that formula down so fast that I wondered how much of it was going to come right back up. I stopped to burp her and when I looked back out onto the street, I saw a mailman walking around the corner. I curled up tighter and checked to make sure the carriage was out of sight.

I sat and watched as he strolled along poking letters in the boxes and slots. More precisely, I took notice of the houses where he didn't stop. I held my breath as he came around the circle and didn't breathe easy again until he moved on to another street. I changed Baby Girl's diaper and rummaged through my bag for the candy bar and soda I had purchased earlier. The candy was a gooey blob and the soda was hotter than the baby bottle had been. I brushed off my backside and mustered up the courage to walk around the circle a couple of times. I wanted to get a better look at the houses that had gotten no mail. On my first time around, I looked for cars in the driveway or lights on in the house. Then I circled around again, listening for dogs and checking to see how close these houses were to their neighbors. I spotted a treehouse behind one of the houses. It might be hard to climb up there carrying the baby, but at least it would give us a roof over our heads.

When Baby Girl started fussing again, I knew it was time to head back toward town. My belly was rumbling as loud as Baby Girl was crying, so we stopped in the Tick Tock Diner. A woman sitting at the counter elbowed the man sitting next to her. He turned, looked at us, and shook his head. The group in the front booth stopped talking and just stared at us.

The cold reception caused me to worry about leaving all of our worldly possessions in the carriage basket. I grabbed our bags and took a seat in a booth in the back. When the waitress sauntered over, I asked for some water. She slapped the glass down on the table so hard the water splashed out of the top. "Is that all you're going to order?" she asked, her words sounding more like a challenge than a question.

I took out the new bottle I had gotten at the second hand shop and mixed some formula for Baby Girl. I looked at the menu and ordered the cheapest thing on it for me. "You want me to heat that up?" the waitress asked, pointing at the bottle.

"No, I don't want to trouble you," I answered.

"Well, you can't be feeding it to her like that," she said, as she grabbed the bottle from my hand.

A head popped through the window behind the counter. "Hey, Dottie," the voice yelled. "This food isn't going to serve itself."

The waitress walked off with Baby Girl's bottle, mumbling the whole way. When she returned she put my plate in front of me and held the bottle out. "You know to test the temperature of this before you give it to her, right?" she said.

I nodded, took the bottle out of her hand, and put it on the end of the table opposite of the waitress. When I finished my meal, I made sure the waitress was watching before I placed a few drops of the formula on the inside of my wrist. Dottie came over with the bill as I fed Baby Girl. I asked her where the library was in town and if she knew how late they were open. I knew that if I was going back to that treehouse, it would have to be after dark. She answered my questions and asked a few of her own. "Are you new in town? Is this your baby? Is it just the two of you? That baby doesn't look at all like you. Does she look like her daddy?"

I answered 'yes' to all of them. That last one might have been another lie, but maybe not. I have no idea what her daddy looks like.

We stopped in the ladies' room on our way out. I got a little shock when I saw myself in the full-size mirror. If people praised my looks back home, I rarely had reason to doubt them. With the number of boys who were sweet on me, I guessed that they were being truthful. The girl looking back at me from that glass didn't look like a girl a boy would take to the church dance on Saturday night, though. My long brown hair was wet and sticking to the sides of my head. My nose was as red as Rudolph's. My legs and shorts were coated with train dust. "Girl," I said to the person in the glass, "no wonder people are looking at you funny."

CHAPTER 4

After we left the diner, we went straight to the library. I settled into a chair and scanned the recent newspapers. I started with the ads in the back of the paper. I was hoping to find a place where Baby Girl and I could settle in for a few days until I figured things out. The few ads I saw were all looking for someone to rent monthly and to pay a whole month's rent up front. I didn't have that kind of money, but I took out my notebook and jotted down some of the addresses anyway. I thought that once I got cleaned up and started my new job, I would look like a better prospect. I hoped then that they would be willing to take a smaller amount up front since they would be getting someone with a steady income.

A group of girls came into the library. Baby Girl was sleeping off her last bottle, so I was worried their giggling might wake her. One of the girls bent over the carriage. "Is it a boy or a girl?" she asked.

"A girl," I answered. "Her name is Georgia."

"Aww, that's so pretty," the girl said. "It suits her." She waved over her friends. "Come look at this baby," she said. "Isn't she the most adorable little thing?"

I watched the girls huddle around the carriage. They all looked to be about my age. One of the girls had moved with the herd without ever taking her eyes off her phone. Her thumbs moved up and down the keys with speed and ease. The librarian took notice of this too, and taking the cell phone warning sign off her desk, she started in my direction. The last thing I wanted was to draw more attention to Baby Girl and me and our problems, so I started wishing real hard these girls would disappear. When the librarian blocked the girl's view of her phone with the sign, the girl shoved her phone in her pocket. As the librarian walked back toward her station, the girl rolled her eyes and muttered something under her breath.

One of the other girls looked at her watch. "Never mind her; we need to get out of here anyway. I don't want to miss the bus. If we get there too late, the movie will be sold out."

"Okay," said the first girl. "Where did Sarah go? Sarah!" she said in a strange combination of a whisper and a shout.

Another girl walked out from between two bookcases with several books in her arms. "What are you doing?" the girl with the pink stripe in her hair asked.

Sarah shrugged her shoulders. "I thought as long as I'm here, I might as well find something new to read."

Pink Stripe shook her head. "First of all, you spend too much time with your face buried in a book. Secondly, we don't have time for this. If we miss the bus, we miss the movie. Drop the books and let's go."

For a second, Sarah looked like she was going to follow this order. Then she said, "Can't we hang around town tonight—maybe go to the diner? My mother said the next time I get caught sneaking out of town I'm grounded for the summer."

The other girls in the group groaned as if on cue. "Your mother is not going to find out and there is nothing to do in this town. We're going to the movies."

"My mother will find out," Sarah answered. "I don't know how she does it. Maybe she has a network of spies or a sixth sense or something, but she always finds out. You all can go ahead, but I'm not going. It's not worth getting in trouble. I don't even really want to see that movie all that much."

The first girl planted her fists on her hips. "Why do you have to be so difficult? If you go home now, our parents will find out and wonder where we are. Then we will get in trouble. A real friend wouldn't get me into trouble."

Sarah sighed. "I'm not going to rat anybody out. I'll just hang around here for a while and then go home." She sat down on the chair across from me and ended the conversation.

The other girls cooed one last time over Baby Girl, I think more because it gave them a chance to turn their backs on Sarah. I thought about asking them if they knew of a place to stay. It seemed they were already inclined to keep secrets from adults, so maybe they wouldn't run off and tell someone what I was asking about. I was just about to ask when one of the girls said, "I love babies. They are the sweetest things on earth."

Her friend answered, "Sweet when they belong to someone else."

"I hear the bus!" one girl shouted.

I watched the girls run out of the library and glanced back at Sarah. She was shuffling the books on her lap and looking like she was going to cry. I didn't need to be dealing with the attention that might bring either, so I decided to try and pull her thoughts from those other girls. I pointed at the book on the top of her pile and said, "I loved that book. I could hardly put it down."

Sarah lifted the book and smiled. "This one?" she asked. "I've read two others by this author and I loved them, too. They were both set in Paris and the descriptions were so good I felt like I was really there. They made me decide to go there someday."

"That one is set half in Paris and half in Rome. When you're done reading it, I bet you'll want to go to Rome, too."

Sarah smiled and nodded. "My name is Sarah, by the way. You probably caught it when my friend practically yelled it across the building."

"I'm Becky," I answered.

Sarah leaned in toward me. "I don't know what my friends said to you while I was in the stacks, but please don't take anything they say personally. Donna's sister had a baby when she was eighteen, and now her life is practically over. She lives in a tiny apartment in town with her baby and her boyfriend. She was supposed to go away to college and have an exciting life. Now a big day is when she goes out for groceries. We all can't wait until we graduate from high school and get out of this dead town. If they said anything to you about having a baby, it's because they think having one young means the same thing for everyone, not just Donna's sister."

I almost told her she was the only one who had shared her opinion of me, but when I looked in her eyes I saw no meanness there. I forced a small smile onto my face. "Oh my gosh," she said. "I just realized I'm the one being awful. I just assumed the baby is yours, and for all I know you could be babysitting. So whether you're her mother or her sitter, please don't be offended by anything I said. I'm suffering from diarrhea of the mouth, because I'm ticked that my friends ditched me for a movie."

She tapped the cover of the book a few times. "Anyhow, thanks for the suggestion," she said. "I'll put the others back on the shelf and if you don't mind, I'll come back here and sit with you and read."

When she walked away, I turned my attention back to the newspaper. There was a picture of the Gateway Arch in St. Louis at the top of the page. I read the caption and thought about what I had learned in history class. I kind of fancied myself as a pioneer. My adventures would take me places no one in my family had ever seen before. If St. Louis was the perfect starting off place for the people heading west more than a hundred years ago, then it seemed the perfect place for me to start my trip across the country. I pulled my backpack out of the carriage and dug out my notebook. I turned to my adventure list and added the Gateway Arch. Those girls didn't know anything about me, I thought. I was going to see places they had never even thought about. I was going to go to college too—and I was going to graduate. I patted Baby Girl on the back. "Don't you worry none," I whispered. "I'm not going anywhere until I find your mama."

I flipped through every page of the paper, searching for any word of someone missing a baby. As my mind went back to our housing situation for the night, I thought again about going to the police. If I did, would they bring me back home to Mama and Daddy? Then what would happen to Baby Girl? I know Daddy wouldn't welcome another mouth to feed into the house. He hardly was happy about the ones he made with Mama.

Rosie knowing my real name was weighing on me, too. She was more than kind to us, but I figured if my name showed up in the newspaper she might call the police first and ask questions later.

"Becky," Sarah said.

I jumped in my seat a little. I had been so deep in my thoughts I hadn't taken notice of her sitting back down. I looked at her and saw her smiling and pointing up at the ceiling. I looked up and saw the lights blinking. "That's the librarian's way of letting us know she is closing up," Sarah explained. "I'm going to check this out. Are you getting anything?"

"Not tonight," I said.

"Well, it was nice to meet you," Sarah said. "I'm sure we'll run into each other again. I think that is something you'll find out about this town quickly. It's hard to turn around without running into someone you know, or someone that someone you know knows."

"Enjoy the book," I said. I pushed the stroller back to the ladies' room. I changed Baby Girl's diaper and took care of myself. The prospect of having to spend the night outdoors caused me to consider hiding out in there until everyone had gone home for the night. If it were just me, I probably could have gotten away with it. But babies draw attention, especially when there is only one baby in the library, and the librarian had peeked into the carriage a few times while I was sitting there. Even if I could find a place to hide the carriage, I was sure the librarian would notice that we hadn't left the building.

I took a deep breath and swung the bathroom door open. I held it there with my backside while I steered the carriage through the opening. The librarian was standing by the front door looking at her watch when I got there. As I walked out the door, I heard the lock click behind me. I shivered despite the heat. Night would be upon us soon, and I still had no sure plan for where we were going to go.

CHAPTER 5

I pushed the carriage up the same streets we had walked down earlier. It was that dozy time of evening that happens in summer, when day is gone but night hasn't quite arrived. Porch lights dotted the dusky air, and neighbors were swatting the mosquitoes and calling out their goodbyes.

I turned the corner and practically tiptoed down Cobbler Court, the street where I had watched the mailman earlier in the day. The two houses on the right of the circle looked empty. I walked around three times to see if anyone would come outside. The big brick house had a tall white fence around its backyard. I held my breath and plowed across the gravel to the gate.

The tree house was the reason I chose this place. Now I gave it a really hard look. I went around the pool and looked at the rope ladder hanging from the tree. The knots in my stomach were bigger than the knots on that rope. There was no way I could climb up there holding Baby Girl.

The screened porch on the back of the house looked more promising. I swear that I never before entered someone's house without the benefit of an invitation. But I couldn't spend all night shooing away the mosquitoes that hovered around us. I reached up and removed a bell that hung from the top of the porch door. I felt sure the family that lived in this house was away, but I didn't want that bell jingling and announcing our arrival to the neighbors. Then I opened that door the way I pull off a Band-Aid—slowly and carefully.

The porch was large, and had everything a couple of girls on the run could ask for. The furnishings were covered with sheets. I lifted one and peeked inside. They had cushions as thick as a loaf of bread, and one of the pieces lay back just like a bed. Against the wall, there was a long cabinet with a sink built into it. Underneath there was a refrigerator no taller than my two-year-old sister, Mary Jo.

The porch had a slate floor, so the first thing I did was take off my shoes to quiet my walking. The cool slate soothed my tired feet. I cleaned Baby Girl up and mixed three bottles of formula. One would be her good night bottle, and the other two would go in the refrigerator for the middle of the night feedings.

Next, I went to work on me. I must have used half a bottle of their liquid soap removing the dirt and grime. I took notice of what kind it was and promised myself I would replace it tomorrow. I wasn't about to add robbery to my list of accidental crimes.

I sat down and started feeding Baby Girl when I noticed a gray cat rub up against the screen. It was too big and healthy-looking to be a stray, so I worried that its owner would come through the gate looking for it. I slipped back out of the porch and carried the cat out to the driveway. I hid behind the gate and watched it run across the street to one of the neighboring houses.

Baby Girl took this opportunity to slip off to sleep without finishing her bottle. I moved the carriage as close as I could get it to the lounge chair that would be my bed for the night. I wanted to be sure that I would hear her right away so she wouldn't have time to wake the neighbors. I lay down and watched her breathing for a little while, but when I closed my eyes it wasn't her sweet little face I pictured. I was thinking about that cat, and wondering what it looked like when it was a kitten. When I was nine, I found a stray kitten down by the main road. She was the same color gray as the dress on the Christmas tree angel, and just as soft. I named her Gray Velvet and couldn't wait to show

Mama and Daddy. But when Daddy looked at the kitten, he didn't see what I saw. "Did you feed this cat?" he asked.

"Yes, Daddy," I said, feeling proud of myself for taking such good care of the kitten.

"She's the runt of the litter," Daddy said. "Even her own mama didn't want her. She's too scrawny to grow into a good mouser. That cat's useless to us and she'll never move on since you fed her. You go out back and drown her now."

Daddy could be cruel at times when he thought there was a lesson to be learned by one of us; still, I couldn't believe the words he was saying. I remember staring at Daddy for what seemed like days. He looked back at me and said, "Get to it now, and don't you be bringing any more strays into this house."

I hid Gray Velvet in my room and fed her with an old baby bottle. A few days later, she escaped into the living room. Daddy took both Gray Velvet and me by the scruffs of our necks and dragged us up to the barn. He handed the cat to me and filled a bucket with water.

"Now, you're going to do what you should have done when I first set eyes on that cat," he said.

I tried to run away, but Daddy grabbed me and forced Gray Velvet and my hands into the bucket. At first, Gray Velvet seemed to hold her breath. Then she tried swimming away. Eventually I could feel her fighting for air and choking. All the while, I tried to help her. No matter how hard I tried to pull my hands and Gray Velvet out of the bucket, I was no match for Daddy's strength. He held tighter and kept my hands under the water until she stopped moving. "This is a lesson you won't forget, Becky. You do what your daddy tells you, or you'll regret it."

I was crying too hard to answer, but Daddy was right about one thing. I won't ever forget.

The next morning, I awoke not to the baby's cries or another nightmare, but to the sound of *plop, plop, plop.* The sun was starting to push itself into the sky, so I knew we needed to get out of there. I slipped out of the porch door and peeked through a knothole in the fence. The *plop, plop, plop* sound I heard was newspapers hitting the neighbor's driveways. I hurried back to the porch and collected our things. Baby Girl was fussing a little, so I had to tend to her needs first or we would wake the neighbors with her howling. A quick bottle and a fresh diaper and we were on our way. Lucky thing for us, folks on that street didn't keep farmers' hours.

The only thing open in town that early was the Tick Tock Diner. I slid into a booth by the window and Dottie, the waitress, sauntered over. She was wearing the same uniform she had on last night. The grease stain on her right hip pocket and the ink stain on her left told me that Dottie didn't spend her after work hours over at the Super Suds.

"Back again?" she said.

"Food was so good last night," I said, "that I had to come back for more."

She shook her head. "What can I get you?"

"Coffee, please," I said. Baby Girl had gotten me up so many times last night that I had to make extra bottles. I was worried about being able to keep my eyes open all day.

Dottie returned with the pot, poured me a cup, and tossed some of the little cream cups on the table. "A young girl like you shouldn't be drinking coffee," she said. "Do you want something to eat with that?"

I looked at the menu, trying to find the perfect blend of cheap and slow cooking. I wasn't enjoying this lady's company but I was too tired to be pushing that carriage up and down the streets until the Second Hand Rose opened. Unfortunately, we were her only customers, so when Dottie brought my breakfast she hung around the booth.

"Where you from?" she asked.

"A little north of here," I answered.

"How long you planning to stay?"

"I don't know," I answered. "Maybe for good. I got me a job over at the Second Hand Rose."

Dottie nodded at Baby Girl. "Will her daddy be joining you soon?"

"No."

"So where are you staying?"

My fingers tightened around my fork. The door opened and a group of old men puffing on cigars shuffled in. "Coffee all around, Dottie," one of them shouted.

I watched Dottie saunter back to the coffee pot. Those eggs were going to be my last hot meal for a while. I needed to stay away from the Tick Tock Diner until I had time to think of some answers for all of Dottie's questions. Since this was the only restaurant I had seen in town, I figured our dining out days were done.

CHAPTER 6

I arrived at work an hour early and waited for Rosie. When she saw me sitting on the step she clapped her hands and raised them to the sky. "You're early," she said. "I knew I did right in hiring you and giving you that carriage. My granddaughter said I'm an old fool for trusting a stranger. But I told her that there are some folks who are never strangers; they're friends right away."

Her kind words struck me like a splash of sunlight. I parked the carriage behind the counter and got right to work. Rosie wanted to go through the boxes of baby stuff herself, so I started moving things around to make room for the new merchandise. I sorted and folded and moved things until it occurred to me that I hadn't heard as much as a whimper out of Baby Girl. I walked up to investigate and found Rosie sitting in a rocking chair feeding her.

"I'm sorry, Rosie. I didn't hear her fuss. I don't want us to be more work for you," I said, approaching them with outstretched arms.

"Nonsense," Rosie answered. She went right on rocking and showed no signs of handing over Baby Girl. "Georgia and I are just fine. Why don't you take a little break? We don't have to finish all of the work in one morning."

I felt a little shook when Rosie called Baby Girl Georgia. That was another one of the lies that would never leave me. I watched the two of them rocking back and forth, and couldn't tell which of those little ladies looked more content. That is why I didn't say anything about the pink dress with white smocking and rosebuds that Rosie had put on Baby Girl.

At lunchtime, I pushed the carriage down to Haystack's Market. I needed to replace the soap, and Baby Girl was going through diapers and formula at top speed. A jar of peanut butter and a box of crackers would be my dinner for the next few days. On my way to the register, I gave in to temptation and picked up a couple of peaches and another bottle of pop.

I walked back to the Second Hand Rose, thinking about how fast my money was going. I wondered when Rosie would pay me, and how much I'd have coming to me after all of this baby stuff.

Rosie was watching for us through the window. I guess a part of her might have been afraid that her granddaughter was right about us.

"I was worried that I'd worn you out this morning," she said as we came through the door.

"Not at all." I smiled back at her. "I'm ready to get back to work."

I grabbed a dust rag and started cleaning off the things in the housewares section. I cleared off one of the shelves and set up a little display with a placemat and napkin set, some dishes, and a coffee pot.

I had just finished when Rosie came to tell me it was closing time. "Will you look at that!" she said. "Why, with you working here, I'm going to end up with so many customers, I won't be able to keep my shelves stocked."

This sounded a little odd to me since Rosie, Baby Girl, and I were the only people to pass through the door of the Second Hand Rose that day. But I must admit I was feeling prouder than a peacock. Rosie's kind words pushed my money worries aside and we all walked out of the store wearing big smiles. Baby Girl and I were going to the library before heading back to our temporary home. Rosie accompanied us down the two blocks to the big stone building.

"I see there's going to be a Fourth of July parade," I said, pointing to the sign nailed to the lamppost.

Rosie nodded. "Every year it comes right down Main Street." She laughed. "Of course in this town, where else would it go?"

"Is it a big one?" I asked.

"In the old days, all the storefronts were decorated and the sidewalks were filled with people coming to hear the bands and wave to the marchers. But I'm afraid that's history. Nowadays people are too busy to be bothered with all that."

"But there's still a parade?" I stopped in the front of the library.

Rosie nodded. "It's not like it was years ago, but we have still one," she said. She took a deep breath and smiled. "Listen to me carrying on about the size of a parade. If there's one thing I've learned in life, it's to spend my time appreciating what is and not worrying about what isn't. See you in the morning," she said.

CHAPTER 7

We slept on the porch every night that week. For me, it seemed more like catnaps. Baby Girl was waking me several times a night to be fed or changed. When I got her settled, I spent more time staring at the ceiling. Worrying about where we were going next kept my brain from ever shutting down and resting. I never seemed to sleep more than an hour or two at a time.

Each morning, I took a new route to the store, keeping my eyes open for any more of those little Room to Let signs. I wasn't used to surviving on so little sleep. Mama usually took care of the night feedings herself. When she did need my help, I would feed and change the little one and fall right back to sleep. It never interfered with me being able to start my day at six in the morning. I knew the lack of sleep must be showing in my face. But you would never know it, judging by Rosie. Every morning, she met us at the door. She smiled at me like I was a ray of sunshine pushing my way through the clouds.

Every day, I straightened the merchandise, dusted, and set up displays. One day I talked Rosie into letting me throw some of the clothes in with my laundry down at the Super Suds. I used an iron from housewares, and before long I had some outfits looking like new. I was getting really good at displaying things to their best advantage.

Rosie oohed and ahhed and kept slipping new baby clothes into the carriage.

Each night at closing, Rosie walked us down to the library. It was a cool, comfortable place to stay while we waited for the night sky to make it safe to return to the porch. I found it curious that she never asked me where we were staying. I hoped it was because she knew there were plenty of places in town that I could call home. It was that idea that kept me scanning the papers looking for a room. I didn't find any cheap housing, but I also didn't find my own name in the paper. Of course, no matter how hard I tried to keep Rosie's words in my head and appreciate what is instead of worrying about what isn't, my feet still felt heavier each night as I pushed that carriage back to Cobbler Court. With each passing day, I found myself worrying more and more.

On Saturday, I decided it was time to talk money. Rosie hadn't brought the subject up and I couldn't imagine where my pay was going to come from. There hadn't been a single customer in all week.

Rosie came walking up the street carrying a basket. "I brought us a little treat this morning," she said.

She poured us tall glasses of sweet tea to wash down the homemade crumb muffins. Every bite tasted like heaven—especially after days of peanut butter and crackers. By the time I licked the last crumb off my finger, I decided money talk could wait until closing.

"You have this great big picture window in the front of the store. Why don't you have a display in it?" I asked.

"Because you didn't put one there yet," she laughed. "You're the artist here."

No one in my whole life had ever called me an artist before. I got right to work. I washed that window inside and out. There must have been three years of dust and dirt built up. I laid out a red, white, and blue quilt and placed a picnic basket and some red dishes on top of it. I cleaned up an old blue bike and put red, white, and blue ribbons streaming from it. I finished the window off with a few patriotic-looking outfits, and I hung some matching curtains in the background. When I was done, Rosie stepped out onto the sidewalk to get the customer's view of my handiwork.

"Why, it looks just like a storefront from a movie," Rosie said. "The customers will be lined up out the door." She seemed so pleased that I hated to raise the subject of money. But I just had to. It was closing time, and I didn't know what I'd do once my money ran out.

"Rosie, you've been so kind to me, to us, that I hate to say anything," I began. "But this little girl goes through a lot of food and diapers, so I was hoping I'd get paid today."

"Where's my head?" Rosie laughed. "Thank you for reminding me." She hurried over to the register, which of course was empty. "Oh dear, I'm afraid I don't have any cash in the drawer. I know what to do. You have that window looking so pretty on the inside. How about we decorate the outside, too?"

I was failing to see how that was going to solve my money problem.

"I have flags and streamers at home. Why don't you come over tomorrow for dinner? You can help me get those things out of the attic and I can pay you. I always keep cash on hand at home," Rosie said as she wrote down her address and drew me a little map. "I go to church in the morning, and you're welcome to join me there, too."

I stared at that paper, wondering if Rosie really intended to pay me for my work. "Thank you for your invitation to dinner," I finally said. "Georgia and I will be pleased to join you."

After closing up, Rosie stood on the walk admiring the window again. "Well, if you aren't the luckiest thing to happen to me in a long while, I don't know what is. I didn't know I was hiring a window artist when you walked in my store."

I'm sure my cheeks turned as red as Baby Girl's hair. My folks weren't prone to lavishing kind words on me. As Daddy always said, "Put praise in my pocket. Compliments won't buy me a new pair of shoes." He surely lived by that. I don't remember him ever praising me, Mama, or anyone else.

"Which way are you headed today?" Rosie asked. "The library is closed by this time on a Saturday."

Shook by the change in schedule, I didn't answer at first. It was too dangerous to try to sneak into that porch in the daylight. "I need to run up to the market for diapers," I said. "Then I'm off to the Super Suds. After that I'll probably stretch out with a good book." I bit my lip and silently vowed to curb my rambling tongue.

Rosie laughed. "You and your books," she said. "I'll see you both tomorrow."

As I watched Rosie walk down Main Street, it was her words that came to mind, not Daddy's. "Some folks are never strangers; they're friends right away."

Rosie had put her faith in me. Now, it was my turn to put my faith in her.

CHAPTER 8

I woke up to the familiar *plop, plop, plop*. It had become a part of our morning routine, just like packing up all of our belongings. Our bags got a little fuller each day, because Rosie kept slipping new baby things in them. I was afraid the heavier our bags got, the lighter my pay would be.

I wasn't sure where we were going to go that morning. The night before, I had made sure to do all of the things I'd told Rosie. I didn't want any more lies between us than were already there. So with all our errands done, we rolled out the gate that morning with no real direction in mind.

Then, I saw it sitting there in the driveway: a newspaper. The message was clear. Vacation was over and the family who rightfully lived here would be back by nightfall. The welcome mat had just been pulled out from under us.

We wandered the streets, my eyes scanning the front of every building we passed. Block after block, I searched for any opportunity to put a roof over our heads that night. The closer we got to Main Street, the bigger the ache in my stomach grew. The night before at Haystack's Market, I was careful not to give in to temptation again. But after paying for the diapers and the formula, I was left with $3.89.

Despair had just about won over me when Baby Girl cooed and stretched. I bent over the carriage and stroked her cheek with the back of my finger. "Of all the temporary mamas in the world, you got stuck with me," I said. "But don't you worry. I don't know how, but I promise I'll keep you safe."

I walked the rest of the way to Main Street, racking my brain for a way to keep that promise. When we reached the center of town, I saw folks entering the Tick Tock Diner in steady succession; I figured church must be out. Rosie's home was on the other end of Main Street.

Rosie's side of town was very different from the one Baby Girl and I had been residing in all week. In that neighborhood where the tree house was, the houses were big and new. The lawns flowed like one giant carpet across the fronts of the homes. In Rosie's neighborhood, the houses all looked tired and worn out. The peeling paint and cracked windows faced overgrown grass and weeds.

I turned down Jefferson Street and stopped at number twenty-one. Rosie's house looked like a calendar picture. It was tiny like its neighbors, but it wore a fresh coat of white paint. The door and shutters were ruby red, and the railing of the front porch was lined with flower boxes. Pansies and ivy crowded the planters with the green vines hanging down to touch the tops of the sunflowers that grew in a straight line in front of the porch. Beams of sunlight reflected off the windows and drew my attention to ruffled edges of the curtains.

I stood there admiring the beauty of it all until Rosie came through the screen door. "You're at the right place," she called.

Inside, the place reminded me of the Second Hand Rose. Every shelf and tabletop was covered with knickknacks and doodads. And each little treasure was shrouded by a coating of dust.

The aroma drifting in from the kitchen reminded me of the hunger growing inside of me. It must have done the same thing for Baby Girl because she started whimpering. Rosie suggested we sit out on the porch to feed her. I settled into one of the rocking chairs and Rosie came out with a pitcher of sweet tea and some glasses.

"Dinner will be at least another hour away," Rosie said. "After Georgia settles in for a nap, we can haul that stuff down from the attic." She took a long sip of her iced tea and closed her eyes.

"Show me how to get up there and I'll carry everything down myself," I offered. "There's no need for you to climb up there."

Rosie reached over and patted my arm. "Aren't you the sweetest thing, looking out for me like that? But I'll be fine. I don't think you could find anything up there without me or a map showing you the way." She closed her eyes again and her rocking slowed to a stop.

I was careful not to sit and rock too long with Baby Girl. I didn't want her falling asleep until she had a clean, dry bottom. Some babies can sleep right through a diaper change, but she isn't one of them. I tried not to wake Rosie when I got up to bring Baby Girl in for a changing and a nap. I wasn't successful. She appeared at my elbow as I struggled with the last tape on the diaper.

"I had John put up the crib in this bedroom," she said, leading us to a room the color of sunshine.

"John?" I asked.

"He comes by to cut the grass and fix things up outside. It was my way of showing my granddaughter there was no need for me to move out of my house. I'm quite capable of taking care of myself. I've been doing it for years now. I figured for what I pay John, he could come inside and do a little work, too," she answered.

"Will your granddaughter be coming for dinner?" I asked as I laid Baby Girl down.

Rosie threw her head back and laughed. "Not likely. I haven't seen her around here in years. I raised her in this house. But ever since she up and moved to Atlanta, she acts like she's too good for these parts. She sends a little cash every week and calls once a month."

I saw such sadness in her eyes that I had to look away. It made me think about being away from my family, and I wondered what Mama and Daddy would tell folks about me.

We walked out into the hall and Rosie took a deep breath. "It smells like those boxes will have to wait," she said. "Dinner is ready."

I set the table with the china she handed me. I had never held such fancy things before and was afraid I would drop something. When I finished, Rosie came in with a casserole. "Will you look at that?" she said. "You set a table as pretty as you set a window."

I was never much of a cook, having been taught by Mama, whose greatest talent is having babies. But after one bite of Rosie's chicken and dumplings, I found myself begging for the recipe.

Rosie blushed. "Next Sunday, we'll make it together," she said.

By the time I bit into the chocolate chess pie, I was wishing every day was Sunday.

After we cleaned up from dinner, we went up into the attic. One look and I knew Rosie had been right. I would never be able to find anything on my own up there. If the Second Hand Rose ever did sell some of its wares, there was enough up here to stock it again twice over.

What looked like a mess to me made perfect sense to Rosie. She pointed to three cartons without so much as a peek inside and led the way down the stairs. By the time I carried the third box down, Rosie had begun pulling flags out of the other cartons. "I think we have enough of these to put some out in my flower boxes and still have plenty for the store," she said.

With an armful of miniature flags, we went to work on the boxes. We must have poked half a dozen flags in between the flowers in each container. The wind was picking up, causing them to flap and wave. It was a pretty sight until it hit me. When the hot, still air is replaced by cool winds, a storm is sure to follow. No quicker did I think it than the black clouds rolled over us. A flash of lightning split the sky and a boom of thunder shook the house. This was too much excitement for Baby Girl. The next sound I heard was her howling. The thunder was no competition for her cries.

I paced back and forth on the front parlor rug, rubbing Baby Girl's back and trying to soothe her. The sky had opened up and sheets of rain coated the windows. Rosie had run around closing everything as soon as the rain began falling. It was the fastest I ever saw her move.

Rosie settled herself into the overstuffed chair in the corner. She rested her head back on the crocheted doily and stretched out her arms. "How about you give Georgia to me for a little bit," she said.

"She's awfully fussy," I answered.

Rosie sat there with her arms outstretched, smiling at me until I handed Baby Girl to her. I stood by the window wondering when the rain would stop and worrying about where we were going from there. When the lights started to flicker, Rosie said, "You should fix Georgia another bottle before the house goes dark."

I was changing Georgia's diaper again when the lights went out. "Looks like you girls aren't going anywhere tonight," Rosie said. "You better carry her. My footing is not so good in the dark."

Still, Rosie led the way with the flashlight. When I laid Baby Girl down in the crib, Rosie handed me the second flashlight. "The dresser and the closet are empty," she said. "My room is right across from this one, and the bathroom is down the hall. You'll find fresh towels and anything else you might need in the bathroom cupboard. I'll let you get to your unpacking and your books."

I opened my mouth, but words failed me. Did Rosie know we had nowhere to go, or was she just offering a practical solution to the rain? I looked over at our bags. I had been carrying all of our belongings everywhere for days. I'd been afraid of leaving something behind on the porch and returning to find the family home. Only now did I realize how that must look to Rosie. If I didn't find a home for us soon, I at least had to find a place to stow these bags while I was at work.

Rosie interrupted my thoughts. "And don't you be worrying about those boxes tonight," she said. "Tomorrow's only the first of the month. We've got a few days to work on them."

When Baby Girl's thumb found its way into her mouth and her eyes fluttered shut, Rosie leaned over the crib and kissed her head. "May the angels watch over you, Georgia," she whispered.

I leaned over the crib, kissed Baby Girl, too, and added, "And keep you safe through the night."

"You sleep well, too, Becky. Tomorrow's a whole new day," Rosie said, as she crossed over to her room.

When I heard the flashlight click off and saw nothing but darkness seeping from under her door, I called over, "Good night to you, too, Rosie." Then I whispered, "And thank you."

CHAPTER 9

I woke up with the sun. Baby Girl had pulled me from my sleep three times last night. My body seemed to be controlled by old habits, no matter how many times my sleep was disrupted. I rolled onto my side and looked over at Baby Girl. She lay in her crib with her back rising and falling in steady succession. I thought about my own brothers and sisters, and my insides twisted. I wondered if they were missing me the way I was missing them. I worried about Mama, too. How was she keeping up with everything without me there to help? I buried my head in my pillow to quiet my tears. I didn't want Rosie thinking I was anything but happy about being here for the night. After a half hour or so, a new sound filled the air around me. The *plop, plop, plop* of the newspapers on the pavement had been replaced with *sizzle, sizzle, snap*. Before long, the heavy scent of the bacon frying caused my mouth to water.

I slipped out from under the sheet and made the bed. I threw on some clothes and walked into the kitchen. "Do you mind me making Georgia a bottle?" I asked. I decided the night before that I had to get used to calling Baby Girl Georgia, at least in front of Rosie. It didn't feel natural, though.

Rosie smiled. "I was going to do it myself, but I haven't made baby formula in a long, long time and I was afraid I wouldn't get it right," she said. "So how about you get her breakfast ready, while I get ours on the table."

After breakfast, Rosie volunteered to sit with Georgia while I showered. As I stood there with warm water flowing from my head to my toes, I thought about this most recent turn of events. Just twenty-four hours earlier, Baby Girl and I were wandering the streets, my head filled with worries about nightfall. But this morning, I woke up in a real bed with this red-headed angel sleeping next to me in the fanciest crib I ever saw. It only takes a few days of going without to learn to appreciate the luxuries of a bed and a shower.

Rosie talked me into leaving our bags behind so there would be room in the carriage basket for the contents of one of the cartons. I stuffed Baby Girl's necessities into a tote bag Rosie found, and we were ready to go. That is when Rosie handed me the envelope. "I wish there was more in this," she said. "Maybe this week business will pick up."

I doubted the Second Hand Rose was headed for an upswing. The only door on Main Street I had seen people passing through belonged to the Tick Tock Diner. Even the library was pretty empty but for us, and that place was free. I slipped the envelope into my pocket without as much as a peek. I knew I couldn't put off looking inside it for long, but I didn't want to do it in front of Rosie.

As I tucked Baby Girl into her carriage, I was reminded of my promise. If I was going to keep my word, I needed to start thinking ahead.

As I lifted the carriage down Rosie's porch stairs, I was struck by the difference an address can make. I was used to getting up and out early. We had started our day when the newspaper boy was the only one awake in that neighborhood besides us. And at that hour, the quiet wasn't broken when we got to Main Street where, besides the Tick Tock, everything was closed up tight. Even the air had seemed different last week, when the heat would gradually creep up on me.

Starting out the day at nine forty-five in the morning, the heat came crashing over me like a wave. We walked down the block to the music of screen doors snapping shut, dogs howling, and radios blaring. When we turned up Main Street, Rosie stopped to say hello to every shopkeeper unlocking a door.

I went right to work hanging the scallops of red, white, and blue fabric on the front of the window. I had gathered a few jars and vases from the shelves and was arranging bouquets of flags in them when I noticed a man standing on the walk, staring in the window.

"He's looking at the bike," Rosie whispered.

The prospect of a real live customer started my insides dancing. "Do you think he'll buy it?" I whispered back.

"Not likely," she said. "That's Pete Garcia from the used bike shop across the street."

I wondered how long he would stand there and if he was mad about us having a bike in our window. Then the most incredible thing happened. A car slowed down and came to a stop by the curb right in front of the Second Hand Rose. A woman and a little boy stepped out and before they could cross the street, that boy caught sight of the bike.

"I want to go in there," he said, pointing at the bike and tugging on his mother's arm.

"Not now, Henry," she said.

"But you promised," he whined. "You promised I could have a bike."

"We will go to Toy World on Saturday," she answered.

Henry let go of his mother's hand and ran into the Second Hand Rose. His mother came chasing in after him. "Now Henry, you know better than to run away from me like that," she scolded the boy.

"But I don't want to wait until Saturday. I want that bike in the window, so I can ride it at the picnic on the fourth," he said, stamping his foot.

I held my breath, waiting to see what would come next. If I had ever spoken to Mama or Daddy that way, it would have been a long time before my bottom would want to be anywhere near a bicycle seat. But Henry's mama had a different way of handling the situation. As she was paying for the bike, she commented on the store window. "I love your window display. It looks like an old-fashioned small town picnic—except for the dishes, of course. I think we're more paper plate people around here."

"I always say just because we live in a small town doesn't mean we have to think small," Rosie said. "I'm sure I don't need to tell you that whereas folks around here have one set of dishes for everyday and one set of dishes for fancy, big city folks have dishes for every occasion. I'm sure you've noticed that very thing in the home decorating magazines."

Now, I would have bet all the money in my pocket that Rosie had never read a home decorating magazine in her life, but Henry's mama was nodding her head in agreement. As I loaded the carton of dishes and glasses and Henry's bike into the back of the car, I thought of Daddy again.

One of my chores back home was selling vegetables down by the road. One day I had a whole bushel of green beans left and Daddy wasn't happy to see it. "But Daddy," I said. "Nobody needed green beans today."

"Becky, people don't know what they need until you tell them," he answered.

When it came to money, Daddy got his sayings right.

CHAPTER 10

I must have found Baby Girl's sweet spot in that crib, because on only her second night in it she managed to sleep through with only one moonlit feeding. I should have slept like a baby, too, but instead I tossed and turned in that bed trying to figure out our good fortune.

Just before closing time the day before, Rosie sent me to the market to fetch some catfish for dinner. As we walked back toward her house, so I could pick up Baby Girl's and my belongings, Rosie asked, "Do you want me to fry up that catfish for us before or after you go to the library?"

I held my breath for a minute and tried to think before I spoke. I had found the nerve to look in that pay envelope earlier in the day and discovered it didn't hold enough to cover rent anywhere. I had thought about asking Rosie if Baby Girl and I could stay in the back room of the store for a few days. But I was afraid if Rosie knew we were homeless, she would have second thoughts about being involved with us at all.

"You do like catfish, don't you, Becky? I don't like to brag, but if you don't it's only because you haven't tried my catfish yet," Rosie said.

I looked into Rosie's eyes. I had been so busy trying to hide the truth from her all week that I had failed to see that she had already seen a big part of it. I gulped down a big helping of air trying to push back the sobs that were fighting their way out of me.

Rosie reached out and rubbed my arm. "If we're going to be roommates, then we need to get to know these kinds of things about each other," she said. "Now, let's get home before this catfish cooks itself out in this heat."

We walked down the street in silence until Rosie said, "You're awfully quiet tonight. Are you tired? I must be working you too hard. A young girl with a baby needs as much rest as she can get. You turn in early tonight."

I wanted to tell her the Second Hand Rose was the best job I ever had. I wanted to tell her that she wasn't working me too hard and that she was treating me better than anyone else had in my whole life. But I was afraid if I said anything, I would burst into tears and hug her tighter than an old woman wants to be held.

When I crawled into bed that night, I stared at the ceiling for hours trying to understand Rosie's kindness. I tossed and turned as I heard Daddy's voice in my head. "Becky, even a snake oil salesman wears a smile, but only a fool would be taken in by it. A smart girl knows better than to trust anyone."

But Daddy didn't know Rosie. He didn't know people like her walked on this earth along with the snake oil salesmen. He didn't know there were people who in an instant could make you feel like their home was your home. I thought about the knowing look I had seen in Rosie's eyes. I went to sleep and left thoughts of Daddy behind.

The next morning, I cradled Baby Girl in the crook of my arm while Rosie and I ate breakfast. "How did our little princess sleep last night?" Rosie asked.

I looked down into Baby Girl's sweet face and answered, "Like a baby—meaning for no more than three hours at a time."

"You must be exhausted," Rosie said. "Do you need some time off from work?"

"No, ma'am," I answered. "I'm fine." The truth is, I was fine. Waking up knowing we would have a roof over our heads that night was a weight off my shoulders. It left me with an energy I'd been missing for days.

When we got to the store that morning, I put that energy to good use and got to work on that front window display. I wanted to fill in the empty spots from yesterday's customer. I found a huge supply of ribbon in the second box of decorations and discovered even a gray steel pail looks holiday-ish when it's wearing a bow.

I stepped out onto the sidewalk to get a passerby's view of the window. As I was admiring my handiwork, some movement across the block grabbed my attention. It was the bicycle man from yesterday. He was lining bikes up on the walk in front of his store. The bikes had red, white, and blue ribbons woven between the wheel spokes and floating from the handle bars. I was trying to decide whether I should feel mad or flattered when Rosie came out.

"Well, will you look at that," she said. "It looks like your work is so good that it's inspiring others. Wait here."

Rosie hurried back into the store. She came out carrying more of the fabric I had draped across the front of the Second Hand Rose. "I'll stay here with Georgia. Why don't you run this down to Pete?"

By lunchtime, the Better Than New Bike Shop was giving the Second Hand Rose some competition in the looks department.

Baby Girl had settled in for her nap and Rosie looked like she was just about to settle into one, too. I decided it might be best if I busied myself in the front of the store where I could keep an eye on the sleeping beauties. I had found some embroidery floss in the back and had a great idea for how to put it to good use. Last week, when Rosie had unpacked those cartons, she'd found two dozen brand new white bibs.

"Will you look at this," she'd said. "Why would anyone want twenty-four of the exact same things?"

Now I decided the floss could best be used by stitching a tiny flag on one of the bibs. As I was finishing, our second customer of the week walked in. The screen door clapping shut woke both sleepers from their naps. "What can we get for you today?" Rosie smiled.

The young woman stood by the door looking like she wasn't sure she wanted to come in any further. I put down the bib and picked up Baby Girl to stop her fussing.

"What a beautiful baby," the lady said, braving a few steps in our direction. "How old is she?"

"She's brand new," I answered, "only a couple of weeks old."

Rosie passed her hand over the pile of bibs. "Do you have a little one at home?"

"Not yet," the woman smiled. "I have a baby niece though. She's coming up with the whole family for the long weekend. They want to have an old-fashioned family picnic, complete with the Main Street Fourth of July parade."

"No better way to spend a holiday weekend." Rosie was on her feet now. "How can we help you with all your party preparations?"

"I noticed the flags in your window. Are they for sale?"

"Sure are. How many do you need?"

"About twenty of them."

"And would you like Becky to arrange them in a container, so that you have a centerpiece for your picnic table?"

"Oh, I like that idea." The lady took a few more steps in my direction.

Rosie smiled. "You'll probably want a few extras, then, so your table doesn't look bare after your guests take a flag for the parade."

"Absolutely." The lady's hand was already in her purse. "When will it be ready?"

Rosie turned to me. "Becky, you can get that done in the next hour or so, can't you?"

"I'll get right on it." I said. Before Baby Girl and I got halfway down one of the aisles in search of another container, Rosie called me back.

"Becky, I know you normally only do this by special order, but I saw the light in this nice lady's eyes when she talked about her baby niece. Do you think you could make an exception to your rule this one time and do one of your special bibs for this lady today?"

I tried to look like I was concentrating real hard. "Rules are made to be broken." I smiled at the lady.

"Of course, here I am creating more work for you, and I don't even know if this nice lady wants to include the little one in the family celebration. She may not even be interested in a personalized flag bib."

"Oh, yes." The lady reached out for Rosie's arm. "I do want the bib." She turned to look at me. "Her name is Jenny, that's J-e-n-n-y. Could you have it ready later this afternoon, too?"

"I'll get to work on your order right now," I answered.

That turned out to be the start of a busy afternoon. We had three more customers that day, but I made sure that when the lady came back her bib and centerpiece were ready and waiting for her.

At closing, I took the time to fill in the open spots in the window display. "You keep that window looking pretty," Rosie said. "This store hasn't had this many customers in years. Business is booming, thanks to you."

I was proud of my work, but I knew it wasn't just me. My displays were drawing people into the store but once they got inside, it was all Rosie. That woman could sell shampoo to a bald man. "It's not me, Rosie. It's us. We make a great team."

"That we do, Becky. That we do."

CHAPTER 11

The next morning we weren't in the store but a few minutes when Dottie sashayed through the doorway. She announced her arrival by letting loose her grip on the door, allowing it to slam shut and bounce against the jamb. Not wanting to open myself to more questions, I busied myself in one of the aisles. Rosie and Dottie kept their heads together for quite some time before digging into the decoration boxes. Dottie walked out with an armload of supplies without stopping at the register. "Don't forget," she called over her shoulder. "You come over right after the parade."

"We'll be there!" Rosie said.

Before I got a chance to ask where 'there' was, a woman came in carrying a baby in one of those portable seats. She lifted the contraption onto the counter. "Is Becky in today?"

Rosie glanced in my direction. "I'm Rosie. Can I help you?"

"My neighbor told me she bought a bib here yesterday. She said that a girl named Becky does them exclusively for your customers. I want to order a set for my Haley."

I took her order for six bibs, each with a different design. She didn't ask about the cost and didn't seem at all concerned about having to wait a couple of days for them. "They will be one-of-a-kinds?" she asked. "My neighbor said that each one was unique."

I could honestly answer, "I've never sold the same design twice."

Rosie took advantage of the time it took me to write up the order by selling the woman a one-of-a-kind birdbath. Once Rosie mentioned that little Haley looked so smart that she probably would be naming all of the local birds by her first birthday, if only those birds had a reason to visit her yard, I knew to slow down my writing. I carried the "birdbath" out to her car.

As I stood there, squinting into the sunlight while the silver car glided down the street, Dottie yelled over, "It's looking pretty good, don't you think? I know it's not as pretty as yours, but I did a fair job, didn't I?"

I looked over at the Tick Tock Diner. Dottie had stretched the red, white, and blue cloth across the front of the diner in an uneven pattern of loops. She must have run shy of fabric by the end, because the last couple of feet were stretched straight across. "It looks real patriotic," I said.

This must have been enough of a compliment for Dottie, because she sent a big wave and a smile my way and went back to tugging on her loops. I went back into the store and started sorting through my short supply of floss. "I might need a couple of other colors to fill that order," I said. "Do you know if there might be more around here?"

Rosie shook her head. "I dug that stuff out of a sweater pocket. I remember that it ruffled my feathers to think that people don't even clean out their pockets before passing things on. I was going to toss it away, but I changed my mind. I must have been having a vision of what was to come."

Rosie got a look on her face like she was having a vision right then and there. She turned on her heels and hurried over to the register. She reached into the cash drawer and handed me ten dollars. "Becky, you go on down the block to the Needles and Notions shop. You buy those threads in every color of the rainbow and anything else you might need, too. And tell Lydie that we'll be giving her a lot of business. The way word of your work is getting around, you'll need fresh supplies on a regular basis!"

Rosie sat back down in her chair. She looked tuckered out from the excitement of the floss, so I decided to take Baby Girl with me on my shopping spree. I was surprised to see Sarah walking out of the Needles and Notions shop. "Hi Becky!" she said. "I loved that book. Thanks so much for the recommendation."

"I'm glad you liked it," I said. "Do you do needlework, too?"

"No," she laughed. "My mother decided today would be a 'girls day out.' My little brother is away at camp for the week. We're going to do our regular mother/daughter stuff, you know—hair, nails, and shoe shopping later, but Mom got this great idea that I should learn something that she enjoyed doing when she was my age. I'm sure it will end up in hibernation in the storage closet with the rest of her arts and craft projects, but whatever. I'll give it a try."

The door to the store opened and a woman walked out. "I'm sorry that took so long, Sarah. It gave me time to come up with another idea, though. Let's go to the library now and you can show me a few of your favorite books. I'll check them out, read them, and we can have our own little mother/daughter book club to discuss them." The woman caught her breath and looked at me as if she just noticed me standing there.

Sarah said, "Mom, this is Becky. Becky, this is my mom, Mrs. Hanson."

"Hello, Mrs. Hanson. It's very nice to meet you," I said.

"It's nice to meet you too, Becky. I always enjoy meeting Sarah's friends. I don't think I've ever seen you at school."

Before I can answer, Sarah says, "Becky is new in town, Mom. You wouldn't have seen her at school."

"Well then, welcome to Watson's Grove. Who do we have in here?" Mrs. Hanson asked as she bent over the carriage. "What a sweetheart! Look at those beautiful red curls. What's her name?"

"Her name is Georgia, ma'am."

Mrs. Hanson stood up and turned toward Sarah. "You could take a lesson from Becky," she said. "You were complaining the other night there were no jobs in town. Babysitting would keep you very busy and provide the spending money you're always asking for from your father and me."

Sarah hesitated a moment, then said, "Mom, maybe you should go to the library ahead of me. Becky and I were just about to discuss a book I'm sure you're going to want to read. We don't want to spoil the ending for you. I'll be there in about ten minutes."

"Spoiler alert!" her mom giggled. "Thanks for the warning! It was nice to meet you Becky. Sarah, I'll see you in a few."

We watched her mother walk down the block, before Sarah said, "My mom and I aren't best buds. I don't spend all of my time with her. Last night at dinner, my dad mentioned that we would be spending most of his vacation days next spring and summer touring college campuses. Then they both started rocking nostalgic. They spent the rest of the meal talking about the things we did when I was younger and all the dreams and plans they had for me when I was born. So now a regular old mother/daughter day isn't enough for Mom. She needs to throw in some of the things she thought we would do together, but never did. Anyway, the book was great. We really should get together and swap some books or book titles. I think we have the same taste in literature. That's not something I can say about the girls you saw me with at the library."

"Okay. Have fun today," I said, as I walked into the store.

I picked out the colors I needed and hurried to the counter. I had already been away from the Second Hand Rose long enough.

"I'm Becky. Rosie asked me to say hi and to tell you we'll be coming to you for all of our floss needs."

Lydie nodded. She didn't smile, but at least her face went from a frown to a flat line. I was ready to pay for my ten hanks of floss and a packet of needles when I spotted the Fourth of July bargain basket. I sifted through the basket and came upon a small music box with a top for stitching. I was looking at the price and wondering if I dared buy it when Lydie spoke her first words to me. "I've got six of those music boxes, if you're interested."

"I don't have enough money for more than one," I smiled.

"Are you the girl that dressed up Rosie's store?"

"Yes, ma'am."

The ends of Lydie's mouth curled into a smile. "Maybe we can make a deal. I'll give you all six of these beautiful music boxes for the price of one—and the sale price at that. And in return you can dress the front of my store for tomorrow's parade."

I hesitated before answering. I was worrying about what Rosie might think of this bargain. Lydie decided to add some honey to the pot. "Each box plays a different tune, and if you come back after the weekend to take the stuff down, I'll throw in three items of your choice from this basket."

And of course, once again, I was overtaken by the thrill of shopping and piled the music boxes onto the counter next to my floss. When I got back to the Second Hand Rose, I discovered that I had been worrying for nothing. Rosie was sure we got the better end of the deal. She helped me gather things to decorate the storefront, and I set off to complete the first half of my part of the bargain.

As I worked, I thought about Sarah and her family. The closest thing Mama and I ever got to a girls' day was spring cleaning. Having someone paint our nails would have seemed as strange as feeding chickens in the house. The truth be told, Daddy wouldn't have put up with us spending money like that. I don't think I ever saw Mama wearing nail polish. As hard as Daddy could be on me, he was ten times worse with Mama. I couldn't even picture Mama and me having a little book club together. I was always sneaking a few minutes alone with a book, but I never saw Mama enjoying the luxury of a novel. I wondered if I had spent a little less time with my books maybe Daddy would have been a little easier on all of us.

When I finished, the Needles and Notions looked as pretty as a picture postcard. Lydie was so happy with my work that she had me set her chair out in front of her store. She started to settle in, but before Lydie's bottom even touched the chair, she sprang back upright. She clutched my arm with one hand and shaded her eyes with the other. "Do my eyes deceive me or is that Miss Lily standing with Rosie?" she asked. "I can't remember the last time I saw her in town. It definitely was before the tragedy. Poor Lily has endured too much pain for a woman her age."

As Lydie settled back into her chair, I turned to look up the street. Rosie stood on the walk in front of the Second Hand Rose, waving at a dark car as it pulled away from the curb. Even from my distance, I could see the sadness in her face. I wondered who Lily was, and what kind of tragedy had caused such pain.

CHAPTER 12

The parade didn't start until eleven, but Rosie wanted to beat the crowd so we could stake our claim on the walk in front of the Second Hand Rose. I carried the chairs out to the curb, parking the stroller between them. Rosie settled into her favorite chair and started slowly rocking the stroller back and forth. She had come to know Baby Girl's love of motion.

"I'm going to see if Lydie needs some help with her chair," I said.

"You go ahead, Becky," Rosie answered. "Georgia and I will be right here, soaking in the excitement of the day."

As I walked back to the Second Hand Rose after helping Lydie, I spotted Rosie coming out of the store. She was toting a bucketful of flags, but what was worrying me was what she wasn't toting. I couldn't see Baby Girl's stroller through the people, so I sprinted the rest of the block.

"No need to run in this heat. I can carry this myself," Rosie said.

I was looking at Baby Girl. She was curled up safe and sound in Dottie's arms. Dottie was gazing down at her with such tenderness that it made me put all my bad feelings about the inquiring waitress aside.

"You didn't think I left Georgia alone out here, did you?" Rosie asked. "I got to thinking that it wouldn't be unpatriotic to do business on the Fourth if that business was selling flags. I waved Dottie on over and she sat here with Georgia while I got the flags out of the window."

I took the bucket from Rosie and placed it by her chair. Before I could take Georgia from Dottie, I heard someone call my name. I looked up and saw Sarah approaching.

"Hi!" she said. "I was hoping I would find you here." She waved a paperback book with its cover on in front of her. "Right after the parade, I have to go with my parents to my aunt's house for a week. From there we are going to pick up my brother from camp and then we're going on to Virginia Beach for vacation. I'll be gone for four weeks, which required a stockpile of books. I started this one on my way home from the store and finished it before I could pack. I thought you might like to read it next."

"Thanks," I said as she handed me the book. It was hard to come up with social words when all I could think of was Dottie holding Baby Girl. I had such a need to hold that baby in my arms at that moment.

Rosie put her arm around my shoulders. "Becky, are you going to introduce us to your friend?"

My cheeks started to heat up. "Yes, I'm sorry. This is Sarah Hanson. Sarah, this is Rosie Perkins."

"It's nice to meet you, Mrs. Perkins," Sarah said.

"Call me Rosie; everyone does," Rosie answered.

Sarah smiled and nodded.

I waved my arm toward Dottie. "This is Dottie, and you've already met Georgia."

Dottie lifted her chin and said, "I've seen you around the diner."

Sarah nodded again. "I have to go. My parents are all the way at the end of the street. I hope you enjoy the book. I also put an invitation in there. When I get back, I'm having a pool party. It won't be over the top or anything, just a few friends. My dad will throw some dogs and burgers on the grill for us. We'll swim, eat, talk, dance, and whatever. It might be the last chance for fun before school starts again. I hope you can come."

"Maybe," I said. "Thanks again for the book. I'll take good care of it and get it back to you after I read it."

As soon as Sarah walked away, I reached down to take Baby Girl from Dottie's arms. "Thanks for your help," I said, as I wrapped my arms around the baby.

"Any time," Dottie answered. "She's a little angel."

Dottie went back across the street, and Rosie and I settled back into our chairs. The flags sold in the flick of a cat's tail. "All gone," Rosie said.

"Yup," I responded.

"Becky, I would never put doing business before the needs of that little girl you're holding. I knew she would be safe with Dottie."

I reached over and took her hand. "I'm just being silly. I know you would never put her in harm's way. Let's just forget about it."

"No. Worrying is what mamas do, and I gave you cause to worry, so I apologize."

Before I could respond a band began to play. "Yankee Doodle" filled the air, and I covered Baby Girl's ears to protect her from the booming drums. I felt a little homesick watching the band in their matching uniforms march by me. They reminded me of the band at my old school. And the majorettes that followed behind the band really tugged at my heart. I'd practiced twirling a broom handle behind the barn for weeks, getting ready to try out for the Tyson Twirlers. Mama and Daddy would have none of that foolishness, though, with so much work to be done at home on the farm. A flash of light in my eyes brought me back to the here and now. A man was walking along snapping pictures of the crowd and the parade. He looked like he was about to ask us something, until I glared at him real hard. He moved along and I returned my attention to the parade.

Veterans dressed in uniforms marched in straight lines, and a horse-drawn wagon was filled with children who were tossing candy out to the crowd. A whole pack of boys zipped down the middle of the street, riding Mr. Garcia's decorated bikes. At the very end of the parade was Mr. Garcia himself. He was walking on stilts, dressed in stars and stripes, and wearing a white wig and beard. Every time Uncle Sam bent over to tip his hat at the crowd, he would sway back and forth on top of those sticks. I wondered if he would make it to the end of Main Street.

When the last note was played and the parade turned from a stream of people to a swirling pool, the crowd wandered off in search of their cars. Baby Girl had managed to doze off in my arms during the festivities. I was debating the merits of putting her back in her stroller when Rosie took charge of the situation.

"I'm going to put this pail back in the store, along with the flag money. When I come back out, we can bring these chairs across the street for the picnic. I can smell that pork barbeque already. It's got my mouth watering."

Rosie pushed the stroller while I lugged the two chairs. She had some difficulty deciding where the chairs should be set. "We want some shade," she said. "But we want to be in the middle of things, too. No sense going to a party and not knowing who danced."

It took about ten tries before Rosie settled on a spot. "I'm going to go down to see if Lydie needs some help again," I said. But when I looked in the direction of Needles and Notions, I saw Mr. Garcia walking up the middle of the road wearing shorts, a T-shirt, and his stars and stripes top hat. He had Lydie on his left arm and her chair on his right arm.

The road in front of the Tick Tock filled with the people who spent their days on Main Street. Even Miss Willis, the librarian, was there. I didn't recognize most of the folks, but Rosie knew each of them by name. Two men had brought guitars, and it didn't take much convincing to get them to start strumming away.

A man cleared a space in the middle of things and started dancing to the guitar music. He spun and strutted as fast as a jackrabbit with a hound dog at his heels. When he wore himself out, he bowed to the crowd and made a sweeping motion with his arm. Folks took up the invitation and found a place on the dance floor. Pete Garcia stood in front of us. He tipped his hat toward Rosie. "Señora, if you please."

I swear Rosie turned as red as the stripe on his hat, but she got up and took his arm. I stood on the side swaying to the music with Baby Girl. I had my eyes fixed on Rosie and Pete gliding and twirling their way through the crowd, so I didn't notice when Dottie first joined me. "Are you having a good time?" she asked.

She startled me so that I lost my rhythm, which of course set Baby Girl off. "Now I've gone and upset the apple cart. I guess you two were having a better time before I came over." Dottie ran her fingers through the swirl of red curls.

"We're having a great time." I kissed Baby Girl's forehead and picked up the pace of my swaying. "Does your boss throw a party every year?"

Dottie laughed so hard, I thought she was going to pee in her pants. "First off, Ray isn't my boss. He's my husband, and if you take a look at him over by the grills you'll see why I keep him tucked away in the kitchen. Secondly, this is the first shindig we've had in the seventeen years we've been here."

"I sure hope it's not the last," I said.

The music turned from a waltz to a two-step. Pete returned Rosie to her chair. She looked flushed, but happier than a kid on her last day of school.

"Looks like you two built up an appetite," Dottie laughed. "How about one of Ray's famous pulled pork sandwiches? A nice big scoop of my coleslaw on the side and you'll be raring to get back on the dance floor."

I followed Dottie over to the food table. In the corner of my eye, I spotted the boy I had plowed into on the sidewalk the day I arrived in town. He was dancing with the two check-out girls from Haystack's, and he must have felt me staring at him because he paused in the middle of the song to wave. Embarrassed to be caught staring, I pretended not to notice.

When I returned to Rosie, carrying her dinner, I saw the boy again. This time he was down on one knee in front of Rosie. "Becky, this is John, the young man I told you about. You'll probably see him someday working in our yard. He keeps everything looking fresh and pretty. We were just talking about a friend of mine, Lily. John thinks she could use some company, and I agree. He brought her by the store yesterday when you were out. We could barely get her to step outside the car, much less come into the store. We had no luck convincing her to come by for the parade or picnic. I think you, Georgia, and I should pay her a short visit on Sunday."

"Lydie mentioned her surprise at seeing Lily on the street. She said something awful had happened."

Rosie's face tightened. "Lydie should be keeping her comments to herself," she said.

John looked like he was about to say something, but decided to swallow his words instead. After a moment or so he smiled, stretched out his hand, and said, "We've run into each other already but we were never formally introduced."

I allowed myself to watch him walk away for longer than was respectable. If Daddy was here to witness my behavior, I would be feeling the sting of his belt on my backside.

When evening fell on Main Street and the mosquitoes outnumbered the people ten to one, everyone agreed it was time to call it a day. I ran into the ladies' room in the diner to change Baby Girl one last time and dress her in a sleeper to keep away the bugs. When I came back outside, Dottie's words pulled the plug on what was left of my celebrating spirit.

"All I'm saying is that when a girl as young as Becky shows up in town with a brand new baby that doesn't look a bit like her, you have to wonder." Dottie threw her hands up in the air as if she thought the answers were going to fall from the sky. "Where is she from? Who are her people? Why is she here?"

Rosie's patience must have been worn thinner than the knees of my favorite jeans, because she let out the only sharp words I'd ever heard pass her lips. "You need to stop sticking your nose into other people's business. You want to spend your time thinking about Becky, then think about how lucky we are she came to Watson's Grove. Do you think any of us would be here today, celebrating together if she hadn't? How many people came to the parade last year? How many people took part in it? How many stores here on Main Street even put up a flag? Becky is taking a layer of dust off this place. Be grateful, it will help you be kinder."

They lowered their voices and their heads and continued their conversation. I only caught a word here and there, but that was enough for me to know this wasn't good news for me. Then Baby Girl let out a howl, causing Rosie and Dottie to look up from their chairs and stare at me.

Rosie and I walked home in silence. I knew she must have been wondering what I had heard. I kept replaying the words I'd caught in my mind. Had Dottie convinced Rosie I wasn't worth the faith she was putting in me?

When we got home, Rosie went straight to bed, but my insides were having such a battle that I knew sleep was a long way off for me. I sat in the parlor with the television turned low and my hands busy with the needle and floss. My heart said to tell Rosie everything. She had been so good to us; she deserved to know the truth. My gut said to wake up early and head back down to the tracks. I had done my best to turn a deaf ear to the questions and comments about me and Baby Girl. That might not have been the best thing—the safest thing—for me to do. Maybe it was time to move on to a town where folks were less prone to ask questions. And my brain didn't agree with either my heart or my gut. It told me to stay put and be grateful for what we had. Sooner or later, even Dottie would get tired of asking questions.

That night I pulled my notebook out for the first time in more than a week. I read my list of adventures from start to finish. My life sure wasn't turning out like the stories in the books I'd read. When I finally turned in for the night, I still wasn't sure which body part to follow.

CHAPTER 13

Baby Girl and I were up and dressed long before Rosie on that next morning. I even made breakfast. I stuck to scrambled eggs, though, not wanting to give Rosie a reason to give up on me on that front. When Rosie sat down at the kitchen table, she was still dressed in her housecoat.

"No work today," she said. "We've earned a day off."

Even after sleeping in, Rosie looked tired. A full day of partying had worn her out. I decided that today could not be moving on day. "Are you sure?" I asked. "I'll go in myself if you like, so you don't miss any of the long weekend shoppers."

"I think folks will be picnicking with their families today. If they are shopping, they'll probably go down the highway to the mall. No, let's enjoy a day off. Maybe later on, we can take the bus over to the Mission Creek Mall. We can do a little shopping ourselves."

I must admit that the prospect of going to a shopping mall did excite me some. I had never set foot in one before; Mama and Daddy wouldn't hear of it. Spending my afternoon surrounded by people wanting to get their hands inside my wallet was high on their list of ways to waste a day. I had to settle for hearing about the shopping center from Tammy Larson, whose texting skills would have put that girl in the library to shame.

"I think I'll just steal a little extra rest this morning." Rosie pushed her chair back under the table. "Do you think you can clean this up on your own?"

After I dried the last of the dishes, I took Baby Girl out onto the porch. I sat there rocking her and thinking. I wondered what

Tammy was doing at that moment. When we were younger, we'd spend hours skipping rocks across the pond, racing through the fields, or making stories up behind the barn. But truth be told, Tammy and I had drifted apart over our high school years. Her time was filled with cheerleading practice, dances, and parties. Daddy, of course, would not give his permission for me to do any of those things.

At first, Tammy prodded me to ask Mama to convince Daddy that it was all perfectly respectable. I explained to her again and again that Mama would never say a word against Daddy. Daddy's word was law in our house and no one, including Mama, had a right to question it. Tammy, whose mama wore red nail polish and went away on business trips, couldn't understand this. Eventually, she gave up on me and concentrated on new friends.

Thinking about Tammy was making me sad, so I moved on to better thoughts. The prospect of window shopping outfits in the mall was positively thrilling. I had been wearing just the few clothes I had packed and some men's colored T-shirts that came in neat plastic packages from a rack at Haystack's. I started imagining myself in some of the outfits the girls back at school wore.

My pleasant daydream was interrupted by the sound of metal clicking. I scanned the yard quickly trying to find the source of the noise. It was John, trimming the shrubs around Rosie's porch. He took the T-shirt draped over his shoulder and used it to wipe the beads of sweat from his face, neck, and chest. My own chest felt like it did when I flew too high in the tire swing back home.

"Beautiful day, isn't it?" he said.

"Sure is," I answered and tried not to stare at the way the pink cloth on his shoulders looked against his tanned skin. He nodded in my direction and bent over to pick up the handles to a wheelbarrow. I forced myself to look down at Georgia so I couldn't watch him push his collection of weeds and cuttings around back.

I sat there rocking Georgia for about an hour. Then the darnedest thing happened. I was singing her a lullaby when she looked up at me and smiled. Now, I know most folks will say it was just a belly bubble causing her lips to curl up like that. But I swear, she looked me right in the eye and smiled like she knew who she was smiling at. It just about caused my heart to explode. It also brought to mind all of the things her real mama was missing. I put her in the stroller and headed to the library to search the papers again.

I'm ashamed to admit that on my way back to Rosie's, I was feeling relieved about the lack of news in the papers about Baby Girl.

I had been tending to babies that weren't mine for years. I knew better than to start thinking of her as my own. Feeding, cleaning, cuddling, and keeping her safe fell to me for the time being. Dreams for her future, like Sarah's parents had for her, were a gift belonging to someone else. But knowing and feeling are two different things.

Rosie was waiting for us on the front porch. She smiled and started down the street toward us when we were still a few houses away. She gave me a big hug like I was some long-lost relative and scooped Baby Girl right out of her carriage. "I woke up and you were both gone. I wondered where you had gotten yourself off to on a Saturday morning."

"We just took a little walk down to the library. I'm sorry I didn't think to leave a note."

"I should have guessed." Rosie laughed. "How come you never bring anything home to read? I know I tease you some about all of the reading you do but I'm all for it. Bringing the book home to read would be easier than going to the library every day." She stopped, caught her breath, turned to me, and raised an eyebrow. "You're not reading any dirty books, are you? 'Cause I won't have any of that under my roof."

"No, Rosie. I'm not reading dirty books. I just like being in the library."

"You're not thinking of leaving the Second Hand Rose to go work there, are you?"

"No, ma'am."

As soon as we got back to the house, we packed what we needed for our trip to the mall and headed for the bus stop. It took some doing to get onto the bus with Baby Girl's deluxe carriage. As soon as I settled into a seat I noticed how cool the air was in there. I was worrying about Baby Girl getting a chill since I always dressed her for the summer heat. I held her close and kept rubbing her little arms and legs to keep the goose bumps away. When we got into the shopping mall, the air wasn't any warmer. My first purchases of the day were a pair of socks to cover her feet and a new blanket to cover the rest of her.

We walked up and down both sides of the mall and then took an elevator up to the second floor. The walls of the elevator were made of glass so you could see out as you rode the car between the floors. I had never been in one like this before, and was finding the ride to be a mix of scary and exciting. I looked out at the floor sinking below us and the gears holding that car up. It only took a few seconds for me to decide it best to close my eyes until we reached our destination.

At one end of the second floor was the Beautiful Baby Boutique. We stopped and stared in that window for a long time. In the center, there was a whole new baby wardrobe done in yellow, green, and white. On one side of that was a set of mix-and-match baby girl clothes, and on the other side a set for boys. It was the one in front of them all that grabbed my attention. It was an exact match with the baby things we pulled from the boxes in the Second Hand Rose.

Rosie noticed it, too. "Let's go in for a minute," she suggested. She went straight for the newborn table. She picked up a white bib and inspected it closely. She paid even closer attention to the price tag. This of course caused the sales girl to come running over. "Ten dollars," Rosie said. "How many of these do you get for the ten dollars?"

"Each one is ten dollars," the girl answered. Her smile looked frozen on her face. "They're made of the softest cotton. We wouldn't want anything less for our babies, now, would we?"

"Do you have a boy or a girl?" Rosie asked, locking a smile onto her face, too.

"I was referring to our customers," the girl answered. A phone rang and she looked happy for an excuse to walk away from us.

Rosie continued her price checking and I looked around the store. In one corner they had a stack of diaper bags. The one on top had a name written on it in paint. The sign said that they charged two dollars a letter to personalize the bags. A bell went off in my head. I hurried back to Rosie, because my new idea was ready to burst out of me like those wire snakes in a fake can of nuts.

Rosie had moved from the clothes to the furnishings and was standing next to Baby Girl's stroller twin. She lifted the price tag and pointed it my way. It knocked the wind out of me. I hoped Rosie wasn't regretting the fact that the stroller was in my hands and not in the window of the Second Hand Rose.

"It's a good thing Georgia is a little princess, because her carriage was made for royalty." Rosie laughed. "What were you so excited about when you came over here?"

That price tag might have curbed my energy some, but my idea still came out of me like steam from a kettle. My sputtering start quickly became a whoosh of words that had Rosie laughing out loud again. "Becky, I'm going to die a rich woman with you in my life. You have a lot of great ideas in that quiet self of yours. Just hearing them has me tired out. How about I treat you to dinner out at that restaurant down there? These old bones of mine could use a little rest."

First I saw John in the morning, then a trip to the mall, and now dinner out. What other surprises could today spring on me?

CHAPTER 14

The restaurant was busy. Rosie sat down on a bench while I waited in line. When I finally got to the front, a girl asked me, "How many?" When she saw Rosie coming over with the carriage, she rolled her eyes and started snapping her gum. "This way," she said and led us to a booth in the back.

Despite the chilly reception, I was enjoying myself. Before the Tick Tock, my only restaurant experience had been on a school trip in the eighth grade. We stopped for lunch on the way home from the caverns. Mama had ignored the teacher's note and had sent me without any money. I had worried all morning about the stop and planned to hide out in the bathroom while everyone else ate. Mrs. White came into the ladies' room looking for me.

"You were taking so long in here, I had to order for you. It will be my treat, since you didn't get to choose for yourself. Let's get back to the table now."

One look into Mrs. White's eyes and I knew that she guessed my pockets were empty. For the rest of the year, I brought her baskets of beans and tomatoes and jars of jam. She deserved a better thank you, but it was all I could do at the time. Even that gave me cause to worry about Daddy tanning my hide if he found out.

Rosie cut my trip down memory lane short. "What looks good to you?"

The menu at the Tick Tock was just the front and back of a piece of paper. This one was a whole little book and I didn't know where to read first. I looked over at Rosie, who was flipping through the pages and nodding and decided to do the same. "I don't know. What looks good to you?"

The waitress came over and took our orders. When Rosie asked for the special of the day, I decided to follow her lead. Over dinner, Rosie and I talked about where I might be able to buy the paint markers I saw behind the sales counter back at the Baby Boutique. Neither of us was sure about what kinds of things they would work on, and Rosie pointed out our lack of diaper bags.

While we waited for the waitress to bring us our dessert, I fed Georgia her bottle. She had been as quiet as a mouse throughout the meal and had seemed to enjoy all of the attention she was getting from passersby. She was wearing one of her little white outfits, and I had tied a pink bow in her hair. Before seeing the clothes in that baby store window, it hadn't occurred to me that it was odd for such things to be in the Second Hand Rose. "Rosie, where did all of these baby things come from?"

"You saw me unpacking the box," she answered.

"I know," I said. "But where did the box come from? Who gave you a whole box of brand new expensive baby clothes—and a carriage and crib to boot?"

Rosie didn't answer at first. She looked down at the peach cobbler that the waitress had just set before her and started tapping her fork against the side of the plate. "I don't want you to be upset about Georgia having these things when I tell you . . . well, when I tell you about the awful thing that happened."

I looked over at Rosie. I wanted to know, now more than ever, where the things came from, but Rosie's eyes were filling with tears just thinking about it. "It's okay, Rosie, you don't have to say."

Rosie took a sip of her tea and took a deep breath. "When my granddaughter was younger she was a real spitfire. She didn't like coming to work with me, and she turned her babysitter's hair from gray to white. I couldn't leave her on her own, so I hired a girl to come stay with her after school. That girl was as special as the flower she was named for—Lily. She was in high school and Jenny, my granddaughter, thought she was something special. That girl worked magic with Jenny. She really helped to keep her out of trouble."

"Is that the same woman you and John were talking about?"

Rosie nodded. "Yes. After high school, she gave up babysitting and went off to college. Unlike my granddaughter, she didn't forget where she came from. She married a boy she met at the university and they bought some land on the edge of town. He was a handsome young man with a good head for business. They built a house the size of a hotel on that land, but she is still the same sweet girl I met all those years ago. Before the accident, she came by the store almost every week to say hi and offer me a ride somewhere."

I wanted to stop Rosie and ask her what kind of accident, but I could tell by the look on her face the story was hard enough to tell without me rushing her.

"I remember the excitement in her voice when she came to tell me about the new addition to their family. They had been trying for years to have a baby. But as she said, it wasn't *having a baby* that was important to them, it was *raising a child.* The poor girl never had any brothers or sisters, and her mama and daddy had passed on by then. Her husband's family was the same. They wanted a family of their own. Her husband had a lawyer friend. He knew about a young girl about to give birth. The girl wanted to find a family for her baby. It seemed like a miracle for everyone."

I reached across the table and wrapped my hands around Rosie's hand. Thinking and talking about this was filling her with such pain that it filled me with dread. Rosie glanced at Baby Girl and took a deep breath before continuing.

"Last April, their dreams came true when a healthy baby girl was born. They named her Beatrice Virginia, for her two grandmas in heaven. The hospital Beatrice was born in was up by Timber Creek. Coming back home on the highway, there was a horrible accident. A trucker fell asleep driving, and his sixteen-wheeler came across the highway and into the family car. Her husband and baby were killed. The new mama was broken body and soul, and ended up spending a month in the hospital. First thing she did when she got home was to have her help pack up all of the baby things and bring them down to me. I guess it made her too sad to see them. Her body is healing now, but she barely leaves her house and never accepts callers. I send notes to her every week in a prayer basket the preacher sends to her house, but I wish I could do more. John lives up on her property and takes care of the grounds for her. He knows how close we are, and thinks she may be up to seeing me now.

"When I told you those things had just arrived, I wasn't being completely honest. I just hadn't had it in me to open those boxes until you and Georgia walked into the Second Hand Rose."

We sat quiet for a while. Sadness had come over me like a wave blanketing the shore. I didn't even know these folks, yet my heart felt heavy from hearing the story. I could only imagine how hard it was for Rosie to share it with me. When we got up to leave, I gave her a big hug.

When we stopped at the register to pay for our feast, Rosie let out a little squeal. "Will you look at that," she said, pointing at a newspaper clipping hanging over the register. "That man taking pictures at the parade must work for the newspaper. That's you, Georgia, and me! It's a mighty flattering photo, if I do say so myself."

I felt my heart starting to race again as I stared at the clipping. It was surrounded by a half dozen other shots of people celebrating the Fourth. Still, Rosie noticed it right away. How many others would? I tried to force a smile on my face, as Rosie patted my arm and continued to heap on the compliments about the picture. Her comments were drawing attention our way, and I wished the girl behind the register would hurry and finish with us. A few minutes later, I was relieved to be walking out of the establishment.

We made three more stops in the mall. The first one was at an art supply store, where the boy behind the counter was happy to take some time to show me how to use those markers and tell me about all the things I could use them on. Our next stop was at a store that only sold things that cost one dollar. Mama and Daddy would love that place.

Our last stop was Rosie's idea. We walked into a department store so big I couldn't see the other end of it. Polished squares of floor tile formed a path through a jungle of racks packed with clothes. Rosie put her hand on my arm. "You've been working so hard; you've earned a little bonus," she said. "I want you to pick out a couple of new outfits for yourself. It will be my treat."

I started to protest, but Rosie took charge of the stroller and said, "I don't want to hear any arguments. Don't be looking at those price tags, either."

I snaked my way through a few racks, stopping to feel fabric with my fingertips. I was afraid of ruining something I didn't own. "Those clothes won't bite," Rosie said.

I turned in her direction. It looked like the carriage was holding her up. I picked up two tops, a skirt, and a pair of pants and hurried back to Rosie. "These are a great start," Rosie said, "but you're forgetting something."

"What?" I asked, looking at the clothes in my hand.

"Why, a new bathing suit, of course. You can't be going to a pool party without a swimsuit."

"I'm not going to the party. I don't know any of Sarah's friends."

"Nonsense, you need a little time to be you without worrying about little Georgia. You'll get to know her friends at the party.

Don't you worry any. I'll have Dottie come to help me with the baby. You are going to go and have some fun. Now, I see the bathing suits right over there. Let's go."

Her words sounded more like an order than an invitation, so I did as I was told. When I chose a swimsuit, Rosie took all of the clothes from my arms. She insisted on going to the register herself, and came back looking proud of her purchases.

We boarded the bus home feeling tired but satisfied. Both of my companions fell asleep as soon as the bus pulled away from the curb, leaving me alone with my thoughts. Hearing about that awful tragedy made me think about how much I missed Mama and my brothers and sisters. Mama must be taking on so much extra work with me gone. Maybe I should go home before the new baby arrives, I thought.

One look into Baby Girl's peaceful face brought me back to reality. Even if Mama and Daddy took me back in, they would never welcome this little one into their home. I had searched the papers for a sign of her rightful mama since the day I found her. Truth be told, I'd guessed a while back that no one was looking for either one of us. We were a couple of castaways, and Rosie was now the island we called home.

CHAPTER 15

Despite our big shopping adventure, Rosie was up bright and early the next morning. I decided to lay low in the morning to avoid any talk about me going to church with her. I was doing the best I could, but I knew in my heart that my every day was a lie. I couldn't imagine standing next to Rosie in church and still keeping my secrets from her.

I decided to try and push back my guilty feelings by making a batch of muffins for when she got home. I had watched Rosie make them and it seemed simple enough. I started measuring and mixing before realizing I was missing a few of the ingredients. I gave the cupboards and refrigerator a quick tour and picked out a few things to add in place of the missing ingredients. I was soaking in the sweet smell floating from the oven and giving Baby Girl her bath when Rosie walked in the kitchen. "What smells so good?" Rosie asked.

"I made us some muffins," I answered. "They won't be as good as yours, but I hope you like them."

"They smell better than mine," Rosie said, handing me a towel. "I'll take them out of the oven for you while you get Georgia dressed."

When I came back into the kitchen, Rosie was sitting at the table with John. The basket of muffins sat in the middle of the table and Rosie had already poured a round of orange juice. I was busy studying the way the napkins were folded, trying to avoid staring at John, when Rosie said, "John came to take me up to see Lily. I invited him to join us for some of these delicious muffins. It's not every day a young man gets to spend time with a young lady who is pretty and can bake, too."

Rosie can say some of the kindest things my ears ever heard, but she also can turn my face redder than anyone else. It took all my strength to keep from running out of the kitchen and hiding out until John left. John got up, pulled a chair out for me, and nodded.

I sank into the chair, and played with Baby Girl's ringlets until I could catch my breath. When Rosie served the muffins, I stopped thinking about Rosie's comments and started worrying about how the muffins would taste. I was feeling a little less sure of those new ingredients the closer the muffins came to being eaten. Rosie took the first bite. "Mmm mmm," she said. "This time you're going to have to give me the recipe."

I didn't want to admit in front of John, but I couldn't even remember what I put in the batter. When we finished, Rosie asked, "Why don't we bring some of these up to Lily? They sure will sweeten her day."

Before I could even nod, she said, "I know you're nervous about meeting Lily, but I think once you get to know her, you'll love her as much as I do. I'm sending John over to the store to get a baby car seat from the back room. We aren't taking any chances with this little one."

When John returned, he and Rosie had another chat. When they were both nodding their heads, Rosie said, "John is going to bring me up first, then he will come back for you and Georgia."

She didn't say it like a question, so there was nothing to say. I just nodded and followed them out onto the front porch. Baby Girl and I sat out there watching the birds hop from branch to branch on the tree by the road. "Today will be your very first ride in a truck," I said. "It will be a real adventure for you."

My words got me to thinking again about my own adventures list. I closed my eyes and tried real hard to picture the words in my notebook. It had been some time since I had pulled it out and read the list. Back when I first found Baby Girl, I spent time picturing how it would go with Baby Girl as a traveling companion. But it didn't take long for me to know I wasn't prepared for all sorts of things that could go wrong with a baby on the road. I was starting to realize I might never have any of those adventures. I tried to stay far from those thoughts, so I kept the notebook buried in the bottom of a drawer.

The truck's horn pulled me out of my little pity party. John hopped out and hurried up the walkway. He scooped up the car seat with one hand and said, "This should only take a minute."

I didn't need to worry about what to say to John during our ride. Neither one of us could have heard a spoken word over Baby Girl. She did not take to this new mode of transportation as well as I'd hoped. My brothers and sisters had always fallen asleep as soon as the truck hit the gravel. No such luck with Baby Girl. She started howling the minute John turned the key. I sat rocking and wiggling the seat trying to get her to calm down. She cried herself asleep about two minutes before we reached our destination. I had been so busy trying to quiet Baby Girl, I hadn't had a chance to look around yet. John pointed to the house half-hidden by a stone wall and iron gates. Two giant poplars stood guard at the entrance, their arms, heavy with leaves, reaching out to warn strangers away.

John hopped out of the truck and swung the gates open. A bad feeling washed over me when I looked past the gates. I half wanted to grab Baby Girl and run, but I couldn't coax my body into movement. John smiled when he climbed back into the truck. "It isn't half as scary as it looks the first time you see it," he said.

The truck rolled to a stop in front of a pair of doors. They were practically the size of the doors on Daddy's old barn, but a whole lot fancier. John walked us up to the door and rang the bell. A woman opened the door. Her hair was pulled back in a tight bun at the back of her head. She had a look on her face that fell halfway between sad and angry. She wasn't what I was expecting from Rosie's description. I took a deep breath and said, "Good afternoon, Miss Lil . . ."

John put his hand on my shoulder and interrupted. "Mrs. Harper, this is Becky and Georgia. They're here for a visit with Miss Lily."

I hadn't even stepped into the house and I was already embarrassing myself. I followed Mrs. Harper into the front parlor. The drapes on the windows were pulled tight, blocking every sliver of the daylight that filled the outdoors. A single dim lamp was lit. It cast a soft shadow across the room. Rosie sprang from her chair when I walked in. She put her arm around the small of my back and guided me toward the woman sitting by the empty fireplace. At first glance, I wouldn't have guessed there was any kind of problem. She was neatly dressed with matching jewelry and there wasn't a hair out of place on her head. On closer inspection, though, I noticed her pale skin, thin frame, and lifeless blue eyes. Her face had an expression that made me feel like her body was here but her mind was far away. Even though she was seated, she kept one hand draped over a cane that looked like an old-fashioned walking stick.

"Becky, this is Lily," Rosie said, nodding her head in the direction of the chair. "Lily, this is Becky. She's the girl who baked those wonderful muffins and does all the work at the store I told you about. You saw the beautiful window displays she did for Fourth of July. You have to come back into town soon to have a peek for yourself at all of the changes she's made. My words don't do them justice. And this little one in her arms is Georgia. There is more sweetness in this baby than in a whole field of sugar cane. Why don't you hold the baby for a bit?"

Lily's hand had been sweeping back and forth as if to keep us away as Rosie spoke. She shook her head and whispered to me, "Hello."

The hours dragged on like the times I had to stand in front of Daddy while he thought about what punishment was harsh enough to fit my latest crime. Rosie progressed from talking about the weather to church to all the happenings in town. It was as if she feared something awful might happen if she left room for a moment of quiet. Lily looked like she was trying to swallow a sigh. I suspect she was taught not to show her lack of interest in someone else's words. As for me, I sat, spine straight, hoping Lily couldn't hear my stomach growling over Rosie's nonstop chatter. The muffin I'd had for breakfast hadn't filled me up, and my insides were letting that be known. Lily didn't seem to notice, though, as she sat there staring at Baby Girl. When the doorbell rang again and I heard John's voice, I felt like I had been saved.

It was agreed that Georgia and I would go first, but Lily found her voice. "There is no sense in you taking two trips into town, John. Take my car, and they can all leave together."

While John fetched her car from the garage and moved Baby Girl's seat, Rosie ignored the "here's your hat, what's your hurry" we'd just gotten, and filled in the quiet. "Next week, why don't you come down by us for a visit?"

A half smile pushed its way across Lily's face. "Thank you, but I don't think so."

"You give it some thought," Rosie said.

In the car on the way home, Rosie turned toward the back seat and said to me, "Lily was always a song in the wind. She just needs a little time to get back to herself. A little time and a whole lot of us, and she will fill up with life again."

I thought about the sadness I had seen in Lily's eyes. I had never known Rosie to be wrong about a person yet, but I was having a hard time believing she was right about Lily only needing a little time.

CHAPTER 16

July slipped away and August showed no mercy with its heat. People were taking pride in their places on Main Street again, and the once empty sidewalks now hosted a steady stream of shoppers. The thick air was causing everyone to move a little slower than usual; everyone but Georgia. The more she grew the less she slept, leaving me with fewer minutes for creating merchandise for Rosie's customers.

Rosie was spending most of her days sitting behind the counter and most of her nights sitting in front of the television. I attributed Rosie's dwindling pep to the sweltering summer air. I swear some days the temperature got so high even a stone would sweat.

The Second Hand Rose was benefiting from the extra Main Street traffic. And the more sales we had, the more money Rosie put in my pay envelope each week. I sent half of my money back to Mama and Daddy every month, along with some suckers for the little ones. The rest mostly got eaten up by Baby Girl's neverending need for diapers and bigger clothes. But I did manage to save a little, and so on one of the hottest days of the season, I took my savings down to the hardware store and bought two of the strongest electric fans they sold. I set one up by the register to keep Rosie and Georgia cool at work, and I put the other one by Rosie's bedroom door.

One afternoon, I heard a thud coming from the front of the store. I hurried up the aisle and discovered Rosie had thrown a small ball at the door. She was sitting in her chair, cradling Baby

Girl, and waving someone in. As I got closer, I saw Sarah coming up the steps. She opened the door, bent over to scoop up the ball, and said, "Hi! You've got a great aim, ma'am."

Rosie laughed.

"I'm sorry, I don't have your book here," I said. "I left it at home, but I can get it to you."

"Just bring it to my pool party tomorrow night."

I looked down at the floor. "I appreciate the invitation, but I can't go."

Rosie said, "Of course, you can make it. What time would you like her there?"

Sarah looked from Rosie to me and back several times. "Any time after five," she said.

"Perfect," said Rosie. "We will be closing up at four tomorrow, so that gives her plenty of time to get ready."

"Great! Hey, I'm going down to the market to grab a Coke, do you want to walk down with me?"

Rosie reached over to the drawer and pulled out a few dollars. "That's an excellent idea. Becky, why don't you buy a couple for us, too? Georgia and I will entertain each other while you're gone."

Since the last minutes were spent talking about me instead of to me, I shoved the money in my pocket and followed Sarah out without a word.

When we got back, Georgia was in the carriage sleeping and Rosie was in the chair, on her way to dozing off. "That didn't take long," Sarah whispered.

I placed the drink within Rosie's reach and pointed toward the door. We sat on the front steps and sipped the cold, bubbly liquid. "How was your trip?" I asked.

"Fun!" Sarah said. "There's nothing like sleep-away camp to make a girl miss her ordinarily annoying little brother. I actually was glad to see him and spend time with him." She pulled out her phone and showed me pictures of her with her family. They were smiling and laughing and acting silly in the pictures. I tried to picture Mama, Daddy, and my brothers and sisters and me acting like that. I couldn't do it.

"Are you okay?" Sarah asked.

I coughed. "I'm fine, thanks for showing me your pictures."

Sarah stood up and slid the phone into her pocket. "I can't believe school starts in another week," she said. "At least it's always preceded by days of school shopping. New clothes are the best part about going back to school, don't you think?"

I stood up, too, and smiled. I didn't want to tell her stocking up on new clothes was never a part of my back to school routine. I was hoping she wasn't going to ask about me going to school at all this year.

"Gotta run!" Sarah said. "I promised my mother I would go to the store with her to pick up supplies for the party. I'll see you tomorrow."

True to her word, Rosie insisted on closing the store at four the next day. As we made our way out the door, Dottie came out of the Tick Tock and yelled, "I'll be at your house before five."

"It's always good to have an extra pair of hands around with a baby," Rosie said, "but I hope she doesn't think she is going to hog Georgia all night."

The look on Rosie's face reminded me of my brother Thomas. He always wore that face when he was determined to beat one of the bigger boys at a game. I wondered how he was doing without me there to nudge the older ones into giving him a chance at victory.

When we got home, I gave Georgia a bath and fed her. Then I showered and slipped into my bathing suit. As I walked down the hall toward my bedroom to grab a pair of shorts, I heard Georgia fussing. I passed my door and called out, "Is everything okay?"

Dottie was reaching down to the baby seat to pick up Georgia when I got to the living room. She stood back up with her in her arms and started the swaying and patting dance. "Do you want me to take her?" I asked.

Dottie waved me away, but Rosie called out. "Come on in here and let me see you in that new bathing suit. You didn't try on any of those clothes before we bought them. Does it fit?"

I inched my way into the room. "I think it fits well enough," I said while tugging the seat down a bit.

Rosie looked me up and down. "I'd say better than that. You'll have to bat the boys away."

My arms crossed my middle. I could feel myself going red all over. "Now I'm just teasing you, Becky. I know you're a good girl."

I forced a little smile on my face and glanced at Dottie. She didn't look like she agreed with Rosie. "I'm going to put some shorts on. I'll be back in a minute."

As I walked out of the room, I heard Dottie in a half-whisper say, "I'm sorry, Rosie, but that is not the body of a girl who just had a baby."

I stood in front of the mirror looking at myself. This was the first time since coming to Watson's Grove that I'd worn anything but baggy clothes. It was probably the first time since I was twelve I'd worn anything but baggy clothes in front of anyone other than Mama and the little ones. At the store, I had picked the most modest suit I could find. I pulled on the shorts and wondered if I should cover it with a loose T-shirt, too. I had woven a cloak of lies since I'd gotten here, and this bathing suit just might be the loose thread Dottie could tug on to make the whole deceitful cloth unravel. I sat on the edge of the bed. Putting on a shirt now wasn't going to make Dottie unsee whatever it is she saw. It was too late for that. Maybe it was time for Baby Girl and me to move along.

Dottie yelled my name and pulled me from my thoughts. I jumped up and ran to the living room. "What's wrong?" I asked, looking at Baby Girl.

"There's nothing wrong. John is here to drive you to that party. You're bringing a towel with you, aren't you?" Dottie said, nodding toward the door.

I looked at John, who was leaning against the doorjamb. When I turned to face him, he stood up straight. "I can walk there," I said.

Rosie pulled herself up out of her chair. "Nonsense, John's happy to do this. It's a long walk, and you have those brownies you made last night to bring with you. In this heat, they would be chocolate soup by the time you got there. He will go back to fetch you after the party too, so just tell him what time to be there."

Sitting in the front seat of the truck, I could feel John looking at me every few minutes. I just kept staring ahead. When he stopped in front of the house, he said, "You're going to a party, not a funeral. This is supposed to be fun."

I couldn't tell him my current state of being was because my brain was clouded with worries about where Baby Girl and I should go next. I just let him think it was me worrying about a party.

John looked at his watch. "How about I come back between eight-thirty and nine, and if you want to stay later I'll make myself scarce for another hour or two?"

I nodded, even though I had never stayed out to eleven o'clock in my life and I was certain today wasn't going to be the first time. I slid down from the seat, grabbed the plate and towel, and began to walk at snail speed up the driveway. I wasn't even halfway up when I heard whooping and hollering coming from the backyard.

When I was almost to the gate, the girl with the pink stripe in her hair raced by me. She stopped, turned around, and looked at me. "Hey, I know you. You're the girl from the library. I didn't know you were coming." She opened the gate and held it for me.

Sarah ran over to us. "I'm glad you're both here! Mickey, Amy is telling us about a guy she met on her cruise this summer. You have to go listen. The story is so funny! Becky, those brownies look delicious. Let's go put them in the kitchen."

She led me across the patio. "That's my dad," she said, pointing to the man behind the grill. "Dad, this is Becky," she shouted. The man raised a long fork in my direction. I waved back. Her mother was standing at a counter in the kitchen wrapping ears of corn in foil. "Mom, you remember Becky. She brought brownies." She picked one up and took a bite. "They taste as good as they look, too."

Her mother rolled her eyes. "Thank you, Becky. That was very thoughtful of you. I'll put them out later." She looked at Sarah. "Some people actually eat dessert *after* they eat their dinner."

Sarah hugged her mother. "Don't worry, Mom. I'll have one then, too!"

I looked around the room. Every surface glistened in the light. Mama and Daddy would approve. Sarah let go of her mother and grabbed my arm, leading me outside. As I looked around the yard, I wondered if Sarah really thought this crowd was just a few friends. There were about a dozen boys at one end of the pool, trying to get the attention of the girls by acting as silly as my little brothers do when they are down at the pond far from Mama's and Daddy's eyes. The girls were doing their best to look like they were ignoring them. They formed a circle on the patio, some stretched out on lounge chairs, some sitting cross-legged on towels. My worries about being seen in a bathing suit disappeared in a flash. You could cut up my suit and make a half dozen of the tiny suits some of those girls were wearing. Mama and Daddy approving would surely have ended at the kitchen.

We joined the circle of girls. Each of them had a story to tell about their summer vacation. Having never been on a vacation, I had nothing to add, but I enjoyed hearing about all of the places they saw and the things they did. Each of those places deserved a spot in my notebook. When the conversation changed to movies, one of the girls got up and announced she was going for a swim. Several other girls trailed after her. I pulled off my shorts and got into the water, too. A few of the girls sat on the steps, half in and half out of the water. A couple of them floated around in chairs. I swam laps. As I glided back and forth in the water, my brain seemed to escape my worries. When Mrs. Hanson rang a cowbell to call us all to dinner, I realized I was truly hungry. I got out of the pool, wrapped myself in a towel, and joined the others.

The boys huddled around the grill, talking football with Mr. Hanson as they ate. The rest of us sat around a long table. Mickey was sitting next to me, and Amy was on the other side of her. Amy leaned over Mickey and said, "I'm surprised you two are sitting next to each other."

"Why?" I asked.

Amy pointed at a boy standing with the others. "Drew has not been able to take his eyes off you since you went into the pool. Mickey is in love with Drew."

"He doesn't even know me," I said.

Amy laughed. "Don't worry, he'll make sure you know him before the party is over."

Mickey got up and moved to the other end of the table. I stared at my plate. The boys came over to the table when Mrs. Hanson placed the dessert platters in the center of it. The conversation quickly changed to school. Everyone exchanged information on which teacher they had for chemistry, what period they had English, and horror stories they had heard about the history teacher. I sat back and hoped no one would ask me about my schedule.

After dessert, the group splintered. I went back to the pool. It was the one place I felt comfortable. I swam around for a short time, but when a dark cloud rolled overhead I pulled myself up onto the side of the pool. I was still sitting there with my legs in the water when Drew swam up and grabbed hold of the edge, to the right of me. The side of his arm scraped against my thigh. "Hi, I'm Drew," he said. "You're Becky, right?"

I nodded, but before I could speak I heard the *thwack, thwack, thwack* of flip-flops on concrete. I looked up and saw Mickey standing over me. "Oh, Becky, I forgot to ask about your baby earlier. Is she home with the Baby Daddy?"

"What?" said Drew.

Mickey tilted her head. "Didn't Becky tell you about her little family yet? Maybe she has some pictures of her baby she can show you later."

Drew swam to the shallow end of the pool. He whispered to the other boys there, and they all turned and stared at me. I stood up and walked past Mickey. I wrapped my towel around me. A rumble of thunder rolled across the sky. Sarah came over and shouted, "Everybody out of the pool. The party is moving inside. Grab something to carry in on your way."

"I'm going to go home now, Sarah," I said. "Please tell your parents thank you for me."

"No, don't go. The party is just getting started. Besides, you might get stuck in the rain if you leave now."

I shook my head and tried to blink away the tears forming in my eyes. "I really have to go."

Mickey put her hand on my arm. "I hope it wasn't something I said," she said before sauntering away.

Sarah looked at me like I was a lost puppy. "What did she say?"

"It isn't important," I answered.

Sarah chewed on her bottom lip. "Mickey can be a real jerk sometimes, especially if it involves boys. This is my home and you are my guest. I hope you'll stay. I'll talk to her and she won't bother you again."

"It's okay. I really just want to go home."

The gate swung shut. I looked over and saw John standing there. "Are you ready to go?" he asked.

I nodded. Sarah said, "I'm really sorry about whatever happened. We can still be friends though, right? I don't want to lose my book buddy over this. We'll get together soon and talk books."

"Soon," I said. I knew that was just one more lie. Sarah was going back to school and would be spending what free time she had with her school friends. The problem wasn't just Mickey. I didn't fit into that world.

I waited to pull my shorts on until I was in the truck. The thunder gave way to lightning on the way home. I knew Baby Girl was going to need a whole lot of cuddling that night. Both Rosie and Dottie looked real glad to see me when I walked into the house. Georgia, who had no appreciation for Mother Nature's concert, let out an ear-piercing scream after every drum roll.

For the first time since we moved in with Rosie, our nightly routine was broken when Rosie gave in to her need for sleep before I could put Baby Girl down in her crib for the night. It was midnight before the sound of windows rattling was replaced by the steady rush of water through the drainpipes. When I laid Georgia down she felt a little warm to me, but I guessed it was from being held close for hours nonstop.

I had no sooner slid between the sheets than my eyes closed and the rest of the world slipped away. Sleep didn't last long. I knew something was wrong the moment I opened my eyes. The rain had stopped but the room was still dark. A quick glance at the clock told me it would be hours before the sun came up. I was used to waking up to Georgia wailing for a bottle or a clean diaper, but this was different. Instead of a demanding cry, I heard short sputtering puffs of breath. The steady pattern was broken with slow, sad whimpers. I pulled myself out of bed and leaned over the crib. I gently kissed her forehead, trying not to wake her. She was hot to the touch, causing my heart to race.

Back home, I had seen plenty of medical emergencies. There were more broken bones, head bumps, and split knees than any one family should have to endure. But I couldn't recall any of us ever getting sick with fever, so I didn't know how to tend to Georgia now. My first thought was to wake Rosie and ask her what to do. But it was the middle of the night and I didn't want to disturb her only to learn that babies just sleep away their fevers. I rested my backside on the edge of the bed, wrapped my fingers around the crib railing, and leaned forward, pressing my forehead into the slats. I listened to Baby Girl breathe and watched her back rise and fall. When her mournful whimpering grew to a heartbreaking moan, I lifted her from the crib and banged on Rosie's door.

"Rosie, I need you. Georgia's sick."

I heard a click and saw light spread out below her door. The door opened and Rosie came out, squinting into the bright hall light. "What's wrong?" she asked, and reached out to touch Baby Girl's head. "This baby is burning up with fever."

Rosie moved with more determination than I had seen in her in weeks. "This way," she said and headed down the hall to the kitchen. "You get her out of her clothes, and I'll fill the sink."

I did as I was told and a few minutes later, Georgia was soaking in a bath. I scooped water with my free hand and let it run over her. Baby Girl always loves bath time, and kicks and splashes so much that I end up as wet as her. But not this time. Now she lay limp in the water, her arms hanging by her side.

Rosie stood near me. "She didn't want her bottle when we tried to feed her. Did she take one for you?"

"She only took an ounce or two."

"We need to get something in her," Rosie said. "I'll warm a bottle of sugar water while you finish up here."

While I sat rocking Baby Girl and trying to coax some water into her, Rosie called the drugstore. It was only the crack of dawn, so no one was there to answer. Wasting no time, she called the pharmacist at home and demanded he do his civic duty and bring us some baby fever medicine. Less than an hour later, he was knocking on the door.

Getting those medicine drops in Georgia was a bigger struggle than the water. So much of it came dribbling out of her, I couldn't be sure she got the right dose. I spent the rest of the morning rocking, pacing, and trying to get some water into Georgia. When her body started to heat up again, Rosie told me it was time for more medicine and another bath. While I held her in the sink, Rosie examined the bottle to see how much Baby Girl had drank.

Rosie picked up the phone again. "A fever is one thing, but not drinking is something else altogether. It's time to call Doc Richards and have him come over to take a look at Georgia."

I could hardly hold back the tears. Why was Rosie calling a doctor to the house? Even when my brother broke his leg falling from the tractor, Mama and Daddy just tied it up, put him in the back of the truck, and took him into town. The only time I ever heard of a doctor making a house call was when Doc Pritchett went to Old Lady Miller's. They buried her the next day.

What had I done to this little girl? Was that fan too strong for a little one? Why hadn't I found a clinic for her to get shots, the way Mama did with us? Was God punishing her for me being such a bad daughter and a dishonest friend? Maybe Dottie was right to question my ability to care for this sweet child. My tears started to splash into the bath water. Rosie put down the phone and came over and gave me a hug.

“Everything’s going to be all right,” she said. “Babies get sick. It’s a part of growing up. I’ve known Doc Richards his whole life. He’ll have Georgia feeling good as new in no time.”

Rosie went back to the phone. It seemed like the nurse who answered the call didn’t see eye to eye with Rosie. But Rosie didn’t back down. “We will not bring a sick baby out into the world. You tell the doctor who is calling. You remind him that I was his mama’s best friend on Earth, and I still remember changing his diapers. Tell him I expect to see him at my door shortly.”

Rosie hung up the phone and shook her head. “I’m going to have a talk with that boy after he tends to Georgia. No house calls? Whoever heard of such a thing? His daddy always paid us a visit whenever anyone in the house took ill. Young Doc Richards might know more about modern medicine than his daddy, but Old Doc Richards knew more about taking care of people.”

She walked over to the sink and felt the water. “Get Georgia dressed, and try to get some water into her while we wait for him. And Becky, when Doc does get here, I’ll do the talking. That boy always is asking questions.”

Georgia and I barely got settled into the rocking chair when there was a knock at the door. Rosie swung open the front door. A soft voice spoke. “My nurse said there was an emergency. Are you having trouble breathing, Mrs. Perkins? Are you experiencing much pain?”

“I’m fine,” she answered. “That fool nurse of yours doesn’t listen. I told her it’s the baby who’s sick.”

“Baby?”

They walked into the parlor and I got my first look at Doc Richards. He was a tall, thin man who towered over Rosie. His hair was silver, and his face lined with creases and folds. For a moment, I thought the young doctor had sent his father in his place.

"Your mama was your daddy's nurse," Rosie said. "*He* knew how to hire good help."

Doc Richards laughed and gently patted Rosie on the back. "So this is my patient today." He leaned down and lifted Georgia from my arms. "What's her name?"

I started to answer but remembered Rosie's warning so I sealed my lips.

"Her name's Georgia," Rosie answered.

"How old is she?"

"About two and half months."

"When was her last checkup?"

"This is the first time she's been sick. She didn't need a doctor before now."

The doctor looked at me and asked, "You've been here more than a month and you haven't taken the baby to see a doctor yet?" I couldn't control the muscles in my face when the corner of my lips began to twitch. How did he know we had been here for a while? As if he read my mind, Doc Richards said, "There was a picture in the county newspaper of you at the Fourth of July parade. In these parts, that makes you a famous celebrity of sorts." Then he laid Baby Girl on the sofa, sat next to her, and stared at me. "Don't you speak?"

"Of course she speaks," Rosie answered. "She is exhausted from taking care of this little one, so I'm answering your questions so that you get the right answers. You know how flustered a tired mama can get."

Doc stared at me for a minute, and then returned his attention to Rosie. "Has she had any of her shots?"

Rosie looked at me. I shook my head. "Not yet," she said.

"Can you bring me my bag?" he said to me, nodding in the direction of the rocking chair.

I walked over and picked up his bag, and brought it to him. He took Georgia's temperature and checked her over from head to toe, all the time asking questions. Finally, he handed her to me and walked into the kitchen. When he returned, he told us that he had called down to the pharmacy and that someone would be dropping off some medicine for Georgia. He said she had an ear infection and she would feel better in a day or two.

"Keep giving her that medicine until it's all gone. Try to feed her a little something every hour until her appetite returns. We want to keep fluids in her. And promise me that you'll bring her in for a checkup next week." He closed his bag and stood up straight. "As a matter of fact, why don't you both come in next Wednesday? You are overdue for a checkup too, Mrs. Perkins."

Rosie started to protest, but Doc Richards put up his hand. "No arguments," he said. "I'll have my nurse give you a call with the time. And be nice to her, Mrs. Perkins. She works very hard."

We spent the next few days at home. I took care of Georgia. Rosie took care of Georgia and me. After that first trip out to see Lily, we had taken to having weekly visits with her. Each trip seemed like the first. When words did pass through Lily's lips, they always seemed to be in regard to Baby Girl and my apparent inability to tend to her properly. *Is that baby drinking enough? Is she drinking too much? The summer sun is awful hot; I do hope you're making sure she's wearing a proper hat outdoors.* Her tone let me know what words she was leaving unsaid. Rosie always tried to change the subject quickly, but once a bee stings you can't just rub the hurt away.

When Sunday rolled around, Rosie decided it was too soon for Baby Girl to be out and about, so she called up to Lily's to let her know we wouldn't be around for our weekly visit. I did my best to convince Rosie she could go without me, but truth be told I was relieved when she didn't take me up on it.

I was more than a little surprised when Lily showed up on our doorstep. John had driven her into town, and Lily had insisted they stop by the store to make sure everything was as it should be. He had noticed a letter wedged between the door and the jamb of the Second Hand Rose and gave it to Lily to pass along.

"John thought it might be important," Lily said as she handed the folded paper to Rosie. "I had heard the doctor had paid you a call, so when you phoned to say you weren't coming, I was concerned. How are you feeling?"

Rosie raised an eyebrow.

"I wouldn't be surprised to learn everyone in town knew about Doc Richards's house call, but I didn't think it would travel all the way out to you. No need for concern, though; it was Georgia who was in need of a doctor, not me, and she is on the mend now."

Rosie guided Lily to a kitchen chair. I looked at the paper in Rosie's hand. I was curious about its contents, but didn't want it to show in front of Lily. Rosie made a show out of carefully folding the paper back up and tucking it into her housecoat pocket for safekeeping.

"If the baby was sick, why didn't you call her pediatrician? Why call Dr. Richards?" Lily asked.

"She doesn't have her own doctor," I said.

Lily turned and stared at me long and hard. I wished I could pull back my words. I walked over to the refrigerator, took out a pitcher of lemonade, and placed it on the table in front of Rosie along with three glasses. "Is the paper important?" I asked, trying to change the subject.

"Nothing that can't wait until we're ready to go back to work," Rosie answered, as she poured the lemonade. "Why don't you put out a plate of cookies, too?"

I brought the treats to the table and began babbling on about them, but Lily was set on her subject and wouldn't be distracted from it. "Why doesn't she have her own doctor? It's best to use a specialist for children," Lily said.

"Now, Lily, Doc Richards took care of you growing up and look at how fine you turned out," Rosie said, patting Lily's arm.

The look on Lily's face softened a bit. "So he has been giving Georgia her checkups and shots?"

"Not yet, but he'll get started on that soon." Then, before Lily could get another word in, Rosie launched into the Hollywood version of the story of Baby Girl's illness. Of course in Rosie's version, I starred as Florence Nightingale. I was about to correct Rosie when Baby Girl started to cry. I was happy to hear her sad little moan was back to a demanding ear-piercing howl. I excused myself and went to rescue her from her crib.

Rosie and Lily had their heads together when I returned to the kitchen, and the discussion seemed less than friendly. When I heard Lily whisper Doc Richards's name, I stopped in my place and stood there trying not to make a sound.

"All I'm saying is that if that girl is old enough to have a baby then she's old enough to know," Lily said.

"Age has nothing to do with my decision. I'll decide when the time is right," Rosie answered.

And that was when they noticed me standing there in the doorway. They both turned and stared at me in silence. I felt like I had just walked into a crowd with my skirt tucked in my pantyhose. Even unintentional eavesdropping is shameful behavior.

The three of us stared at each other for what seemed like forever. Baby Girl broke the silence when she let out a happy coo. "Well, look who's here," Lily said. She stood up and walked over with her one arm outstretched. "I'll take her. Becky, please go write down the information about Rosie and Georgia's checkups. I'll be sending John down to take you, so there is no chance of you missing the appointments."

I tightened my hold on Baby Girl and looked at Rosie. Lily never made any attempt at holding Baby Girl, so I wasn't entirely comfortable with the situation. I looked down at her cane and chewed my bottom lip.

"I'll sit down," Lily said.

I glanced at Rosie. She nodded, so I placed Georgia in Lily's arms. I stood there watching for a minute, half expecting Baby Girl to kick up a fuss about being in a stranger's arms. "She's fine," Lily said. "Please get me the information I asked for." I reached for a pencil and a pad of paper.

"Thank you," Lily said as she started swaying back and forth with Georgia. "This little girl is ready to take on the world. Why, look at how bright her eyes are and how pink her little cheeks look. I really don't think the store is the proper place for a baby to be spending her days, though."

I reached over and pulled Baby Girl from Lily's arms and shoved the note in her hands. "There's the information you want," I said.

Baby Girl squeaked at being pulled from her comfortable resting spot. I buried my face in her curls. Rosie got up and said, "Her mama takes good care of our little Georgia, no matter where she is."

Lily gathered her things and headed for the front door. "Regular checkups are important for a baby," Lily began. "Make sure you make appointments for all of her shots and visits, and give the information to John. He'll see to it that you arrive at the appointments on time."

I watched Rosie close the door behind Lily. The last thing I wanted was to talk about my eavesdropping, so I was ready with words when Rosie turned around. "I think Lily is right about Georgia looking like her old self, and Doc Richards said she would be good as new by now. Besides, I don't want you missing out on any more business because of us." I stopped for a split second to catch my breath. "Was the letter Lily brought from a customer needing something from the Second Hand Rose? I could go down there today by myself if that would be helpful."

Rosie put her hand up like a traffic cop before I could rattle on any longer. "Slow down, Becky," she said. "Nobody's going anywhere today. The letter is from a woman looking for you to help her with a christening gown. A bunch of moths had a party with the family heirloom and the new mama wants you to try to repair it somehow. If that's something you want to take on, then I can give her a call from here and have her bring the gown in when we decide to go back to work."

"I can call her," I offered. "That way I can get a better idea of what she's looking for and whether or not I can do it."

"Suit yourself," Rosie answered. She pulled the letter from her pocket. "Lily has a good heart, Becky; I know her words seem harsh sometimes, but she only wants what's best for us."

I took the letter in my right hand and shifted Georgia to my hip. The first thing I noticed on the letter was the date. The woman left the letter two days ago. "I better call now, before she finds someone else to do the work," I said.

"I wouldn't worry too much about that," Rosie said. "Did you read the whole note? She got your name from somebody at a Mommy and Me class. They were talking about your stitch work on the baby clothes. What kind of mama needs to go to a Mommy and Me class? What do they do there, anyway?"

I smiled and shrugged. Rosie was catching my bad habit of rambling on when her nerves got rattled. I picked up the phone and dialed.

Rosie stood in front of the sink pretending to not listen to my conversation. When I placed the phone back on the cradle, I said, "She'll drop by the store in the morning. I hope I can fix it in time for the christening. If not, this baby will be the first child in five generations of that family not to be christened in the family gown."

"A christening is a very important thing in a person's life," Rosie said. "To be wrapped in family roots during it is extra-special. I hope you can help them."

That night as I lay in bed, I wondered about the conversation I had walked in on. What did Lily think I was old enough to know? I didn't doubt for a second that she would be criticizing me. I pushed my thoughts as far out of my mind as I could. Tomorrow was a workday and I needed my rest. The last thought that stirred in my brain wasn't about Lily or Rosie. It was about Doc Richards and his comment on the photo in the newspaper. Thinking about how many people might have seen us in the paper made me feel like a storm was brewing, and I needed to find a safe shelter before it hit.

CHAPTER 17

The sun shone extra bright the next morning. At least that's how it felt when I walked outside for the first time in days. There were none of the usual hellos as we walked down Main Street. Rosie thought it wise for us to go in early and air out the Second Hand Rose before the customers started arriving. When Rosie swung the front door open a full hour early that day, I knew that once again she was right. The hot musty air rolled out at us, and Rosie and I sounded like we were having a sneezing contest.

Despite our early start, Mrs. Jeanie Applewood arrived at the store shortly after we opened. She was carrying her brand new baby in one arm and a cardboard box in the other. A young man paced back and forth on the sidewalk in front of the store with a cell phone pressed to his ear. I took him to be Mr. Applewood.

Mrs. Applewood shoved the box at me. "This is it," she said. "The gown. The christening gown. The christening gown that has been in my husband's family forever. The one my mother-in-law bestowed upon me the day we returned from our honeymoon. The one I stuck up in the attic, because I didn't appreciate her interfering. Not that she interferes—she would be the first one to tell you that she never does that. And not that I'm judging, because I'm really not the kind of person who jumps to judgments. It's just that . . . Can you fix it?"

Mrs. Applewood looked more nervous than a bird in a roomful of cats. I opened the box and examined the gown. The Applewood's attic was home to one hungry batch of moths. When I looked up Mrs. Applewood was pacing the floor in step with her husband pacing outside.

"Well?" she asked. "Is there any hope?"

Rosie walked over and stood beside the woman. I think she wanted to be ready to catch the baby in case I said the gown was a lost cause.

I pointed to the paper taped to the cover of the box. "Do you know if this is a list of everyone who wore this gown?" I asked.

Mrs. Applewood nodded. "The Applewoods are very organized people. I'm sure the list is complete."

"Well, I can't make it look like it used to look, but I can try something a little different," I said. The poor woman looked like she was about to melt into a puddle on the floor, so I started talking faster. "I could cover the holes with embroidery. I could stitch the name and baptism date of everyone on the list onto the gown. I'll stitch your baby's name on it, too. It will look like you wanted to do something special for the family. No one will ever have to know about the little moth problem."

Mrs. Applewood bit her bottom lip. Her eyes filled with tears. Rosie put her arm around her. "Can you imagine how impressed your dear, sweet mother-in-law will be when she sees the gown? The history of the whole family will be a permanent part of that dress. And you can always come back and have the names of any future Applewood members stitched onto it, too."

Mrs. Applewood sniffled. "Mother Applewood will love the idea," she said.

"And she will love you for doing this," Rosie said.

I held baby Chloe while Rosie took care of the business end. Chloe felt light as a feather compared to Georgia. I brought her over to Georgia's carriage and let Baby Girl have a peek. Baby Girl looked so big compared to the baby I was holding that I doubted she would still fit into a christening gown.

I waved to the Applewoods as they drove away. I decided to do a little housekeeping around the store before starting in on the gown. I pulled out a dust rag and got to work.

"Becky, I can do that. You need to get to work on your stitching," Rosie called out without lifting herself from her seat.

I walked back up the aisle and looked at Rosie. The day I met her, she moved up the aisle like a steam engine chugging down the tracks. Today, less than three months later, she reminded me of a car on its last drops of gas. My chest ached with worry that living with Georgia and I was the cause of this change. When Rosie leaned forward and tried to pull herself up, I said, "You just sit there and keep an eye on Georgia. Cleaning frees my mind and it will give me a chance to think through this project. I can bring the gown home with me to work on, and I have a few days to finish."

After lunch, I opened the box again to take another look at the gown. The white thread I had would look too bright against the fabric. "I need to go down and see Lydie about some floss for this project. I'll take this with me," I said folding the dress back into the box. "And I'll bring Georgia along. I think she would like to go for a little stroll in the sunshine."

"Tell Lydie I said hi," Rosie said. She turned her chair slightly, so she could soak in some of the warm sunshine that poured through the window.

I explained my project to Lydie when I got to Needles and Notions. She looked at the gown and found the perfect floss. It was the color the dress would be, if a tea bag had been allowed to steep a little longer. And it had a shimmery finish that made it pop out against the gauze-like cloth. Lydie was impressed by my idea for the project, and I felt myself getting excited just talking with her about it.

"Becky, I'd be happy to put a sign up right here in the Needles and Notions advertising your services. You would enjoy more business, and I would enjoy having more business from you," Lydie said.

I was flattered, but I was pretty sure Rosie would not like the idea. "I have all the business I can handle over at Second Hand Rose. Thanks for offering, though."

I waved to Rosie when I reached the sidewalk in front of the store, but she didn't wave back. That worried me a little so I picked up the pace and was huffing and puffing by the time Georgia and I got back inside. A customer stood at the counter with a pile of would-be purchases in front of her. Rosie was slumped in her chair, sound asleep.

"I hope you haven't been waiting too long," I said.

The lady jumped a little. I think she had been staring so hard at Rosie, trying to will her awake, that she hadn't noticed Georgia's and my arrival. I wrote up a receipt and helped carry her bags to her car. When I came back in I contemplated waking Rosie, but decided instead to push the stroller over next to Rosie's chair and let the two ladies nap together. I settled into the chair and threaded my needle.

Baby Girl woke first and served as Rosie's alarm clock. Rosie seemed a little confused by the time. "You shouldn't have let me sleep so long," she snapped.

I chose my words carefully. "It has been quiet in here all afternoon. I was thinking that maybe we could close up early today."

"Why, of course, Becky. We can close early. You and Georgia must be tuckered out from your first day back. I told you we shouldn't rush back to work," Rosie said. "I'm sorry if I seemed a little impatient with you a minute ago."

"No need for an apology," I said.

We got about halfway down the block when Rosie stopped. "I forgot to pick up something to make for dinner. I checked the freezer this morning and there was nothing to defrost," she said.

"We have plenty of leftovers. Why don't I heat them all up? It will be like buffet night at the Tick Tock," I suggested.

After dinner, I played with Georgia until it was her bedtime. She was looking lively again and enjoyed the attention. Rosie turned in right after I put Georgia in her crib, and I got back to work on the gown. By the time I turned out the lights, I had stitched a third of the way through the list.

The next morning, the phone was ringing when we walked into the Second Hand Rose. Rosie hustled behind the counter and opened the drawer where she kept the phone tucked away. By the time she accomplished this, the phone stopped ringing.

"What's wrong with people today? Why place a call if you don't have the patience to wait for an answer?" Rosie complained. She closed the drawer and walked over to flip the sign on the door from "closed" to "open."

The phone started ringing again. "I'll get it," I said. I didn't want Rosie rushing across the room again.

Mrs. Applewood was on the other end of the line. I explained to her that I was making good progress, but that I wasn't done yet. "Don't you worry. It will be ready by Saturday afternoon, like we agreed," I said.

"I said Saturday because the christening is this Sunday, but now my mother-in-law is coming up on Saturday to make sure I'm doing everything right. I just know she will want to see the dress," Mrs. Applewood said, her voice rising with every word.

I could practically see her crying through the phone line. "Then we will have to make sure the work is done before she comes visiting," I said. "You go take care of your baby, and I'll take care of the dress. I'll call you as soon as it's done."

I told Rosie about Mrs. Applewood's predicament and we agreed that I would stitch all day while she took care of the customers. By afternoon, I was two-thirds through the list and Rosie was tuckered out. She sat in her chair and asked me to bring Georgia over to her. I had noticed about a month ago that Rosie no longer held Baby Girl when she was standing. I guessed it was because Georgia was growing so fast; she was getting too heavy for Rosie to lift.

When I got them settled, I went back to my stitching. Watching them together made me smile. Georgia had quite a personality now, and the two of them always seemed to share a secret joke. When they both showed signs of needing a nap, I took a break and gave Baby Girl a bottle and a lullaby before putting her down for a rest. Rosie dozed off before Georgia. I sat for a few minutes, watching the two of them sleep before getting back to work. I hoped Mrs. Applewood was enjoying a moment like this in her day.

At closing time, the phone rang again. Two calls in one day must have been some kind of record, since the phone rang so rarely that I worked there for two months without even knowing there was a phone.

"I can guess who that is calling," Rosie said. "Do you want me to talk to her?"

"I'll get it," I answered.

Once again, I told Mrs. Applewood not to worry and that I would call as soon as I finished. She was starting to get me worrying and thinking about all of the things that could go wrong. I double-checked to make sure I had plenty of floss to finish the project without needing an extra trip to Needles and Notions. Rosie volunteered to go up to the market, so I wouldn't lose any stitching time. I considered the offer, but figured my eyes and fingers needed a break before a night of sewing.

When we got home, Rosie made dinner while I fed Georgia and gave her a bath. Rosie volunteered to tend to her after dinner, so I got right to work. It was after midnight when I slid my needle through the fabric for the last time. I was tempted to give Mrs. Applewood a call right then and there.

I know Mama always said it was a sin to be prideful, but I admit to taking a few minutes to admire my handiwork the next morning. Georgia was still asleep, so I gently laid the gown on top of her. Rosie walked in at that very moment. "Doesn't she look like the angel she is," Rosie said. "I've wanted to bring up having her christened at my church, but I was afraid you wouldn't approve. You never want to come to church with me on Sunday mornings. Now that I know we're of one mind, I'll go ahead and speak to the reverend about it."

For the first time in my life, I was so nervous I couldn't speak. Christenings meant paperwork and questions. Questions I couldn't answer truthfully, or didn't want to answer truthfully. And a christening is *permanent.* Since finding Baby Girl, everything I did was *for now.* I changed her diapers *for now.* I named her Georgia *for now.* But a christening is *forever.* I would have to stand before God and promise to always help Baby Girl follow His path. I didn't have the right to make *forever* choices for this baby.

Before I could correct Rosie, Baby Girl woke up. I put the gown back in its box and took care of her. By the time we left for work, Rosie had created a to-do list and was trying to decide whether she should call the reverend or stop by to see him.

I had called Mrs. Applewood from the house before we left, and she was waiting at the door when we got to the store. As soon as we got inside, I took the box from the basket and laid it on the counter. I expected her to rip into it like a kid at Christmas, but instead she just stared at it. It was like she was afraid of what might be inside. I lifted the lid and pulled the gown from the box.

Mrs. Applewood let out a quiet gasp. "It's beautiful," she said, running the tip of her finger over the fabric where Chloe's name was stitched. "It's perfect." And then she started to cry.

Rosie had her arm around her and a tissue in her hand in no time at all. I folded the dress back into the box and tried to avoid Mrs. Applewood's eyes. I had never been around such a teary person before, and I didn't know how to help. A half hour later, the woman walked out of the store clutching the box and smiling from ear to ear. "Thank you again," she said. "And please let me know if I can help you in any way with your baby's christening. I owe you so much; I would welcome any opportunity to repay your kindness."

I stood there with a gaping mouth. I guess Rosie was already getting the word out.

"Becky, would you mind tending the store on your own for a little bit? I'm going to pay the reverend a visit. I'll be back with lunch," Rosie said. She walked out the door without giving me a chance to answer.

I watched her walk down the block. She had a real bounce to her step again, but I felt like I was teetering on the edge of a cliff. I knew in my heart, the only way to stop this christening was to confess to all of my lies. Tugging on that thread might unravel the cloth that held the three of us together. I couldn't take that chance.

"Well, Baby Girl, it looks like you are going to be baptized."

CHAPTER 18

It was half past noon, and my empty stomach seemed to be taking control of me. I should have been taking advantage of Georgia's nap to do some dusting. Instead, I was sitting and staring out the window at the front door of the Tick Tock Diner. A couple of times my mouth actually watered when I saw someone leaving with a carryout bag. My insides jumped a little when I saw a familiar face coming out of the diner. John raised his hand in a kind of salute, shading his eyes. He squinted a little and then smiled, nodded, and waved in my direction. I hoped he couldn't see the blood rushing to my cheeks. I gave a quick wave back and got busy with my dust rag.

It was two o'clock in the afternoon before I caught sight of Rosie again. Staying true to her word, she walked through the door toting a bag from the Tick Tock. My stomach growled as she laid out grilled cheese and tomato sandwiches and a couple of cold root beers. She was smiling from ear to ear.

"It's all set," she said. "The christening will be a week from Sunday. You need to fill out a couple of forms for the reverend."

I could feel the blood rush from my head as I choked down a bite of my sandwich.

"Now, don't you worry about anything. The forms are simple, baby's name, place of birth, that sort of thing. And I'll take care of the rest," Rosie said.

"The rest?" I asked.

"I'll take care of the party and the christening outfit. I've already started inviting folks, and on Saturday we can take the bus to the mall to buy whatever we need," Rosie said.

I should have told her not to go to such a fuss, but my mind was stuck on those forms. Rosie must have taken the look of worry on my face as meaning something else. She said, "Of course, I don't need to make all of the decisions. Why don't you make a guest list, too? Put anyone you think I might miss on there. How about your friend, Sarah? I haven't seen her around since school started. Am I working you so hard you don't have time for friends anymore?"

I rubbed an imaginary stain off the floor. "I have time for everything I want to be doing," I said.

Rosie must have sensed my yearning to end that conversation, because she quickly changed gears. "And we need to find a pretty dress for you to wear, too, Becky. Don't you worry any. It will be my treat," Rosie said. Then she sat down and took a big bite out of her sandwich. "I worked up an appetite this morning."

Rosie didn't leave out as much as a sneeze when she gave me a report of her visit with the reverend. I heard the words coming out of her, but I wasn't listening. I was too busy trying to come up with answers to fill in the blanks on those forms. Rosie didn't seem to pick up on my strange, silent behavior. Thoughts and ideas were shooting out of her like fireworks. One simple little statement, like "We'll need plenty of food," burst into dozens more about what kind of food, where we would put the food, what to serve the food on, and so on and so on. I don't think I could have gotten a word into the conversation, even if I was so inclined.

Georgia was a little fussy that night. I think she picked up on my feelings. The two of us sat curled up on a chair in the front parlor. I had spent much of my afternoon trying to convince myself that there would be a way for me to fill out the reverend's forms without outright lying. But sitting there with Rosie across from us made me realize that lying to a stranger wasn't my problem. It wasn't even God that I feared. I figured He knew I was doing my best to keep Baby Girl safe. It was knowing that I hadn't shown Rosie the respect of telling the truth that filled me with shame.

Baby Girl let out a little sigh that was a sure sign she was giving in to sleep. I thought about putting her to bed, but decided I felt braver with her in my arms. Besides, what I was about to confess I was saying for both of us.

"Rosie, I have to tell you something," I said. "I should have told you all of this a long time ago. You've been so good to Georgia and me. And I haven't been completely honest with you. I can't let you go through all this trouble with the christening without you knowing the truth. I can't stand in a church with all these lies between us."

Rosie set her teacup on the table and leaned in closer. "What kind of lies?"

"About who we are, and where we came from. About how we ended up at the Second Hand Rose," I said.

"None of that's important," Rosie whispered.

"Yes, it is," I said. "Didn't you ever wonder why I never mention family?"

"Becky, we are family," Rosie said. "You and Georgia becoming a part of my life was providence. And if there is one thing I've learned in my eighty-eight years on Earth, it is to never question your blessings. Accept them, appreciate them, be thankful for them, but don't ever question them. I don't care about your past; it's the here and now that's important to me."

I wiped away the tears rolling down my cheeks and gulped in some air.

"And if all these tears have come about because I got a little carried away with the notion of a christening, then we can put a stop to that right now," Rosie said. "But remember, Becky, God knows all of our pasts and He welcomes us into His home all the same."

I looked down at Georgia sleeping in my arms. Maybe Rosie was right about this being providence. When I left Mama and Daddy's house, I never would have guessed the twist and turns my life was about to take. Georgia needed me. I needed Rosie. And in a way, Rosie needed the both of us. "No," I said. "I don't want you to stop. Georgia should have a christening. I'm the bad one."

"You're no such thing," Rosie said. "Why, you don't have a bad bone in you. And you don't owe anyone an explanation. You aren't looking to learn all about my past, are you?"

I shook my head no.

"Then put this little angel to bed," Rosie said. "And let's not talk any more about this. I know all I need to know about the two of you. I know that you walking into the Second Hand Rose was one of the best things that happened in my life. Now, let's get Georgia tucked in for the night. We've got a party to plan."

I knew Rosie couldn't know the truth about us, but when I looked into her eyes it felt like she did. It felt like she knew all of our secrets, all of my wrongs, and it didn't matter. She loved us as much because of it as despite it.

CHAPTER 19

Rosie must have planned a lot of parties in her lifetime. She knew exactly what we needed and where to get it. Best of all, she knew how to have fun while doing it. The only thing that didn't seem to go her way was our trip to the mall.

We found the perfect christening gown in the Beautiful Baby Boutique. It was the softest white cotton with tiny white flowers embroidered all over it. It had a matching cap that the salesgirl kept mentioning as being able to convert into a wedding day hanky. For the life of me, I couldn't imagine why anyone would be thinking about their baby's wedding day when they were planning a christening. There also was a tiny pair of white shoes to match, but Georgia's feet were already too big for them. Rosie tried to use that fact to bargain down the price of the set.

At the Second Hand Rose every price tag is an 'about.' Rosie taught me to answer a customer with, "That's about twenty dollars." If the customer thinks the price is too high then we emphasize the 'about' and work down from there. When we saw the price of the christening set, Rosie was ready to bargain. Unfortunately, the salesclerk was not familiar with this way of doing business.

"How about if we deduct the cost of those shoes," Rosie said. "Since we all know that Georgia can't wear them, it makes no sense for us to buy them."

The salesclerk looked at us as if we were a cup of spoiled milk. "They are part of the ensemble," she said. "I can't sell you only part of an ensemble. Who would buy the shoes without the outfit?"

That evening when I got Georgia tucked in that night, I said, "Rosie, if you don't need anything, I'm going to bed now too."

Rosie looked up at me and said, "I don't want you giving a second thought to the price we paid for that christening gown. We bought an heirloom today, not a dress. It will get passed down from Georgia to her children and grandchildren. It was just the lack of practicality of those shoes and the salesclerk's snippy ways that got my feathers ruffled."

I nodded and said, "Honestly, Rosie, if you want to return it, I understand. Georgia will look beautiful no matter what we dress her in."

Rosie hesitated before saying, "We're keeping the dress. I don't want to upset you any, but I think you and Georgia should come to church with me tomorrow. After services, we can give the reverend the forms you filled out."

I was too ashamed to tell her I hadn't filled out the forms yet, so I nodded in agreement. I closed the door behind Rosie and pulled the papers from the drawer of my bedside table. I stretched out and started writing. It was easy enough to fill out her name without feeling like I was lying. As far as I knew, the only name she had was the one I had given her. The date of birth was a little bit harder. I decided on June 24, the day our life together began. I could feel my body tightening up when I got to the place of birth line. Everyone knew we weren't from around Watson's Grove, and I didn't think telling them my own home town was a good idea. I was stuck on that answer for quite some time before settling on Freedom, South Carolina. When I finished with the rest of the questions, I placed the papers on my nightstand and rolled onto my back. I was trying to picture Georgia in her christening dress, but all I could see was me boarding a bus. I was sure lying to a preacher was the same as buying a bus ticket on the direct line to hell.

Even though we got an early start, almost every seat in the church was full when we arrived the next morning. We found a place in the front row, which made me as nervous as the turkeys must be with Thanksgiving right around the corner. Rosie watched me fidget for a few minutes before whispering, "Do you need to use the ladies' room?"

"No," I whispered back, hoping no one else had heard her question.

Reverend Thompson is a lot younger than I had imagined him to be, and I found myself taking more notice of his eyes than his sermon. There was something real familiar about them that I couldn't put my finger on. Realizing that concentrating more on a preacher's looks than his words might be another big sin, I decided to redirect my attention. I looked over Rosie's shoulder at the songbook and sang with the choir.

When the service ended, the whole congregation moved from the church to the basement. A group of ladies had thrown aprons on over their church dresses and were already busy serving coffee and juice. Long tables were covered with muffins, breads, and pastries. I spotted a number of familiar faces, some I could put names to, some I couldn't.

"There's the reverend," Rosie said, pointing across the room. She grabbed my elbow and steered me through the crowd.

I let Rosie do all the talking when we caught up with the reverend. I couldn't help but stare at him. I was trying so hard to place him in my mind that I lost track of the conversation. The next thing I knew Rosie was digging her elbow into my ribs and the reverend was standing there with his hand out. I reached out and shook it. The reverend looked bewildered.

"Becky," Rosie said. "Reverend Thompson is waiting for you to give him the papers."

When I handed over the papers, the reverend skimmed them. He opened his mouth, but before the first word came out, Rosie interrupted. "I'm sure you'll find everything in order," she said. "And as someone who has been a member of this church longer than you've been alive, I want to thank you for all you do to welcome new members into our church family."

The reverend opened and closed his mouth several times and then just seemed to give up on whatever he had planned to say. He smiled and nodded.

Rosie said, "We've been hogging all your time. We'll move along now, so you can say good morning to everyone."

"Yes," the reverend said. "It was good to meet you. I look forward to the baptism next week. I hope to see you all here every Sunday."

When we left church, Rosie said, "Now that you're coming to church with me, there is no one home baking us muffins. How about we go by the house to meet up with John, and then we hurry on over to the Tick Tock for breakfast before going to visit Lily?"

CHAPTER 20

The next week flew by. I woke up at five on the morning of the christening, fed Georgia, and put her back down for another couple of hours of sleep. I was too wound up to sleep myself, so I slipped on my jeans and a T-shirt and tiptoed past Rosie's room into the kitchen. I was about to put the kettle on when something caught my eye outside the window. I leaned over the sink and looked into the yard. Green and white striped fabric was stretched across four poles. Underneath the canopy, John was setting up folding tables and chairs.

I slipped out the back door, trying to not wake anyone inside. I hadn't taken the time to put on shoes, and the grass was wet with the morning dew. I forgot my discomfort as soon as John turned and flashed me a smile.

"You sure are here early," I said.

John shrugged. "I wanted to get this done before Rosie woke up. Otherwise, she would give me more directions than I would want to hear. I hope I didn't wake you."

"No, I was up with the baby. She's asleep again, but I decided to stay up. Can I help you?" I asked, hoping I didn't sound too eager.

John smiled again. "I don't know if Rosie would like that," he said.

"Rosie is asleep," I said. "Besides, if you want this all done before she wakes up, the work will go a lot quicker with two of us doing it."

I didn't wait for an answer. I picked up a pair of chairs and set them up at a table. We worked in silence for a while. When all of the tables and chairs were up, John said, "I'll be right back."

He returned carrying a sack full of tablecloths. As we spread the cloths open on the tables, I asked, "Is working for Rosie your only job?"

"No," he answered. "Remember, I work for Miss Lily, too. And I go to college part-time."

"You go to college?" I asked. "Is there a college in Watson's Grove?"

John laughed. "This little town doesn't have a college. Heck, it doesn't even have a high school. I drive forty-five minutes out to Barton every Tuesday and Thursday for classes. I even take one class at home on my computer. I'm studying to be an engineer," he answered. "How about you? The only thing I see in your hands more often than a book is your baby. Are you planning to go to college when she gets a little bigger? Heck, if you can talk Rosie into getting a computer, you can take a class online now when the baby is sleeping."

I could feel myself turning red, so I looked down and studied my toes. Taking a college course would require two things of me: a high school diploma and time. I still had another year of high school to finish, and if there was one thing lacking in my new life, it was free time.

"How old are you?" John asked.

"I'm sixteen. I'll be seventeen next Tuesday," I said. As soon as the words passed through my lips I was full of regrets for saying them. The less that people knew about Georgia and me, the safer we were. But like I said before, I have a real weakness for good-looking boys, and I don't always act with reason around them.

"Then you probably haven't even finished high school yet," John said.

I raised my eyes to table level and scanned the yard. "It looks like we're done here," I said, trying to end the conversation.

"Not quite," John said. "I'll get the rest from my truck."

I thought of taking this as my chance to escape. I looked at the back door, but before I could act on my thoughts John was back with a carton full of heavy glass bowls filled with pink and white carnations. He took the bowls out one at a time, wiped away any spilled water with a small towel, and handed the bowl to me. I placed the centerpieces on the tables. When we were finished, I stood by the kitchen door and looked at what we'd created. It took my breath away. I don't think I'd ever seen anything so perfect.

"I'll be going now," John said. "You have a great day."

"Thanks," I said. I sat on the concrete steps leading up to the door and peeled wet blades of grass from my feet. I wasn't about to traipse grass onto Rosie's clean floor.

John smiled, bowed, and said, "Allow me." He pulled the towel out of his back pocket and wiped off my feet. When he was finished, he gave my foot a little squeeze and said, "All done."

I felt like my insides were exploding. I sat on the step with my hand wrapped round my foot where John had held it and watched him walk out of the yard. I closed my eyes and listened to his truck engine roar and fade as he pulled away from the front of the house. I was in the exact same place and position when Rosie opened the door.

"There you are," she said. "I peeked in your room and saw an empty bed. I wondered what you were up to."

My behind was numb from the concrete, so I stood up slowly. "Doesn't it look like something out of the movies?" I asked.

Rosie smiled. "It looks like a slice of heaven," she said. "But we better start getting ready. Georgia will be up soon, so why don't you take your shower first."

Baby Girl woke up happy while I was dressing. She was content to lie in her crib studying her fingers and toes while I finished. I put my robe on over my dress while I got Georgia ready. I had enough stains on my clothes to know better than to wear a new dress while feeding her. When it was time to leave for the church, I pulled off my robe and slipped the christening dress onto Georgia.

Rosie and I took a few minutes to admire her. That was when Rosie noticed what I had added to the gown. Just above the hem, I had embroidered *Georgia Rose* and today's date. Rosie ran her finger over it and hugged me.

As I stood in the church holding Georgia with Rosie right beside me, I thought about how it seemed like most of my life had happened in the past five months. When Reverend Thompson christened Baby Girl as Georgia Rose, it felt right.

The backyard was filled by the time we got home from church. Rosie must have invited everyone who worked on Main Street. I realized our guests were more a tribute to their affection for Rosie than for us, but I was overwhelmed by the sight of them just the same.

Dottie and Ray were busy arranging food on a couple of long tables on the far side of the yard. Lydie, who had somehow beat us home from the church, was telling everyone what a perfect angel Georgia had been. Pete Garcia was setting up a music system toward the back of the yard. I was about to point out the dancing potential to Rosie when someone popped up and shouted, "They're here!"

In a heartbeat, we were surrounded by our guests. The commotion was too much for Georgia, so she let out a wail.

"Back up, everybody," Rosie yelled. "You're frightening the baby. Let's give these ladies a little room. We'll be here all day. Everyone will get a chance to see them."

The crowd behaved exactly as I had come to expect whenever Rosie gave an order: they did as they were told. Rosie and Georgia and I made the rounds. At each table someone would comment on Georgia's beautiful dress. I would tell them that Rosie was spoiling the baby with such extravagances. Rosie would follow with, "There's nothing too good for our Georgia Rose. Did you know that we both have Rose for our middle name?"

About half the way through the tables, I suggested Rosie take a rest. She had been on her feet all day and I was worried about her. But Rosie wouldn't hear of it, so we turned to the next table. I was surprised to see the Applewoods sitting there. "Hello, Mrs. Applewood, thank you for coming," I said.

"Please, stop calling me Mrs. Applewood. I'm Jeanie and this is my husband, Donald. You never formally met him, did you? Donald, this is Rosie and Becky. And this little beauty is Georgia."

Rosie interrupted, "Georgia Rose."

Mrs. Applewood smiled and nodded. "Georgia Rose," she repeated. "I know she and Chloe will be great friends growing up."

Mr. Applewood looked like someone had forced his feet into a pair of too small shoes. I caught sight of the toe of Mrs. Applewood's pump smashing into Mr. Applewood's shin. He stood three quarters of the way up and gave us a little bow. He said, "I'm happy to meet you. My wife has been more excited about your baby's baptism than she was about ours. I appreciate the help you gave her with Chloe's christening gown."

Mrs. Applewood frowned. "It's not that I wasn't excited about Chloe's big day. It's that I had too much to worry about." She turned her attention back to me. "After you eat," she said, "I'll help you with your gifts. I'll record everything as you open it along with the name of the giver, so it will be easier for you to write thank-you notes."

It hadn't occurred to me that folks would have brought Georgia gifts. I looked around and saw a long table overflowing with wrapped packages.

"Thank you, Jeanie. I appreciate your offer," I said. "I'll see you later."

After we visited the last table, I suggested Rosie sit down and eat while I fed and changed Georgia.

I left Rosie in Dottie's hands and went into the house to take care of Georgia. Dottie was just managing to get Rosie seated at a table when I returned. About three bites into dinner, someone suggested it was time to open the gifts and dragged a chair in front of the table. Jeanie Applewood came bouncing over to us.

"Whenever you're ready, everything is set up for you," she said. "Would Rosie like to hand you each gift to open?"

"I need some more lemonade," I said, draining my cup dry. "Have you tried the lemonade yet, Jeanie? Why don't you come over with me and try a glass?" I put Georgia in Rosie's arms. It was the one way I knew to make Rosie stay put. "We'll be right back," I said.

I waved Dottie down to the lemonade and the three of us stood there with our heads together. "I need help from both of you," I said. "Rosie has been going all day. I think she must be sorely in need of some rest. Jeanie, can you have someone put up another chair for Rosie? And Dottie, Jeanie will record everything to keep us organized. Could you bring the gifts to be unwrapped? I don't want Rosie getting up and down so many times."

Dottie looked like she had been crowned queen for the day. I think for a moment she forgot it was me she was helping. Then a cloud crossed her face. "What will Rosie say about this? She won't be happy having a job taken away from her."

Dottie, of course, was right. "I'll tell her I need her to do a much more important job. She'll be holding the belle of the ball, so everyone can see Georgia," I said.

Rosie was happy with my plan and settled into the center seat, holding her arms out until I deposited Baby Girl in them. Rosie reacted to every gift I opened in a similar way. "That dress will look mighty pretty on our Georgia Rose. Georgia Rose can never have too many bibs. Georgia Rose is going to love that doll."

She said Georgia Rose so many times that I knew I had made the right decision filling in that blank on the reverend's forms. I was surprised by how generous our guests had been. It made me feel good to know so many people went out of their way for us. The look on Rosie's face made me feel even better.

Rosie and I stood by the gate saying goodbye to our guests. Dottie, Ray, and Pete walked up together. "We are your clean up committee," Ray said. "Where would you like us to get started?"

"You'll do no such thing," Rosie said. "John is coming back to take care of everything."

"Where was John today?" Pete asked.

"He had something to do for the reverend this afternoon," Rosie said. "But he was at the church this morning."

Dottie wasn't wasting time waiting for directions or Rosie's permission to clean. She had an armful of gifts and was heading for the kitchen door. I ran over to help her and everyone else followed me. In no time at all, the kitchen table was covered in tiny little dresses, sippy cups, and toys. Pete lugged in Baby Girl's brand new highchair. When the chair was settled and the last of the leftovers were wrapped, the doorbell rang. I hurried to answer it, and was surprised to once again see Lily at the door.

My stomach churned at the sight. I knew Rosie had all but begged her to come to the christening, and I had seen the disappointment in her eyes when Lily didn't show. To me, showing up after the party was like rubbing salt in the wound. Lily didn't wait for me to invite her in; she just sailed past me and into the kitchen, scraping my ankle with her cane as she passed. My attitude toward her softened a bit when I saw Rosie's eyes light up.

The kitchen quieted when one by one our guests noticed the new arrival. Lily handed Rosie a small wrapped box and said, "I don't want to interrupt your party. I just wanted to drop off this gift."

"This isn't the party," Rosie laughed. "This is the clean-up! I thank you for coming, but you should be giving this to Becky."

I unwrapped the gift, a silver rattle with Georgia's name engraved on it, and thanked her for her kindness. A hush dropped over the kitchen again, until Pete suggested we call it a night.

"Pete, thank you so much for the music today," I said. "Everyone was tapping their toes."

"You can't have a party without music," he answered. "I plan to have plenty of music at my Thanksgiving celebration. I hope your family will join us. It won't be much of a celebration without you, Rosie, and little Georgia Rose."

I was too busy swimming in the words "your family" to answer. Rosie didn't waste a minute though. "Of course we'll come. Thank you for inviting us."

Pete turned to Lily and said, "Of course, Miss Lily, you're welcome too."

Lily nodded, but said nothing. The crowd started moving toward the kitchen door. Dottie paused and hugged Rosie, and then she did an amazing thing. She reached out and hugged me—a real hug, not one of those polite hugs you see on television. "Thanks for letting me be a part of things today," she said.

When the last guest had left the yard, I left Rosie alone with Lily. Baby Girl was tuckered out from her big day, so I got her ready for bed and put her in her crib. Lily followed Rosie into our bedroom and watched as Rosie gave Baby Girl a kiss good night. For a moment, I thought Lily was going to do the same, but instead she reached into the crib and gently stroked Baby Girl's hair and back. Rosie seemed to get real comfort from seeing Lily with Georgia, but I didn't share those peaceful feelings.

I said my good night to Baby Girl after Rosie and Lily left the room. By the time I came out Lily was gone, and Rosie had settled into her favorite chair and turned on an old movie. I offered to make her a cup of tea. I put the kettle on and stared out the kitchen window. I wondered if John was coming back for the tables and chairs before it got too dark out there. I brought Rosie her tea, but by the time I got to the front parlor she was sound asleep in her chair. I turned down the television and covered her with an afghan.

I went back to my room and stretched out across my bed. I pulled my notebook and pen from the door and wrote a letter to Mama.

Dear Mama,
I've been sending Daddy money every week for the barn, but I've failed to keep you up on my life. I got a job and have been working real hard at it. I miss school, but know I will go back some day. I've met some special people, Mama. I know you will love them as much as I do, if you'll give them a chance. I miss you and the kids. Is the new baby a boy or a girl? Does Daddy talk about me ever? Is he hoping I'll come home soon? I've done some things that are too hard to put in a letter. But I want you to know that I try hard every day to live in a way that will make you and Daddy proud. I'll write again soon and maybe I will find the right ways to tell you about the special people I mentioned.
Love,
Becky

I folded the paper in thirds and slipped it inside an envelope. I addressed the envelope and for the first time put Rosie's address in the left corner. Tomorrow, I would walk to the post office and send it on its way.

CHAPTER 21

Rosie suggested we skip work and catch up on our rest the next day. The offer was mighty tempting, but with Thanksgiving only a few days away, there was too much work to be done. I convinced Rosie to stay home and let me work by telling her I was finishing the decorations for the store's Christmas tree, and I wanted them to be a surprise for her.

The folks on Main Street had decided they were tired of waving the white flag in the battle to bring in shoppers. The time had come for them to give the malls a little competition for some holiday customers. On Wednesday, Pete and a couple of other guys would set a bare tree in front of each business on Main Street, and every shop would decorate their own tree. On the Friday and Saturday following Thanksgiving, customers could vote for their favorite tree. I didn't know if it really would bring in more customers, but I was having fun making the decorations.

It worried me some when Rosie didn't even put up a fight the next morning when I suggested she stay home again. I decided I would come home at lunch to check on her and make sure she ate something.

It was my birthday and I was expecting it to pass without notice, since I hadn't told Rosie about it. When I walked onto the front porch at lunchtime, I was surprised to see a package waiting for me. I sat on a rocker and opened it right away. It was a book and a note. *Happy birthday, Becky! Study hard and let me know when you're ready for the exams. I'll drive you there myself. —John*

I looked at the cover of the book—*Everything You Need to Know to Pass the High School Equivalency Exam.* I was feeling so many different things all at once that I couldn't see straight. I sat there for a minute, deciding whether to be angry at his interference or grateful for his concern.

Georgia tired of waiting for her lunch and leaned forward, smacking me hard on the knee with her new silver rattle. I rubbed my knee. "I can't wait till you have your words to tell me what you want," I said. She laughed and flung the rattle at my head. I caught it mid-air and stuck it in my bag. "I'll have none of that, little lady. I knew you were too big for a rattle. We'll just put this away in your keepsake box."

I stuffed the book and note into my bag, too. I didn't want to explain anything to Rosie at the moment. When we went in the house, Rosie was dozing in her chair. Georgia babbled our hellos and woke Rosie. "Is it closing time already?" she asked.

"It's lunchtime, Rosie. We came home to have lunch with you," I said.

"Oh, dear," Rosie said as she struggled to lift herself from the chair. "I haven't made lunch."

"You stay right where you are. Georgia has been missing you all morning," I said. "How about you sit here with her, while I heat some soup for us? There's a chill in the air today."

"I can feel it in my bones," Rosie said, sinking back into her seat. She stretched out her arms and said, "Bring her to me. Maybe she can give me some clues about that tree you're decorating."

I laughed and set Baby Girl on her lap. "I'm not worried about that. This little one isn't giving any secrets away."

"Don't be so sure," Rosie kidded. "We have our own way of communicating. We don't need conversation."

Looking at the two of them together made any bad feeling I still had from finding the book from John on the porch disappear.

Rosie was right. They did have a special way of communicating. Baby Girl was growing strong, and when she sat in my lap she never stopped moving. But when she settled into Rosie's lap she was real quiet and calm, as if she knew Rosie's body wasn't as strong as her spirit. I left them playing peek-a-boo, and went to warm our soup.

When Georgia and I got back to the store, I settled her in for a nap. I had seen a piece on the news a few days earlier about the vintage rage. According to the reporter, buying pretty much anything vintage was a big thing. She'd showed old clothes, furniture, jewelry, and knickknacks. I'd been thinking about that story since then. I was sure there were plenty of vintage items at the Second Hand Rose. I looked around the store, trying to decide what items could be called vintage instead of just plain old used. I was concentrating so hard on my task that I didn't notice the door opening behind me. A cough startled me out of my thoughts. I turned around and saw John standing there.

"Happy birthday, Becky," he said.

It's amazing how good those words can feel when you're not expecting to hear them. "Thank you."

John took a couple of steps closer to me and handed me a bouquet of flowers. "I decided a school book probably wasn't the best birthday gift. I hope you know, though, I gave it to you because I believe you can do it. Anyway, I hope you like these."

Now, I know I should have taken this opportunity to let John know I wouldn't have appreciated that book any day of the year. I should have made it clear I just wanted him to forget what I had told him. Standing that close to him made it impossible for me to have any harsh feelings or words, though. Instead, I took the flowers, and before I even knew what I was doing I was hugging him. The next thing I knew he was hugging me back, and instead of being embarrassed by my behavior I was feeling like I could stand there past closing time.

It was John that let go first and took a couple of steps back. "I might have crushed your flowers there," he said.

I looked down at the bouquet. "They still look beautiful to me."

John smiled and shoved his hands in his pockets. "I need to get back to work. Enjoy your special day, Becky."

I looked out the window until John's truck was too far down the street for me to see. Then I found a vase for the flowers and put them on the counter. No one had ever given me flowers before. I wasn't the kind of girl people made a big fuss for. I pulled a daisy from the vase, then got some tissue paper and the biggest book I could find on the shelves. I put the flower in the paper and slipped it into the middle of the book. I put the book under the counter. I don't like taking Rosie's merchandise off the sales tables, but I wanted to save this moment forever. Besides, it wasn't like I was expecting a truckload of people in there looking for a chipped vase and an old copy of the unabridged dictionary.

The next day, Dottie watched me open without Rosie for the third day that week, and she could not contain her curiosity any longer. I hadn't even gotten Baby Girl's coat off when Dottie came through the door. "Where's Rosie been?" she asked.

"She's a little worn out from the christening," I said. "So she's taking a little vacation time to catch up on her rest."

"Does that mean we won't be seeing you girls at Pete's house for Thanksgiving dinner?" Dottie asked.

"We'll be there. I offered to make dinner at home, but Rosie wouldn't hear of us backing out of his invitation," I said. "I think she's looking forward to seeing somebody other than Georgia and me." I laughed.

"Ray is afraid Pete will skip the turkey and make us a Mexican feast," Dottie said. "I had to put my foot down to keep him from bringing a turkey with us."

"I don't think it will matter to Rosie what he serves," I said. "She hasn't had much of an appetite lately."

"Maybe all she needs is some good cooking," Dottie said. "I see you go home at lunchtime. I'll bring you over some of Ray's famous chicken and dumplings to take home with you. That will stir Rosie's appetite."

I forced a smile on my face and thanked her for her offer. I could feel a little steam building up inside of me. On the one hand, it was real nice of her to want to help Rosie. On the other hand, she didn't need to insult me doing it. I still wasn't a great cook, but I'd picked up a few things from Rosie over the past months and I was capable of cooking a decent meal.

Before Dottie left, she stroked one of the flowers in the vase. "These are mighty pretty," she said.

"Yes, they are," I said. I walked past her and opened the door. I wasn't about to give her a chance to ask any questions about their origin. Dottie's questions always seemed like mice in a kitchen. You know as soon as you spot one, there's a dozen more just waiting to pop out and scurry across the floor. "Thanks again for your offer to help. I'll see you at lunchtime."

When she left, I got busy with work. By the time lunch rolled around, I had decided to take after Rosie and concentrate on the good in people, not the bad. I reminded myself about how kind Dottie had been to me at the christening. When Dottie came across the street with a big bag of food, my thank you was genuine.

I met up with the mailman at the bottom of the porch stairs. He stooped over to say hi to Georgia; she is a beautiful baby and not many people can pass her by without wanting a closer peek. When he stood up, he handed me a stack of envelopes and wished me a happy Thanksgiving.

There was a letter addressed to me on the top of the stack. There was no return address, but I recognized the writing as belonging to Daddy. Looking at that envelope filled me up. I had hoped to hear from Mama for my birthday. It would be like a gift—forgiveness wrapped in an envelope. When my birthday came and went without a word from home, I laughed at myself for being afraid to let them know where I was all this time. Even giving them the address didn't land them on Rosie's doorstep. But the envelope with my name on it filled me with some kind of expectation. I couldn't tell if it was excitement or dread. "Now don't be silly," I reminded myself. "Mama and Daddy never were much for letter writing, and Daddy was always economical with postage. It is just like them to send a letter right between my birthday and Thanksgiving, so they can send me all kinds of good wishes for the cost of one stamp." I stuffed the letter in my pocket, picked up Georgia and the food, and practically danced into the house.

Rosie was up and moving that day. "I was going to start lunch," she said.

"No need," I answered. "Dottie sent a treat home with me. Chicken and dumplings," I said, pulling the container from the bag. "And for dessert, some apple cobbler."

We sat down and dug into lunch. I was happy to see Rosie eating some today instead of just rearranging the food on her plate. She asked for a scoop of ice cream to go with the cobbler, but I noticed her slipping more of it into Georgia's mouth than her own. She seemed a little unwilling to be left behind when it was time for Georgia and I to leave. I reminded her of how disappointed Pete Garcia would be if we had to cancel at the last minute. She decided to stay home and bake some apple and cranberry breads to bring to the dinner.

As soon as I got Baby Girl settled in for her nap, I pulled out Daddy's letter. I couldn't wait a moment longer to read all the news from home. I unfolded the white sheet of paper. Daddy didn't waste words.

Dear Becky,
No need for you to write anymore. The barn is paid for.
Yours truly,
Joseph W. Miller

I can't even tell you how long I sat there staring at those words. The next thing I knew, Georgia was crying to be picked up from her nap. I held Baby Girl tight and paced a bit. Then I crumpled that letter and threw it in the trash.

I closed a few minutes early that day and stopped at the diner on the way home. "Thanks so much for lunch," I said. "Rosie cleaned her plate for the first time in days."

Dottie smiled from ear to ear. "I didn't think she would be able to resist Ray's chicken and dumplings," she said. She leaned in closer, lowering her voice. "He's not much to look at, but that man sure can cook."

Not knowing how to respond to that, I sort of half smiled. "I want to ask for a little more help from you and Ray," I began.

Dottie draped her arm around my shoulders. "Of course you do. A young girl like you can't handle all this responsibility. What do you need, darling?" The words rolled out of her like syrup sliding down a stack of pancakes.

I reminded myself this was for Rosie. "I was wondering if you would be willing to come by tomorrow and pick up Rosie on your way to Pete's. She's had a chill for days now, so I think the November air might not be the best thing for her," I explained.

"No problem," Dottie said. "We'll come around about noon to pick the three of you up."

My desire to get out from under Dottie's grip was strong, so I just gave another half smile. "Thanks," I said, separating myself from her. "Rosie is looking forward to tomorrow."

I don't know if it was the extra rest or the big lunch that restored her energy, but Rosie talked on and on through supper.

She wanted an accounting of everybody who passed through the Second Hand Rose door. By the time we moved into the front parlor for the evening, she was trying to decide what items would sell best for Christmas.

"Rosie," I said. "I noticed a sewing machine on the shelf, so I tried it out and it works."

"Of course it works," Rosie said. "Why would I sell a machine that didn't work?"

My mind immediately made a list of the many broken items in the store, but I decided to keep it to myself. "I was wondering if you would mind if I used the machine to make some tree skirts and stockings, and maybe even some doll clothes," I said.

"Where are we going to get the material for those things?" Rosie asked. "Lydie might carry some, but we probably would have to go back to the mall. I wish you would have thought of this the last time we went to there. It's too crowded for me after Thanksgiving."

"I was thinking we wouldn't need to buy fabric," I said. "What if I cut up some of the clothes and ties that haven't been selling anyway? I went through the store this morning and found quite a few things that would work."

"You are too clever for me," Rosie laughed. "I said it before and I'll say it again. The day you two walked into my store was the luckiest day of my life. You use anything you see fit. I won't stand in the way of the family artist."

"We are the lucky ones," I said, and got up to get Georgia ready for bed.

After we got the baby tucked in for the night, Rosie went off to bed, too. I decided to watch a movie on the television, but my mind was too cluttered to follow the story. I gave up and slid into bed, but no matter how heavy my eyelids got, I couldn't fall asleep. I'd thrown Daddy's note away, but his words were etched in my brain. I had spent most of my growing up years helping out at home. Maybe that's why Mama and Daddy seemed to see my leaving as losing a hired hand instead of missing a daughter.

CHAPTER 22

I opened my eyes the next morning and looked over at the clock on my bedside table. When the time, nine-fifteen, registered in my brain, I bolted upright. I had never slept this late before. Why hadn't Baby Girl demanded attention before now? I looked into the crib and there she was holding onto her feet and rolling from side to side with this big old toothless grin on her face. I stood there watching for a few minutes and laughing at myself for being such a worrywart. When the ammonia smell drifted up from her diaper, playtime was over.

"Good morning, sleepyheads," Rosie said as we walked into the kitchen. "I thought I heard you up and moving, so I started breakfast. I made us something substantial today just in case dinner is a long way off."

I put Georgia in her baby seat and set the table. "I need to stop by the store for just one minute this morning," I said. "Dottie and Ray are going to come by and drive you over to Pete's. Georgia and I will meet you there."

"You'll do no such thing," said Rosie. "Today is a holiday. We don't do business on holidays."

"I'm not opening the store," I explained. "I just have to pick something up. I made a little gift for Pete to thank him for inviting us today. I forgot it at the store yesterday. It will only take me a minute. Georgia and I will probably beat you over to Pete's."

Georgia and I set out for the store about a half hour before Dottie and Ray were expected at the house. This turned out to be the perfect timing. I walked up to Pete's house just as Ray pulled his car into the driveway. When I saw Ray get out from behind the wheel dressed in a suit and tie, I was glad I had worn my good dress.

Back home, we didn't dress up for the holiday. All work on the farm stopped by breakfast on Thanksgiving Day. This, of course, left the whole family packed into our tiny house. Things tended to get ugly fast, and by mid-morning Daddy would send anyone not able to help with the cooking out into the fields to do their whooping and hollering. Jeans and coveralls were more suited for a Miller Thanksgiving than dresses and suits.

I put the basket on the hood of Ray's car so we could arrange the breads inside of it. I was almost too busy concentrating on how pretty that basket looked to notice the corsages Rosie and Dottie were wearing. They were the kind of thing though that once they caught your eye, you just couldn't look away, no matter how hard you tried. Each corsage was an arrangement of red, yellow, and orange flowers and ribbons. Each one was bigger than Baby Girl's head. I stood there staring at them, speechless.

"Don't you worry," Ray said, smiling. "We didn't forget you." He opened his trunk and pulled out a white cardboard box.

I looked at the box, picturing one side of my chest collapsing under the weight of one those corsages. I gulped and prepared my thanks. "You shouldn't have," I said.

"Nonsense. Ray buys me a corsage every year. Your day shouldn't be any less special than mine. I hope you don't mind that your corsage is a little different from ours," Dottie said. "But I didn't think you would want to be wearing a straight pin while carrying the baby."

I let out my breath and smiled, probably more than I should have. "I don't mind at all," I said. "I think it was real thoughtful of you to consider Georgia's comfort and safety." I opened the lid of the box.

"Let me help you with that," Ray said. He lifted the corsage from the box and slid the gold elastic band over my hand. Flowers stretched from my wrist to my elbow.

"Thank you," I said. I'm ashamed to admit that my feelings of appreciation were overshadowed by my trying to figure out how long I had to wear that little garden before finding an excuse to plant it back in the box.

Pete did the holiday justice, giving us all plenty to be thankful for that day. When he brought out the desserts, Rosie asked if everyone could wait a bit before indulging our sweet tooth. "Lily promised me she would stop by for dessert," she explained.

She had barely gotten the words out of her mouth when the doorbell rang. Pete came back into the dining room with Lily and John in tow. His arms were filled with another basket of goodies. He put down the basket and pulled another chair over to the table, so Lily could sit beside Rosie. Ray stood up and said, "We have room for you down here, John," he said, placing a chair beside mine and winking in my direction.

I wanted to disappear into the rug below me. I wondered if there was anyone in town who didn't know John had caught my eye. I was grateful when Dottie started a conversation at the other end of the table. I stayed quiet, and I noticed Lily did too. Much as Dottie tried, she couldn't coax more than a few polite phrases from Lily's lips. After we enjoyed enough desserts to last us until Christmas, Ray stood up and stretched.

"You give one hell of a party, Pete," Ray said. He rubbed his stomach. "That was some spread you put out. I hate to be the wet blanket, but it's time for me to call it a night. I have to get up extra early tomorrow to get a jump on all those shoppers. If I don't keep pouring coffee in them, they might be too tired to keep on shopping." He laughed and bowed to Rosie. "I hope you don't mind us leaving a little early, Rosie."

Rosie accepted his arm and allowed him to lift her to her feet. Dottie was standing by with their coats. I dressed Baby Girl for the trip home, thanked Pete, and leaned over the stroller.

"I think it would be easier to get the carriage in the car without Georgia in it," Pete laughed.

"We're going to walk back," I explained.

"Not tonight," Pete said. "It's dark and it's raining out there. You can't be walking in this. You ladies stay in here, and Ray and I will get the carriage in the car."

"We don't have a car seat with us," I explained.

"The carriage doubles as a car seat, but there's no need to bother with that," Lily interrupted, placing her hand on the carriage.

I was about to speak my piece, when Lily added, "We have a car seat in our car. We can take them home."

Without another word, John folded the carriage, thanked Pete, and went to put the carriage in the trunk. There was a wild exchange of hugs between us all before John returned. I noticed no one gave Lily their usual bear hug. Instead, they treated her like an expensive and fragile china doll.

Once we got to the car, Lily took command. She settled Rosie into one side of the back seat while I buckled Baby Girl into her seat. Then Lily motioned to me to get into the front seat, while she took the position next to Baby Girl. When Baby Girl started fussing, I wished I had spoken up and taken the back seat. Lily asked John to turn on the sound system. At first I thought, she was using a too fancy name for a radio, but when John pushed the button the car filled with a symphony. "That should soothe her," Lily said.

I wanted to correct her, but within two minutes Baby Girl let out a contented sigh.

When we arrived home, Rosie kept thanking Lily for coming and John for making sure she came. I used the wet weather as an excuse to cut the love fest short and to get Baby Girl inside.

Georgia had a hard time falling asleep that night. The truth be told, as great a job as Pete did that day, Baby Girl was the real center of attention. She had been passed from one set of arms to the next all day. She had been bounced, tickled, sung to, and sniffed a hundred times. She wasn't ready to give up the spotlight for bed.

I went to my room and picked up a picture book that I brought home from the library. Rosie almost laughed her teeth out when she saw me bringing books home for Baby Girl. She may be right about Georgia being too young to understand a story, but my reading them soothed and calmed her as well as any music could. I settled us into the rocker and began reading. By the time I turned the last page, Baby Girl was in a place where I could put her down for the night, and Rosie was fast asleep.

After I settled Baby Girl into her crib, I decided to stop by Rosie's room. In all the months we've lived here, I'd never stepped to the other side of her door. But the night before Rosie had gone to bed with the parlor afghan still wrapped around her, and I was afraid she might catch a chill dozing out in her chair without it.

Even my good intentions couldn't keep a bad feeling from creeping over me as I passed through the doorway. It felt like the time when I was in second grade on our field trip to the museum. Mary Louise Horton was scared to death of the mummy they had laying out there. I wanted to show her there was nothing to be afraid of, so I slipped under that big red velvet rope and touched that mummy with both of my hands. It gave me chills, but I didn't want Mary Louise to know that. Before I could even finish saying, "See, Mary Louise. There's nothing to be afraid of," I felt my teacher, Mrs. Lincoln, gripping my right shoulder and the museum guide in the navy blue suit grabbing my left. I spent the rest of the afternoon sitting in the museum office while Mary Louise and the rest of the class finished the tour. To top it off, Mrs. Lincoln wrote my parents a letter telling them how disappointed she was in my behavior. Daddy said I had shamed the whole family.

I only tell you that so you will understand why, even though I had a perfectly good reason for entering Rosie's room, I failed to cross the room and answer the phone ringing on Rosie's bedside table. Instead, I ran out of the room and down the hall to the kitchen phone.

The voice on the other end belonged to Rosie's granddaughter. I woke Rosie and while she chatted on the phone, I sat there thinking. This was the first time I had ever spoken to Rosie's granddaughter, but she didn't even ask who I was or what I was doing answering the phone. I wondered how often they had spoken about me. I wondered if Rosie didn't want me to know what she had to say. I closed my eyes and pictured the black phone sitting on Rosie's bedside table and realized that she probably talked to lots of folks on the phone without me knowing. She wasn't keeping secrets; it was just a convenience.

And then, as it so often happens in my brain, one worrying thought brought me to another. When I closed my eyes and pictured that phone ringing, I saw something else. On the bedside table, right next to the phone, were about a dozen caramel-colored tubes with white labels stuck on them. I closed my eyes and tried to see them again. I guess I was really hoping to *not* see them again. But there they were, medicine bottles lined up like soldiers guarding Rosie's bed.

Rosie came down the hall. "I'm going to pop in your room to say good night to Georgia Rose," she said. When Rosie came out again, she said, "Our little angel is already asleep and I think it's time for me to join her."

I wanted to ask Rosie about the amber tubes on her nightstand. I wanted her to tell me everything was all right. But the words didn't come out of me. Instead, I got up and hugged her tight.

"Now what did I do to deserve that?" Rosie asked, smiling.

"I love you, Rosie," I said. "I couldn't love you more if you were my blood relation. I don't know what would have become of Georgia Rose and me if it hadn't been for you."

Rosie looked up at me and placed her hand on my cheek. Then, without a word, she turned and walked off to her room. I went to the kitchen and put the kettle on for a cup of tea. I thought about the hodgepodge of feelings I'd had in the past weeks. I thought about how I felt holding Baby Girl at her christening. I thought about how I felt when I read Daddy's letter. I thought about how I felt hugging Rosie and realizing that she needed me to take care of her now. I had stopped looking for my name in the paper months ago. I had stopped looking for news about Baby Girl and her real mama. I would never understand how someone could leave her baby the way Baby Girl was left, but it didn't matter to me anymore. Instead, I worried that someone, having recognized Baby Girl's picture in the paper, would spot us on the street and tell the whole world about us. Baby Girl and I were two castaways when we met on that train, but that was behind us. I was Baby Girl's mama now. This was our home. This was our family. It was time to stop looking back, and start looking forward.

CHAPTER 23

I tiptoed through the house the next morning. There was a tree waiting to be trimmed and a window waiting to be changed at the Second Hand Rose. If I wanted to get both of those jobs done before opening time, I needed to get moving extra early. If things worked out the way folks downtown were hoping, the stores would be packed with shoppers getting ready for Christmas. I thought Rosie should sleep in since today was an extra-long workday. I hoped that she might even decide to take the day off rather than walk into town by herself. So I tried to slip out unnoticed—not an easy task when you're in the company of a little girl who has come to love the sound of her own voice.

It had taken me longer to remove the last traces of Thanksgiving from the front of the store than I had anticipated. Folks were walking Main Street with their tree ballots before I finished dressing the window for Christmas. I don't mean to brag, but I do believe I outdid myself with that window. I had found a battery-operated truck in the store and rigged it so it would travel through the little village I was building. I put a little Santa doll and a decorated tree in the back of the truck. I had done my best to copy Main Street. The village had a used bike shop, a miniature Needles and Notions shop, and a tiny little diner. Of course, in the middle of it all was a miniature Second Hand Rose. Someone tapped on the glass, and I turned to see a small crowd standing on the walk watching me at work. I smiled and waved, and the people waved back. Nobody moved on. I felt like a fish in a bowl—a fish on all fours with her behind facing the glass. I repositioned myself so as not to spoil anyone's holiday spirit with the sight of my backside.

Working at that angle went a little slower and I was starting to resent my audience. It gave me a great view of the curb, though, so when I heard John's truck I was able to watch him without being too obvious. Back and forth he went, trying to squeeze his big truck into the little space left in front of the store. He must be part magician, because he got it in there with only inches between his bumpers and the cars that bookended his truck. I heard his door bang shut through my glass wall and watched as he inched, tightrope-style, across his back bumper to get to the sidewalk.

My insides started to race like the time in the sixth grade when I was waiting for Mrs. Purdy to announce the winner of the Harvest Composition Contest. When John hopped down from the bumper and turned to walk up the block, my heart sank into my stomach as fast as when Mrs. Purdy had called Billy Wagner's name. But John didn't go far. He stopped, opened the passenger door of his truck, and reached up to help someone out. Rosie was his passenger, and she waved him away once her feet were on solid ground. He ignored her signal and followed her up the steps.

My heart started thumping against my chest. I scolded myself for having such a reaction. "Don't be silly," I whispered under my breath. "He isn't here for you. He's helping Rosie out." I stood up and waved goodbye to the window watchers. They applauded, so I smiled and took a bow. I thought about how Daddy would have reacted to my boastful behavior. It made me grateful he wasn't there.

Rosie passed through the door that John had reached ahead to open for her. "Now, I told you once already," she said, "just because I asked you for a ride doesn't mean I need you following me around like a guard dog all day."

John laughed. "I'm not following you around, Rosie," he said. "Your store has become famous in this town for its fancy window displays. It's a little slippery out there, and I didn't want your window dresser getting hurt climbing a ladder by herself." He looked at me and said, "You are planning to put lights up outside, aren't you?"

I smiled and nodded.

John turned back to Rosie. "There you go," he said. "You wouldn't want your best employee getting hurt on the job, would you?"

"Just don't you forget that there is nothing wrong with my eyes," Rosie answered. "I'll be sitting right here, keeping an eye on you."

Rosie's words were harsh, but I saw the corners of her lips and eyes curl upward. John carried the ladder, and I carried the lights out. I struggled with the choice of letting him climb the ladder and hang the lights his way, or me climbing the ladder and hanging them my way. I decided I would rather live with his work than with him having the same view of my behind I had treated all of Main Street to earlier.

John suggested we put the lights on a timer to save on the electric bill. I knew Rosie would favor that plan, but I had no idea what a timer was or if we had one. John grinned and said, "I've got one in my truck you can borrow."

I wondered what kind of person drove around with one of those contraptions in his truck, but I held my tongue. When he finished setting up the timer and showing us how to use it, he suggested I walk him to his truck. Baby Girl was fussing a bit, so I hesitated.

"You go ahead," Rosie said. "You'll only be a minute, and I'll keep Georgia Rose happy until you get back." She looked at John. "And remember, I still have two good eyes, so don't you get fresh out there."

I turned redder than a Santa suit. "Now, don't you mind my teasing, Becky. John knows I'm only kidding," Rosie said.

I'm not sure what I was expecting, but I was disappointed when we got to the curb. John turned and said, "I can come back to pick Rosie up so she doesn't have to walk home. What time should I come by?"

"Why didn't you ask Rosie that?" I asked.

Now it was John's turn to feel uncomfortable. He dug his hands into his jean pockets and rocked back and forth on his heels. "If I ask her, she will tell me not to come," he said. "I figured you can talk her into it. I can't take all three of you at once in my truck, but, if you want, I could bring Rosie home and come back for you and Georgia."

I was feeling lower than a snake's belly. I don't know why I was so sharp with him when he was being so kind to Rosie. "Thanks," I said. "Georgia and I will be fine on our own. I'd like to get some dinner in Rosie before she goes home, since I'll be here late. Do you think you could come back early in the evening?"

John opened the truck door and dug through the glove compartment. He pulled out a road map and a pen. He wrote his phone number on the corner of the map, then tore it off and handed it to me. "Give me a call when you are ready for dinner, and I'll come back for Rosie."

I stuffed the slip of paper in my pocket and took the stairs up to the store, two at a time. Georgia's whimpering had grown to a full-blown wail that could be heard from the bottom step. I came in and picked her up, and apologized to Rosie for taking so long.

"She's just exercising her lungs, that's all," Rosie said. "So what did John want?"

"Nothing, really," I answered.

"He's a nice boy," Rosie said. "A college boy, you know. And he seems to have an eye for you. I thought he might be asking you about where these flowers came from. It looks like they need a little more water in the vase."

"I don't have time for boys," I said. "Nice, college, or otherwise. I have enough to worry about with this little one."

I was happy a customer walked in and put an end to that conversation. I would have moved the flowers, if I'd known Rosie was coming in today. Whoever first said, "Oh! what a tangled web we weave/when first we practice to deceive" sure knew what he was talking about.

I should have given that tree committee more credit. Main Street was elbow to elbow with people by noontime. And the best part was that they weren't just lookers, they were buyers. I set the chair in front of the register for Rosie, but she was up and down so often that she decided it was easier to just stay standing. I lost track of time until the colored lights around the front window popped on. I looked out the window and saw a line of hungry customers in front of the Tick Tock.

"Rosie, I think we've earned a break," I said. "Why don't we call across to the diner, order us some dinner, and put a sign on the door telling shoppers we're closed for an hour?"

"A whole hour?" Rosie shook her head. "How about a half hour? That should be plenty of time for us to eat and you to feed Georgia."

Baby Girl had spent most of the day perched on my hip, so it felt good to put her down. She immediately started to fuss so Rosie volunteered to sit down and hold her. I was glad to have a reason for Rosie to sit, so I moved Baby Girl from her carriage to Rosie's lap. I taped the sign on the door and walked across the street. I felt bad passing by the folks in line, so I kept apologizing and explaining that I was picking up an order.

When I got in, I used the pay phone to give John a call. As I hung up, I heard a shriek of laughter. I looked down the row of booths and saw Sarah and her friends packed into one. I didn't have to worry about an awkward moment, though. Sarah never even looked up in my direction. Our dinner was waiting by the time I got back to the register, so I paid and headed across the street.

The food tasted especially good that night. I had been too busy all day to notice how hungry I had gotten. When I stood to clear away our garbage, my napkin fell on the floor. I bent over to pick it up and noticed how swollen Rosie's legs looked.

"How are you feeling, Rosie?" I asked.

"My heart's feeling young, but my body's feeling its age," she answered. "Maybe that hour is a good idea. It will give me time to rest my eyes for a few minutes."

Rosie closed her eyes and drifted off. I was changing Baby Girl into her sleeper when John walked through the doorway. The jingle bells I hung from the doorknob woke Rosie.

"What are you doing back here?" she asked.

"I was driving by and saw your light on. I thought you might like a ride home," John said.

Rosie raised her eyebrows. "You just happen to be down here, driving by?" she asked.

"Why wouldn't I be?" John answered. "I think all of Watson's Grove is down here tonight. I've never seen Main Street so busy. I don't know how Dottie and Ray are handling that crowd over there."

Rosie couldn't argue with that. "Thanks for stopping by, but like you said, we have a real crowd down here tonight. I can't leave Becky alone to take care of everything," she said.

"Rosie," I interrupted. "You could help me more by going home with John now. I need the sewing machine at home, so I don't get behind with our orders. If you and John bring it to the house now, you can show him where to set it up so it doesn't inconvenience you any. That way when I get home, I'll be able to get right to my sewing."

Rosie thought about this for a minute.

"Please, Rosie. I'll really appreciate it. John, do you have time to help with this?" I asked.

John nodded. "No problem," he said. "Where is the sewing machine?"

I showed John the machine and he carried it out to the car while I helped Rosie with her coat. When John came back in, I asked, "Can you do us one more favor? Can you drive Rosie up and down Main Street, so she can see the trees and the decorations before she goes home?"

"Scouting out the competition, ladies?" John grinned. "Sounds like fun."

I stood in the doorway holding Baby Girl. John put his hand on Rosie's elbow to help her down the stairs. Instead of pushing him away, Rosie seemed to sink in toward him using his strength to move her body forward. We waved to Rosie and John as the truck pulled from the curb. I closed the door and started to cry. I guess somewhere deep inside of me, I knew that this was Rosie's last day in the Second Hand Rose.

CHAPTER 24

I carried Baby Girl into the front parlor when we got home that night. "She fell asleep on the way home," I whispered. "Would you like to give Georgia Rose a kiss before I put her in her crib?"

I leaned over Rosie's chair, putting the baby within easy reach. After I settled Baby Girl into her crib for the night, I sat on the footstool next to Rosie. I rubbed her feet and told her about how much business we had done that evening. I showed her the pile of order slips I needed to fill.

"Thank you for getting this all set up for me," I said, nodding toward the sewing machine and table set up in the corner of the room. "But you should have had him stick it in my room, so that you don't have to look at my mess while you're watching television."

"Nonsense," Rosie said. "I want you out here keeping me company. Besides, I was thinking that I might be more useful here than in the store. You have so many orders to fill, and there are only so many hours in a day. I'm no seamstress, but if you give me a pattern to follow, I can cut everything out during the day so it's ready for you to sew at night."

I smiled. "That's a great idea. I was worried I might not be able to keep up with the orders on my own. Maybe tomorrow morning you could sort through these slips and when I come home at lunch, I'll give you some patterns to work from. I'm so tired tonight; I don't think I can do anything else."

"You don't think the store will be too much for you on your own?" Rosie asked.

"I won't be on my own," I answered. "I'll have Georgia with me, and that girl can charm everyone into being patient while they're waiting their turn."

We agreed that we were too tired for television and started off for bed. "I think we should come up with a special name for your Christmas line," Rosie said.

"What kind of a special name?" I asked.

"You know, something like Christmas Cherishables, or Becky's Blessings."

"Or Second Hand Santa's," I suggested.

Rosie raised her hands to the sky. "I have it," she said. "Once Upon a Time." She smiled triumphantly.

I leaned back against my doorjamb. "Hmm," I said. "I like it. Once Upon a Time, as in, our decorations are as magical as fairy tales."

Rosie laughed. "I was thinking more like once upon a time, that stocking was an old flannel shirt and a wine-stained tablecloth. Or once upon a time, that tree skirt was a basket of ties so ugly men wouldn't be caught dead wearing them."

Despite the wearing day, I fell asleep laughing.

The next night when I got home, not only had Rosie found the energy to organize my work orders, she also managed to spread a red or green cloth over every flat surface in the house. Each table was decked out in Christmas colors, and when I went into my room there was even a red bedspread.

"I hope you don't mind my going in your room uninvited," Rosie said. "I thought it could use a little Christmas cheer. I wasn't trying to nose around or anything."

"Of course you weren't," I answered.

Rosie smiled. "I'm glad you know that, because now I can be sure you won't be upset about what I happened upon under your bed."

My bones all stiffened a bit. The book John gave me was tucked safely under my bed. I tried each night and morning to spend at least ten minutes studying it. Progress was coming real slow.

Rosie rested on the edge of my bed. "Now, don't you be embarrassed. There is nothing to be ashamed of. I'm proud of you for wanting to finish your education. I never graduated from high school, and it is the one thing I regret in life. How are your studies coming?"

"I don't have much time to devote to them," I said.

"Of course not, what with you working so hard and a baby to boot. I just came up with a great idea. Why don't you bring your book along on our visits to Lily? She can help you get ready for that test."

I had come to dread our Sunday visits with Lily. I wished Rosie's grand idea was for me to stay home and study while she went and visited.

"Yes, this might be the key to opening that door she has locked between herself and the rest of the world," Rosie said clapping her hands.

The next day we arrived at Lily's front door with my book tucked inside the diaper bag. Lily seemed no more enthused about Rosie's plan than I was. "It has been a long time since I tutored anyone. I will be happy to pay for a more suitable tutor for Becky," Lily said, tapping her cane against the floor to make her point heard. Rosie was hearing none of it, though, and within minutes I found myself sitting alone in a room with Lily. The walls were covered from floor to ceiling with shelves of books. As Lily thumbed through my book, I leaned my head toward the door trying to hear even the faintest sound of Baby Girl fussing. She had taken to crying whenever I left the room, so I wasn't expecting a quiet study time. Of course, now that I was looking for a cause to go pick her up, Baby Girl wasn't letting out as much as a peep.

Lily put me straight to work. Studying on my own, I tended to skip over the parts I didn't understand, all the while telling myself I would go back to them when I had the time, but Lily would have none of that. "It's best to face our enemies head on," she said.

Lily had a knack for breaking big ideas down into small bites, and I must admit her patience pool was bottomless when it came to me not understanding something. "There's more than one path between two points," she said, and then she explained things in a whole new way.

I was surprised when she told me our time was up. I had gotten further in the book than I usually did in a whole week's study time, despite not being allowed to skip the hard parts. Time moves faster when you're busy than when you're staring at that grandfather clock in the parlor, trying to will the hands to move.

The following weeks proved too busy to leave time for thinking. Each morning, Georgia and I would set out for the store. We would come home at lunchtime to visit with Rosie, and then go back to work. At night, after I got Georgia down for the night, I would get to my sewing. The list of stockings, tree skirts, and ornaments waiting to be sewed was growing. I was starting to wish I had concentrated on my paint markers instead of coming up with a way to recycle some of the Second Hand Rose's merchandise.

All this extra work left me with even less time for my studying. I rarely finished my weekly assignments from Lily, so she kept me longer and longer each week. Some weeks Baby Girl was happy enough to stay with Rosie in the parlor, but other times she had to come into the little school room with me. She sat balanced on my knee while I solved math problems and wrote essays. One week she was especially feisty, and I could not keep her from pulling my book every time I tried to write something. Finally, Lily took her from my lap and balanced Baby Girl on her knee while I worked. Georgia took to Lily immediately. Before long, she was ignoring me altogether in favor of playing with Lily's necklace. After that meeting, Lily insisted Georgia come in to the study room with us all of the time. "There is no sense in starting a session only to have to stop because this baby is fussing," Lily explained. "It makes much more sense for us to bring her in from the beginning than to lose our momentum by having to start again."

I didn't believe a word she was saying. It was clear to me that she wanted an excuse to hold Baby Girl. Rosie, of course, thought this was a wonderful idea. "Perfect," she said. "That way Becky will get the most she can out of your tutoring, Georgia Rose will be happy, and I'll get in a little rest time."

For a reason I couldn't put my finger on, I was not entirely comfortable with this arrangement. I had to remind myself every week to count my blessings and to abide by Rosie's wishes.

Rosie was having her good days and her bad days. Some days she would accuse me of taking it easy on her and not leaving enough work to keep her busy. Other days Baby Girl and I would come home for lunch, only to find Rosie still in bed. There was no predicting what kind of day the morning would bring.

Rosie never spoke of missing the folks on Main Street, but she always wanted to stay late after church. I was happy to wait while she visited with old friends. Giving up going into the store every day had left her with no one to talk to but Baby Girl and me. We still made our weekly trips to visit Lily, but Lily lived out of town, so she couldn't help keep Rosie up on the gossip.

One day we came home a little early for lunch, and I saw Doc Richards's car pulling away from the curb in front of Rosie's house. I asked Rosie about it, but she just said something about an early Christmas visit. Another day, I came home to find the reverend and another man leaving the house.

"Hello, Becky," Reverend Thompson said. "Rosie's expecting you home now. She was saying how hard you work all day and night, and that she feels bad about you coming home to make her lunch."

"I'm happy to come home and see her," I said. "She worries about me too much."

"I could get some of the church ladies to help you out," he said. "They can stop by with lunch and keep her company for a little while."

"Did you talk to Rosie about it?" I asked.

"I thought it best to talk to you first," he answered. "You know Rosie doesn't like admitting she might need some help."

I nodded. The man with him reached out his hand. "It's good to meet you," he said. "I've heard so much about you."

Rosie swung open the door. "Now, you gentlemen know better than to keep a young girl standing out in the cold with a baby," she said. "Shame on you."

The men gave their apologies and went on their way. Over lunch, I asked Rosie about the visit. "Reverend Thompson came by because I told him last Sunday that I might have to take a few weeks off from church. This weather is hard on my old bones. He wanted to make sure I wasn't taking time off from praying," she said.

The only times Rosie had left the house since Thanksgiving had been to go to church and Lily's. I hated seeing her give up church, too. "Maybe we can get you a ride to church," I said. "One of your neighbors, or I can ask John or Dottie."

Rosie reached over and rubbed my hand. "Maybe," she said. "But for now, let's take things one day at a time."

That day turned out to be a big one for visitors. After dinner, while I was sewing and Rosie was dozing in the chair, there was a knock at the door. I was surprised to see Jeanie Applewood standing on our front porch.

"Look who stopped by for a visit," I said to Rosie, ushering Jeanie into the parlor.

"I'm sorry to drop by uninvited," she said. "But I've come bearing gifts, so I hope that will make up for my showing up at your door unexpectedly."

"We're always glad to see you," Rosie answered, without getting up. "Becky, can I trouble you to put on the kettle? I think our visitor could use a nice cup of tea to warm her up."

"I don't want to put you out," Jeanie protested.

"You're not putting anyone out," I said. "We were about to have our evening tea anyway. Please, have a seat and visit with Rosie while I get the tea."

Rosie said, "Do you need me to help you get the china down?"

I looked at her for a minute not really understanding what she was saying. She turned to Jeanie. "Tea always tastes better when it's served in a proper china cup, don't you think?"

I went to the kitchen and put the water on to boil. I went to the Sunday china cabinet and took out a tray, teapot, and three cups and saucers. I found the white linen napkins in the drawer and tied each one up with a bit of red ribbon. By the time I carried everything into the parlor, the tray looked fit for a queen.

Jeanie made a fuss over how pretty everything looked and Rosie seemed pleased. Our guest had brought a tin of homemade Christmas cookies and Rosie suggested we have some with our tea.

"I didn't think it was possible for these cookies to taste as good as they look," Rosie said. "But I was wrong. They are delicious. You could open a bake shop."

Jeanie blushed. “I can’t take all the credit for the cookies,” Jeanie said. “This being Chloe’s first Christmas, I insisted we spend it at home. You know, start our own family traditions. Don was worried about his mother. This will be the first Christmas he doesn’t spend at her home, and he didn’t know how she would take the news.”

Jeanie closed her eyes and savored a sip of tea. “She seemed to take it well,” Jeanie continued. “But Don warned me it could be the calm before the storm. Of course, he was right,” she said, forcing a smile. “Last week, a car pulled up to the house and out popped Mother Applewood. It took her driver five trips to carry in all of her luggage, boxes, and bags.”

A groan slipped out from me. Jeanie shook her head and sighed. “Mother Applewood decided I needed her help to get our family traditions off to the right start. She plans to stay through New Year’s Day. Anyway, most of the credit for the cookies belongs to her.”

Rosie smiled and leaned forward, pointing at Jeanie. “But you brought the cookies to us, so you deserve our thanks.”

Jeanie put down her teacup. “I almost forgot. I hope you don’t mind, but I brought a little gift for Georgia.” She pulled a box out of the bag at her feet. It was wrapped in shiny red, green, and gold plaid paper, and tied with gold ribbon and a big gold bow.

I held the box, admiring the wrapping, until Jeanie said, “Please, open it now.”

I slipped the ribbons off the box, careful not to undo the bow. I slowly removed the tape from the ends and peeled away the paper, folding it neatly before opening the box. Inside, I found a red velvet dress as pretty as the box it came in. I lifted it up to show Rosie. “Why, that dress is almost as beautiful as the little girl that is going to wear it,” Rosie said.

Jeanie beamed. “I’m so glad you like it,” she said. “I hope it fits her.”

"It looks like the perfect size to me," I said. "Thank you so much. This is the first Christmas present Georgia has ever received. I'm going to put the card in her keepsake box tonight, and she will remember you forever for it."

When Jeanie decided it was time to go, I walked her to the door. "How is everything going between you and Lily?" she asked.

I shrugged my shoulders. "Sometimes when we're working on my studies, I think I'm really lucky to have her in my life, and there is nothing that makes me happier than seeing Rosie light up when Lily smiles. But the truth be told, it still gives me an uneasy feeling seeing Lily with Georgia. It shouldn't, I know that—Lily can soothe Georgia as well as I can, and I know she wants what's best for her—but I always get the feeling she doesn't think I'm worthy of tending to a baby."

Jeanie put her arm over my shoulders and gave them a squeeze. "Don't take it personally," she said. "I'm sure Lily doesn't feel that way about you. I think it's just that she has no baby of her own, yet she still has all that mothering inside of her. Life can play some cruel tricks like that. I don't want to think of how I would feel if I suffered the loss she suffered."

Shame came over me like a curtain dropping onto a stage. Thinking about what Lily had lost made my resentment of the joy holding Baby Girl brought Lily seem even more selfish and unkind. Jeanie seemed to sense my dark feelings and changed the subject. "She's a real fighter," Jeanie whispered, nodding in the direction of Rosie. "I'm sure you want to spend as much time with Rosie as you can now. I'll come down to the store for a few hours every day this week to cover for you so you can come home. Mother Applewood will love the time alone with Chloe."

As much of a talker as I am, it seems that I can never find words when I need them the most. I stood and watched Jeanie walk out to her car. The cold night air that I swallowed hurt my chest, so I leaned for a moment against the door after closing it. Rosie and I were going to have to talk about her health. I stepped toward the parlor and was greeted by the purr of Rosie's snoring. Any talk of illness would have to wait until morning.

CHAPTER 25

I no longer looked at Rosie's bedroom as the forbidden land. This was due to practical necessity, not any loss of respect for her privacy. The closer Christmas got, the earlier I left for the store in the morning. That allowed me time to get any housekeeping and bookkeeping chores done before opening for customers. Rosie's schedule was going in the opposite direction of mine. With each passing day, Rosie got out of bed later. I took to bringing a tray in to her before I left in the morning, so I could be sure she had some breakfast.

Each morning, I would stand by her door and knock three times. I would close my eyes and listen to the sound of the drawer in Rosie's bedside table scrape open. It was followed by the sound of the plastic vials plunking against each other as they were swept into the drawer. Finally, the drawer would scrape shut again and Rosie would call out for me to come in.

That morning when I knocked, there was no sound of pill containers scurrying into hiding. Instead, Rosie called out her welcome right away. When I walked into the room, I noticed that Rosie had already been up and about. The window shade was already pulled up, inviting the light in. Rosie, with a quilt drawn tight around her shoulders, sat in a pool of sunbeams that collected on her bed. "I'm getting used to you spoiling me," she said, smoothing the blankets around her.

I set the tray down on her bed. "You deserve a little spoiling," I said. "You're looking fine today."

"Since I was up early anyway, I decided to make a shopping list for our Christmas dinner. Why don't you look it over and add anything special you might want," Rosie said, handing me a piece of paper.

"I'm sure you remembered everything," I said. "I'm glad you're wide awake this morning. I wanted to talk to you about Jeanie."

Rosie shook her head. "That poor girl. Her husband has to learn to stand up to his mama. Coming in and taking over their home the way she does. It's a shame, a real shame."

I nodded and said, "Jeanie offered to come to the store for a few hours each day to help out," I said. "If she does that, then I won't have to close the store at lunchtime every day. I didn't give her an answer one way or the other; I wanted to check in with you first. How would you feel about her helping out? Would you mind her being alone in the store while I came home for an hour at noon?"

"I think it's a great idea," Rosie said. "You could use the company down at the store. She could use a reason to get out from under her mother-in-law's thumb. And like you said, we wouldn't have to close the store for an hour in the middle of the day."

"Then I'll accept her offer," I said.

Rosie laughed. "I doubt that you will have to say anything. Dollars to doughnuts she shows up today without any word from us. She'll probably put up a fight on this, but I want you to pay her for her time. The store is doing real well, and every girl should have a little pocket money all her own."

I looked at the caramel-colored tubes lined up on her table in parade formation. "Rosie," I said. "What are you taking all of those medicines for?"

"At my age, it's quicker to list what parts don't need medicine," Rosie laughed. "Where is our little princess?" she asked, changing the subject. "You weren't planning to go off today without giving me a chance to spend a few minutes with Georgia Rose, were you?"

I took the tray away and brought Baby Girl in for some hugs. I arranged some pillows into a little chair on the bed and sat her next to Rosie. I left them together for a few minutes while I gathered what we needed for our morning at the store. I went into the last place in the house I considered 'Rosie only' territory: the kitchen drawer where she kept her money, papers, and phone numbers. I quickly copied down a number and stuffed the scrap in my pocket.

The first thing I did when we arrived at the store that day was pull that scrap from my pocket. I took a deep breath and dialed the number I'd scribbled on it. A young woman answered the phone, so I started in right away, thinking I had reached Rosie's granddaughter. "I'm Becky Miller, the girl who works and lives with your grandmother," I said. "I'm worried about Rosie's health, and think it might be best if you come visit her."

The young woman on the other end of the line cleared her throat. "I'm sorry miss," she said. "You must be looking for Jennifer Perkins. I'm her assistant. Ms. Perkins is not available at the moment. May I take your number, so she is able to return your call at a more convenient time?"

I gave her the store number. A minute after I hung up, I picked the receiver up again. This time I reached the party I was hoping to get. "Hello," John said.

I looked at the clock. It was almost nine in the morning. Why did he sound like he was still asleep?

"Hello?" John said again.

"Hi," I answered. "This is Becky. Did I wake you?"

"I was up late studying," John explained. "I have my last final later this morning. Do you need something?"

"I'm sorry. I shouldn't have bothered you," I said.

"You're not bothering me," John answered. "You must have called for some reason. What do you need?"

I hesitated. John had important things to do today. I shouldn't be bothering him with this.

"Becky? Is Rosie all right?"

"Yes," I said. "At least I think so. I called because I was wondering if you have the time to bring a Christmas tree over to the house some day this week. I'll pay you for the tree and your time, of course."

"You don't need to pay me for anything," John said. "I'll stop by later today after I finish my exam."

"I don't want to trouble you today," I said. "You concentrate on your schooling. The tree can wait."

"It's no trouble," John answered. "What time do you close tonight? I'll swing by and pick you and Georgia up, and we can go buy Rosie a tree."

The day kept getting better from there. Just as Rosie predicted, Jeanie arrived at the Second Hand Rose with no prompting from me. "Where should I put my coat?" she asked.

I had gotten used to seeing a lot of grumpy people in the last few days. The closer the holidays came, the more people seemed to feel like they were falling behind. But here was Jeanie, just a few days before Christmas, and her words came out of her like a song. I showed her to the back room. "I hope spending time here doesn't cause you to lose some of that Christmas spirit," I said.

"I'm not worried," she said. "I used to work as a store clerk. I loved it."

"Did you stop when Chloe was born?" I asked.

"No," Jeanie said. "I worked my way through college. My freshman year I worked in this cute little boutique. The clothes were fabulous, which is why the next year I wised up and went to work at the Yarn Barn. Not much chance of my spending my whole paycheck there!"

As I followed Jeanie up the aisle, it occurred to me that there was much more to Jeanie Applewood than met the eye. Baby Girl, who had taken to spending her awake time riding my hip, squealed with wide-eyed delight at the pace that was needed to keep up with Jeanie. We reached the front of the store and Jeanie threw up her hands. "Where is my mind this morning?" she asked. "I forgot something in my pocket." She turned and hurried back to her coat, her feet barely skimming the surface of the wood floor planks. A split second later, she stood in front of me smiling with her arm stretched out. "For you," she said, nodding toward the envelope in her hand.

I took the envelope and looked inside. "Pictures!" I said.

"I took them at the christening," Jeanie said. "I thought you might like a copy."

I spread the pictures across the counter and looked from one to another and back again. Growing up, I had my picture taken in school every year. Mama and Daddy never bought them. One year, the girls in my class exchanged the little pictures with one another. I begged Mama and Daddy to buy mine. I promised I would do extra chores to pay them back. But Daddy said, "Why would we go and spend good money on those? We look at that face for free every day, whether we want to or not. You know what they say, 'the pennies go to the wise and the foolish get a pounding.'"

I told everyone at school that I didn't care for school photos. It wasn't entirely untrue. I think everyone looks like a statue in those pictures and the cloth they put behind you is usually a color too ugly to be found in a box of crayons.

The pictures lying on the counter were nothing like that. Lined up the way they were, they told a story. And I might sound a little crazy saying this, but they didn't just show how people looked that day. They showed how people felt. "They're beautiful," I said. "Where did you learn to take pictures like this?"

Jeanie's face gave meaning to the word 'glowing.' "Thanks," she said. "I majored in photojournalism in college. Now, I mainly take pictures of Chloe."

I looked at the pictures again, zooming in on one of Rosie, Georgia, and me. I pulled a frame I'd stitched for Rosie out from under the counter. The photo was a perfect fit. "I made this for Rosie for Christmas," I said. "I thought I would have to give it to her empty but, if it's okay with you, I'll give it to her with this picture in it."

"Mind? I'm honored. The frame is beautiful," Jeanie said. "I would love to learn embroidery. Maybe after Christmas you can give me a few lessons."

I'd never thought of myself as a teacher, but I agreed. "And maybe you can teach me a little about photography," I said.

"It's a deal," Jeanie said, and reached out to shake my hand. "What else do you have under there?"

"I made her an ornament, too," I said. "I plan to go to the little booth in the drugstore to get a picture of Georgia and me for it."

Jeanie looked at the ornament and the photos again. "This one would be perfect for the ornament," she said.

"It's way too big," I answered.

Jeanie waved her hand in the air. "We'll just crop it," she said, grabbing the scissors from behind the counter. "I can give you another copy tomorrow."

Now, I saw that picture as a piece of art and trimming it seemed no different to me than going into a museum and shaving a little off of a statue. But before I could stop her, Jeanie had started snipping away. When she slid it into the ornament, I couldn't argue her choice. Rosie was going to love it.

The morning got busy and when lunchtime rolled around, I knew there was no need to worry about leaving Jeanie alone in the store. Baby Girl and I headed home when the church bells starting ringing. Every day at noon on the dot, those bells rang, and as soon as I heard them my stomach would start to growl. It was like that scientist and the dog I read about in school. Rosie had the table set when I walked into the kitchen. I put Baby Girl in her highchair and fed her while our soup cooled a bit.

"Was I right about Jeanie?" Rosie asked.

I smiled. "You know you were," I said.

"Like I said the first time I met you, God gave me a sixth sense about people," Rosie said. "She's a good person, and she'll be a good friend to you over the years if you let her."

After lunch, I packed up the sewing machine and worktable to make room for the tree. I had stopped taking special orders days ago and only had some hand stitching left to finish. Rosie didn't complain about the lack of work for her. Instead, once everything was cleared, she asked me to move one of the chairs so she could sit and look out the front window. I wanted to keep the tree a surprise, so I did as she asked and left her at her window post, watching the neighbors pass by.

Jeanie was ringing up a customer when Georgia and I got back to the store. Once we were alone, she gave me the rundown of what I had missed. "There's a camera crew in town from the local TV station. They were filming all the decorated storefronts and streets for a Christmas in Our County series they're airing on the evening news. They stopped by looking for you. The reporter said everyone in town told them it was you who brought back the town spirit. I told them they certainly had the right store, but that you were out at the moment." I wondered if Jeanie heard my sigh of relief at that last remark. "I think they will probably be back later." Then she looked at her watch and said, "I hate to run out on you so quick but I need to get home. It's time for Chloe's afternoon nap, and I don't think she'll go down for her grandmother."

"Don't be driving too fast," I warned. "It's actually snowing out there."

Jeanie looked out the window and clapped. Flakes drifted from the sky and melted as they hit the pavement. "Naptime can wait. I'm going to take Chloe out to dance in the first snow of the season."

I must have looked as puzzled as I felt. Back home, the only thing snowflakes meant was that an ice storm was on its way. There was no celebrating that.

Jeanie grabbed my hand. "C'mon," she said. "Let's get Georgia out there dancing."

I scooped up Baby Girl and followed Jeanie onto the sidewalk. I stood there and watched Jeanie twirling about with her arms spread like an eagle's wings and her face tipped to the sky. She was giggling like a cheerleader when the quarterback brushes up against her. She grabbed hold of my arms and started dancing us in circles too. Baby Girl started giggling right along with Jeanie, which got me to giggling, too. Finally, we collapsed on the steps and breathed in the magical air.

"You must think I'm the silliest person you ever met," Jeanie said. "Here I am, thirty years old and still dancing in the snow. It brings such happy memories back to me. My mother took me outside at the first sight of snow every year. We would dance about until I got too dizzy to stand anymore. Do you and your mother have any silly traditions like that?"

I stood up. "It's getting too cold out here for Georgia. I'd better bring her in the store now."

"I didn't mean to pry," Jeanie said as we walked back inside.

I smiled at her. "You've been so much help here at the store," I said. "Rosie and I want to pay you for your time."

"No! It's been fun," Jeanie said. "I'm looking forward to tomorrow. If you want to do something for me, then keep your fingers crossed that the snow lasts until I get home and that

Mother Applewood is so tuckered out from watching Chloe that she needs a long afternoon nap, too!"

Jeanie rushed out the door and down the steps to her car. She started the engine, then suddenly stopped and got back out of the car. She opened the back door of the car and pulled out a car seat. It was bigger than the one Baby Girl's carriage turned into. She ran back up the stairs with it. "You're going to think I'm as flighty as a bird," she said. "I forgot I put this in the car this morning. I received three car seats as gifts for Chloe, and we only have two cars. What am I going to do with three car seats? I thought Georgia might be growing out of the baby car seat she had been using. If you don't already have a bigger car seat, can you use this one? Even if you have another one, could you use a backup?" Then without giving herself as much as a moment to catch her breath or me a moment to answer, she said, "Gotta run! I hope the car seat works for you!"

I watched Jeanie bounce back down the stairs and into her car. I wished I had her energy. I removed the jingle bells from the doorknob and hoped that nothing else would disturb Baby Girl's nap this afternoon. She was back to her pattern of waking up every few hours in the night, so we both were sorely in need of sleep. After I laid Baby Girl down for her nap, I carried the car seat to the back room. I wasn't sure about accepting such a generous gift. She was already helping us out by being here. She didn't need to be giving up Chloe's things for us.

While Baby Girl napped, I rested my eyes. In my half sleep, I saw Jeanie dancing in the snow. I had never paid Jeanie's age much mind, but at thirty she was closer to Mama's age than mine. I couldn't picture Mama dancing in the snow. Truth be told, I couldn't picture Mama doing anything but housework and laundry. She was married by the time she was my age and had me less than a year later. She had run off with Daddy when she was seventeen to get away from her own daddy's harsh temper. I never saw Mama's family. I guess Mama was a castaway, too. Tears started to well up in my eyes and spill over. I wiped the sleep and tears from my eyes, and made Mama and myself a promise. That night I would dig out my notebook and pen and add *Take Mama somewhere far away from the farm* to my list.

CHAPTER 26

It was the first quiet afternoon since Thanksgiving, with only a handful of people wandering into the store. I decided to stay away from my thoughts by tending to the stock and doing some of my stitching. I wanted to be ready to go, without red eyes, whenever John arrived.

I had just finished a piece when I looked up and caught sight of the news people Jeanie had told me about. They were making a beeline for the Second Hand Rose. I leapt up and raced to the door. I quickly locked the door and flipped the sign so it read Sorry, We're Closed! Then I took Baby Girl and hid out in the back of the store. My insides churned while I listened to the banging on the front door. When the noise stopped, I peeked up the aisle.

The crew had stopped banging on the door, but they hadn't left. They were setting up the cameras right in front of the store. Baby Girl was losing patience with the whole situation and started fussing loudly. I ducked into the back room and opened a tin of cookies. I picked out a plain sugar one and broke off a tiny piece for her. I kept bribing her to be quiet with cookie bits until the news folks left. I knew that wasn't a good thing to do, but desperate times and all. I couldn't risk our faces being plastered on TV screens all over. Baby Girl had changed lots in the six months she had been on Earth, but one thing hadn't changed. She still had that billowy cloud of red ringlets. That would be cause enough for someone to recognize a baby.

Once the coast was clear, Baby Girl and I inched our way back up to the front of the store. I saw the news truck pull away from the curb and head down Main Street. Even though I saw them go with my own eyes, I still felt rattled. I was glad to see John's truck pull up a half-hour before our regular closing time. I wanted to get far away from the store, just in case they came back.

John buckled Georgia's car seat into the passenger seat, thinking that was the safest place for her. This left the middle spot for me, and my close proximity to John caused my train of thought to derail.

"Do you have a place in mind?" John asked.

"What?" I asked.

"Do you have a place in mind? A place to buy the tree."

"No," I answered.

"Let's go to Knotty Pine Farm. They always have a good selection at a fair price," John said.

We rode out of town in silence. John's hand brushed across my leg as he reached over to turn on the radio. A shiver rode my spine, and John asked, "Are you cold? I can turn the heat up."

"I'm fine," I said.

John started tapping on the steering wheel out of sync with the music. I wanted to say something, but was afraid once the first word came out the dam would be broken and the words would flood out of me nonstop. I was grateful when we turned off the main highway and rolled down the narrow road that cut through the trees. The darkness swallowed us whole as John wove the truck along the twists and turns.

"Wow!" I said as we came around the last curl in the road. The North Pole couldn't be more decorated than the Knotty Pine Farm was. The house and barn were covered with thousands of colored lights. Whatever land didn't have trees sprouting out of it played host to blinking snowmen, reindeer, candles, and toy soldiers. In front of the barn, a huge star seemed to hang in the sky, and below it was a nativity. "Are those real people?" I asked.

John smiled. "They've had a living nativity here since I was a little kid."

A woman, who looked like she had eaten more than her share of Christmas cookies over the years, was dressed like Mrs. Claus. She welcomed us to the farm and suggested we have a picture taken of Baby Girl and Santa before we hunted for our tree. I watched a couple of little ones burst into tears when they were placed on Santa's lap. I was having second thoughts about this idea when the lady with the camera said, "Your turn." She must have seen the worry in my face. "She'll be fine," the woman said. "If you're worried then you can stay up there with her."

I took a deep breath and handed Georgia to Santa. She looked right at his face and laughed. I slowly backed away and waited for the camera click. As soon as the woman said, "Got it," I hurried back to fetch Georgia. I was more worried about Santa than Baby Girl. Georgia had gotten ahold of his long white beard with both hands and was tugging with all her might.

I found myself singing along with the Christmas music that was floating out of the speakers hidden along the paths. Our breath was forming little white clouds as it mixed with the night air. I pulled Georgia's hood up over her hat and covered her hands with a pair of baby knee socks. I couldn't keep mittens on her, so I took to carrying the socks with me. I would have taken the first tree we saw but John was pickier.

"Where do you want to put the tree?" he asked.

I knew exactly where I wanted it. "In the front parlor," I said, "in front of the window."

"Then you need a tree that looks good from all sides," he said. He circled every tree I stopped in front of, and pointed out its flaws. "Big gap in this one. Too thin. These branches can't hold anything heavier than a feather." Finally, he nodded his head. "You won't find a better-looking tree than this one," he said, letting out a whistle.

I buckled Georgia into her seat while John tied down the tree in the back of the truck. I was glad I had bundled Georgia from head to toe. My thin coat was no match for the wind, and my hands stung from the cold. When John climbed in beside me, I was trying to rub away the pain in my hands.

He cupped his hands over his mouth and gave a few strong puffs. Then he took my hands in his and started rubbing them. "Sorry this took so long," he said. "I'm sure Rosie will approve of the tree, though."

"Rosie!" I said. "What time is it? I didn't tell her we weren't coming straight home today. She'll be worried sick."

"Nothing to worry about," John said. "I dropped something off for her before I picked you up. I told her that we had plans for after work and would pick up something for dinner on the way back."

We rode along in silence for a little while. Georgia had gotten accustomed to car travel with our trips to Lily's and had stopped howling like a trapped animal whenever she was strapped into her seat. But unlike the silence on the way to the tree farm, this quiet had a kind of warmth to it—a coziness. I was replaying the words "we had plans" in my head for about the hundredth time when John pulled the truck off the road. We were in the parking lot of a restaurant located on the edge of town.

"I hope you don't mind, but I ordered ahead. I'll run in and pick it up," John said. He left the engine running and sprinted across the lot.

I sat the rest of the way home with the heat from the bag of food burning its way through my jeans. I thought about all John had done for us that day, and started feeling guilty about the drain on his time. "I didn't realize you had chores to do for Rosie today," I said. "And with a big exam to boot. I'm sorry I asked you about the tree."

"Like I said before, don't worry about it," John answered. "I'm glad you asked me."

Rosie was perched on the edge of the chair looking at the television when we got home. John had left the tree on the porch so we could eat before setting it up. When we walked in the house, Rosie started talking excitedly. "Watson's Grove is on the news! Look! There's the Second Hand Rose! Turn it up, Becky!"

The woman I had seen banging on the door was talking into a microphone. "Well, Jim, it seems like this Becky is a little camera shy. What's that? Yes, more of a Secret Santa. It seems like the whole town is keeping her secret, too. Everyone around here was quick to credit her with reigniting the town's spirit, but no one was willing to part with any information about her personally. I think if the town wants to keep the secret, we should let them!"

Rosie broke out in applause. John grinned and said, "Who knew I would be dining with a secret celebrity tonight?"

John's comment reminded me of the food I was still holding. I went to the kitchen and set out the food and dishes. The hot food warmed me from the inside out. It put me in a calmer state of being and made me look forward again to putting up the tree. When we finished, I piled the dishes in the sink and warned Rosie away from them. I changed Baby Girl into her sleeper, but knew putting her in her crib was pointless. Her car nap was going to push bedtime back for sure. Rosie put some Christmas records on and sat rocking back and forth to the music with Baby Girl on her lap. "Look at Georgia Rose," she laughed. "This little girl is dancing already."

John and I stood in front of them, watching Baby Girl waving her arms and bouncing to the music. I couldn't tell how much was Rosie and how much of the action was Baby Girl, but they made quite a team. When the song ended, Rosie said, "Didn't I hear something about a tree a little earlier, John?"

John carried in the tree, filling the house with the scent of pine. Under one arm, John had tucked a tree stand. I hadn't noticed it in the truck and was grateful he had thought of it. I held the tree with one hand and turned to face Rosie. She looked like a child on Christmas morning. John crawled under the tree to put the trunk in the stand. "Is it too tall, Rosie?" he asked, from under the branches.

"It's perfect," she said.

"Can you hold it a minute longer, Becky, while I get this tightened?"

"Yes," I said, but as I was saying it I turned to face the tree and got a branch in my face. "Ouch," I said, pulling back from the tree.

The tree started falling forward, and John and I both grabbed it before it got completely away from us. "Sorry," I said.

It was unlikely John heard my apology, because Rosie was having herself a good old belly laugh and Baby Girl was joining in. "I'm sorry," Rosie said. "I'm not laughing at you. It's that you two remind me of my second husband and me, and our first Christmas together. Only we didn't catch the tree. It went right through the front window. We had to return the gifts we bought each other to pay to replace the glass. It was a wonderful Christmas, though. It was so long ago."

Rosie sat quietly for a few minutes. When John climbed out from under the tree, she said, "Yes, it's perfect. I'm a lucky woman." She kissed Baby Girl's nose. "How about some decorations?" she asked.

John and I climbed into the attic and searched for the boxes. When we came back with everything, Rosie looked like she had gotten her second wind. She sat up in her chair and directed us to the right spot for each decoration. When we hung the last shiny ball on the tree, I stepped back to look. "Once again, you're right, Rosie. This tree is perfect."

Rosie said, "I don't think I've ever had such a beautiful tree."

"We still haven't tried the lights," John said. "Rosie, do you want to do the honors?"

I took Baby Girl, and John helped Rosie out of the chair. "I plugged everything into here," he said, handing her a switch. "One click and your tree will be lit."

Rosie looked at the switch in her hand. "You're not trying to fry me, are you?" she said. "You're not in my will, you know."

"Rosie!" I said. John just laughed. Rosie clicked the switch, and the tree sparkled with a spider web of colored lights. I looked at the naked bottom of the tree.

"Our things are still in your truck," I said. "Can I go get them?"

"Becky, you're not trying to chase away our company, are you? We haven't had any of the Christmas cookies yet."

"No, of course not," I said. "I made a skirt for the tree, and it's in my bag in the truck."

Rosie returned to her chair and put her arms out for Georgia. John and I went to the truck to fetch my things. When we came back in, I pulled the skirt from my bag and crawled under the tree. I stood up and stepped back.

"Now it's perfect," Rosie said.

I shook my head. "Not yet," I said. I dug back into my bag and pulled out a tiny package. "For you," I said, handing the package to Rosie. I picked Georgia up, freeing Rosie's hands for unwrapping.

"It's not even Christmas yet," she said. "I should wait to open it."

"This is a pre-Christmas gift," I said. "I want you to open it now."

Rosie removed the colored tissue paper. At first, she stared at the snowflake ornament in her hand. Then she passed a finger across the surface of the beads I had added to my stitches. Finally she pressed the ornament against her chest and spoke. "Becky," she said. "This is the most precious gift any human has ever given me. Thank you."

She popped up out of her chair without any help. "I want to find the perfect place on the tree for this," she said. "I want it right in sight when I'm sitting in my chair."

John tried to leave after the tree decorating was officially finished, but Rosie wouldn't hear of it. She insisted he stay for cookies and tea. After I brought out the tray, I excused myself. I'd gotten a peek at the kitchen clock and knew that no matter how late a nap Baby Girl had taken, it was time for her to go to bed. It took some time to soothe her to sleep, so by the time I was ready to join Rosie and John, teatime was over.

I stopped and looked myself over in the mirror before returning to the front parlor. I grabbed my hairbrush and quickly pulled it through my hair a few times before giving up and pulling my hair back with a ribbon. I had never worn makeup—Mama and Daddy wouldn't allow it—but I was wishing I had a little something to put on my face at that moment. From my bedroom, I heard John wishing Rosie a good night. "The shutters on this side look a little loose," he said. "I'll come by tomorrow to fix them."

"You sure you don't want to wait and say good night to Becky?" Rosie asked. "I'm sure she will be right out."

"I don't want to overstay my welcome here," John said. "Are you sure you can put up with me for a few more minutes?"

I hightailed it out of the bedroom before Rosie could answer. I walked out to the porch with him. "Thank you again," I said. "I couldn't have done this for her on my own."

John tilted his head. "You worry too much," he said. "Rosie's done a lot for me. She stopped me from getting into some real trouble a few years back. I'm happy to be able to help her in any way. She is not a burden at all, and in case you haven't noticed, I like spending time with you."

Then he bent down and kissed me. It was a soft, gentle kiss on the lips, and it caused all thoughts to leave my mind. John rubbed my arms and said, "It's too cold to be out here without your coat. This is the coldest winter for as long as I can remember. You better get inside."

I nodded my head, but I wasn't feeling a bit of cold. I watched John walk down the porch steps. As he drove away, I started to regain my senses. I thought about how shocked John would be to learn his had been my first real kiss.

I went back into the living room. Rosie wanted to sit in her chair and admire the tree a little more before bedtime. I went to the kitchen to wash the dishes. I stood in front of the sink, working and thinking. I wondered what kind of trouble John had been skirting with when he was younger. Realizing I was doing exactly what I wished other folks wouldn't do to me, I gave myself a good mental scolding. *Girl, don't you go poking your nose in his business. If you want to keep your secrets, then you have to let him have his.*

I pushed John out of my mind and concentrated on Rosie. She was moving a lot slower these days, but her spirit tonight was as bright as the day I met her. Her granddaughter had never returned my call, and at that moment I was feeling foolish for making the call in the first place. For all I knew, Rosie may have been taking those pills forever. If she was sick, she would tell me. Mama always said I was the kind of girl who saw a tornado in every breeze.

CHAPTER 27

The next morning, I walked down Main Street like I had sacks of wet sheets tied to my ankles. My special order stitching was keeping me up later and later. On top of that, tree shopping must have been more excitement than Baby Girl could handle, because she'd been awake for more than half of the night. That, of course, meant I had been up more than half the night. I was starting to appreciate Mama's need for me to tend to the little ones so much.

I decided my first chore of the day would best be completed on my backside. I sat down and called customers to let them know their items were ready for pickup. Then I tried my best to concentrate on sorting some bills that needed Rosie's attention. Instead, I found myself clock-watching and hoping Jeanie would arrive soon.

Ten minutes before opening time, Jeanie arrived with the energy of a jackrabbit in spring. She placed two bottles of cola on the counter. "I don't know if you drink regular or diet, so I brought one of each," Jeanie said.

"Which do you like?" I asked.

"Depends on the day," she answered. "If I'm really dragging, I go for the regular. If you don't mind my saying so, you look like you should go for the sugar today."

We sipped our colas as we worked. Jeanie was right about it giving me an energy boost. My walk home for lunch took half the time the trip into town had taken in the morning.

We had been so busy with the tree the night before that I'd never shown Rosie the christening pictures Jeanie had taken.

I decided to show them to her at lunch, knowing they would brighten up her day. Thinking of the smile they would put on her face made me move even quicker.

John was on the front porch, hammering away at the shutters. "I heard you came home around this time every day," John said.

I smiled. It was nice, thinking he had timed his chores to fit my schedule. "What else has Rosie been telling you?"

"Nothing today. I haven't seen Rosie this morning," John answered.

My spine stiffened. "You've been out here pounding away on those shutters and Rosie hasn't come out to check on you?" I asked.

I pulled Baby Girl from her stroller and hurried toward the door. John was at my heels when I stepped inside and heard the needle from her old hi-fi hitting the inside rim of a record. The *tap*, *tap*, *tap* of the needle against the vinyl echoed in my ears. I stepped toward the parlor. The first thing I saw was Rosie's favorite pink and green china cup lying on the tea-stained carpet.

It seemed like I was staring at that cup forever, afraid to look up into the chair, afraid to move. John whispered, "Stay here."

I forced myself to look up. Rosie's white snowcap of hair rested half on the chair and half in mid-air. Her hand hung open over the arm of the chair. I watched John kneel in front of Rosie's chair. He reached out and felt her wrist, and then her neck. "I'm going to call the doctor. You need to sit down."

I stood there while John made some phone calls. I didn't cry. I didn't speak. I didn't listen. I kept thinking I should be doing something, but my body didn't move. I held on to Baby Girl as tight as I could and stared at Rosie. I was shaking so hard, I was afraid I would drop Georgia. John came back to us and took Baby Girl from my arms. He put his other arm around me and said, "You need to sit down."

I was still sitting when the others arrived. First through the door was Doc Richards. The reverend wasn't more than a few steps behind him. The sight of the reverend got me moving. I put Baby Girl in her crib and hurried into the parlor. The doctor was putting away his stethoscope, and taking out a bottle of medicine and a needle. Rosie's eyelids were fluttering, but she wasn't putting up an argument. I was so glad to see her even half-awake that I forgot my fears and knelt on the floor close to her chair. I balanced there, petting her hand like it was a newborn chick. I kept hoping to hear her say that everything was going to be all right.

"You're doing fine, Rosie," Doc Richards said in a half whisper. "We're going to move you to your bed now. The shot I gave you is going to make you a little drowsy; let it do its job, and take a good long nap."

I watched as they lifted Rosie from her chair and carried her into her room. Baby Girl had done as much waiting as she was able. She was demanding attention, so I hurried to her before she woke Rosie. Doc Richards was waiting for me when I came out with Georgia perched on my hip. "She is a real fighter, but not even Rosie can have complete control over her body. Her heart is weak, so spells like this one can come at any time. She's lucky you came home when you did, but we need to make some other arrangements for her. She needs to have someone around her all of the time. Can you stay here with her until we can make other arrangements?"

I nodded and stared at Rosie's door.

"She needs her rest now, but I left the door open a crack so you can hear her if she wants anything."

I followed the doctor into the kitchen. He sat down and wrote a list of instructions. He sat there tapping his pen against the tabletop for a few minutes before handing me the paper. After I looked over the list he asked, "Can you read it? Do you have any questions?"

His words took me back some. "I can read," I said.

"Of course you can," Doc Richards said. "I was referring to my penmanship, not your reading ability." He patted my arm.

I walked the doctor to the front door. John and the reverend met us there, and the three men walked out together. Baby Girl and I watched from the window as the men stopped on the walk. They had their heads together like hens gathered around feed. I wished I could hear the words coming out of those bobbing heads.

I brought Baby Girl into the kitchen and parked her in her highchair while I fixed her lunch. After I fed and changed her, I tucked her into her crib for her nap. "I'm sure you will have a better nap here than you have in your carriage at the store," I said as I bent over to kiss her.

As I closed our bedroom door behind me, I remembered Jeanie. I picked up the kitchen phone and called the store. I explained what happened and was surprised to hear my voice filling with tears all over again. "Close the store and go home to Chloe," I said, and told her where we hid the extra front door key.

"Do you need anything? How can I help? Do you want me to open tomorrow?" she asked.

"No," I answered. "Tomorrow's Christmas Eve. We don't need to open, and I think we have everything we need for now. Doc Richards is sending some new medicine over for Rosie."

"You call me if you need anything—food, diapers, company—anything you need," Jeanie said.

When I hung up the phone, I commenced with my pacing. Up and down the hall I walked, worried that if I was more than a few feet away from Rosie's bed, I wouldn't hear her call me. Lucky thing our room was right across the hall. That way my pacing took care of two problems at once. I knew I would hear Rosie, and I would hear Baby Girl before her fussing filled the house.

The day dragged, but by evening Rosie was awake and looking for some soup. Her skin pinked up a bit after eating, but the activity seemed to tucker her out again. "Bring Georgia Rose over here for a few minutes, Becky," she said, patting the bed beside her.

I sat on the edge of the bed and settled Baby Girl between us. Looking at those ladies together caused me to fill up again. I've never been a teary person, so I didn't know how to lock that salty river inside. Rosie rubbed my arm. "Now, don't you be crying on my part," she said. "Everything is going to be fine."

I was getting Georgia ready for bed when the phone rang. I bolted down the hall trying to stop the racket before it shook Rosie. I slammed my big toe into the table leg as I skidded across the kitchen floor. The phone stopped ringing as I reached for it. I curled up into a ball on the floor and started crying again. I think I must have let out all my tears, because just as fast as it started, the crying stopped. I limped over to the kitchen sink and threw some cold water in my face. I was looking at the reflection of my sorry self in the toaster when I heard Rosie call my name.

I hobbled down the hall and tapped on Rosie's door. "Do you need something?" I asked Rosie.

"That was Lily on the phone," Rosie said. "News spreads like a wildfire in this town. Even nothing news like me taking a little too much of a nap makes the rounds. She wants to come for a visit tomorrow. If it was anybody else, I would tell them to stay home, but I'm so happy knowing she'll be leaving that house of hers. John will be driving her, so I thought maybe we could have a little lunch. Would you mind staying home tomorrow to help? It's Christmas Eve, so you really shouldn't be working anyway."

I looked at Rosie. Getting all those words out had wiped her out. I couldn't picture her sitting at the table tomorrow hosting a lunch. I thought it best to keep that idea to myself. I nodded my head. "Can I get you anything before bed?" I asked.

"Can you help me to the bathroom?" she asked.

I was afraid I would sleep too soundly to hear Rosie that night. I made sure both of our doors were open when I crawled into bed that night. As I lay staring at the ceiling, I thought about what the doctor said about a change in Rosie's living arrangements. A change in Rosie's situation would surely mean a change in living arrangements for Baby Girl and me, too. Between those thoughts and my throbbing swollen toe, I had no cause to fear sleeping through Rosie's call. I had no cause to worry about sleeping, period.

CHAPTER 28

I gave up trying to sleep before morning broke. Baby Girl had made it straight through the night without so much as a peep. I wanted to slip out without breaking that spell, but there would be no tiptoeing for me. I rested my right foot on its heel as I stood outside Rosie's door, listening. I didn't hear anything, so I stuck my head in the doorway to grab a peek. The glow from the streetlight slipped through the opening in the curtains and shone on Rosie's pillow. When I was sure all was right as could be, I felt my way down the hall to the kitchen. I turned on the little light over the sink, grabbed a dishtowel, and filled it with ice. I sat down and propped my foot up on the chair across from me. I swear my toe was as big as a pig's hoof. I set the ice on my foot, glad the towel was hiding the damage.

I was still sitting there when I heard Rosie call my name. I must have finally dozed off for a piece, because the ice was now a puddle on the kitchen floor. I hurried as best I could to Rosie's bedside. I had hoped a night's rest would have restored some of her energy, but it wasn't meant to be. I helped her to the bathroom and then right back to bed. "How about some toast and tea?" I suggested.

"You don't need to be waiting on me hand and foot," Rosie said. "You have a baby to take care of. Where is Georgia Rose?"

"The little lazybones is sleeping in today," I answered. "Why don't I get your breakfast before she wakes up?" I asked it like a question, but I didn't wait for an answer. Back in the kitchen, I cleaned up the floor and wrung out the towel while I waited for the kettle to boil. While the tea was steeping and the bread toasting, I scouted out the refrigerator and cupboards. I had never gotten to the market, but there was enough in there to put together some soup and biscuits for lunch.

I wanted to run and clean myself up while Rosie ate, but she looked too shaky to leave alone with hot tea. I found myself having to coax her to take bites of her toast, the way I have to coax Baby Girl to eat her cereal mush. On my way back to the kitchen, I poked my head into my bedroom. Baby Girl was wide awake and rolling around in her crib. Lucky thing she hadn't caught sight of me, so I was able to deposit the tray in the kitchen before picking her up.

I wasted no time getting back to Baby Girl, so she wouldn't fuss any. After I changed her diaper, I got to thinking that maybe I should have taken Jeanie up on her offer to go diaper shopping. Our supply was running low and I couldn't leave Rosie alone. Even if I could slip out when Lily was here, I didn't think I would get far with that big toe of mine.

After feeding Georgia, I decided to worry about my more immediate problems. I gave Baby Girl a quick bath and got her dressed. I pulled my hair into a ponytail and slipped into some clean clothes. I couldn't squeeze my foot into my sneaker. A quick peek into Rosie's room told me what I already knew. She was fast asleep again. I picked up Baby Girl's highchair and moved it near the bathroom door. I grazed the top of my toe with it. I would have given my last dime for an empty field to scream in at that moment. Since Rosie's house lacked any real open space, I bit down hard on my lip instead. I sat Baby Girl in her seat and put a few toys on the tray. A hot shower would have helped wake me up for the day, but between Baby Girl and Rosie there was no hope of that. I had just finished washing my face when the doorbell rang. I lifted Baby Girl onto my hip and limped to the front door.

Doc Richards was standing on the porch, carrying his bag. Although I was expecting him, the blow to my foot must have affected my head, too, because the sight of Doc at the door threw me some. I tried to calm myself. I needed to look like I could be trusted with Rosie's care for now.

"How is she today?" he asked.

"She didn't eat much this morning, but she got a good night's sleep," I reported. "She's napping again now."

I followed him down the hall to Rosie's room. Doc Richards tapped on the half-open door and slipped through the opening. I peeked around him and saw Rosie's eyes flutter open. "How are you feeling this morning?" Doc asked.

Instead of answering the question, Rosie set her eyes on me and said, "Why don't you go out to the front room? Let our little Christmas angel soak in all that Christmas spirit hanging on that tree."

I took the hint and limped back to the kitchen. I was stirring the pot, breathing in the soup steam when Doc joined us in the kitchen. Georgia greeted our visitor by throwing her teething ring at him. He caught it in one hand and put it on her highchair tray. He ruffled her curls and a big belly laugh rolled out of her sweet lips. "How is Rosie doing?" I asked.

"She is doing as well as can be expected," Doc answered. "We can talk more about that after I take a look at your foot."

I didn't even have the energy to protest his order. I sat down in the chair Doc pulled out for me and rested my foot on the chair across the way. He started poking, pressing, and turning my foot and ankle. It hurt so much I had to bite back my tears. I was questioning the term "healer" when he finally rested my foot on the chair. "I think you have a broken toe and some bruised foot bones," Doc said. "I can tape up your toes here, but you should go to the hospital for x-rays."

He opened his bag and got to work wrapping and taping, while I got to thinking about what excuse I could give for not following his medical advice. I wasn't about to leave Rosie when she needed my help so badly, and a hospital visit would cost money I didn't have. I had no intentions of telling him about my money situation, and I wondered if I was making myself sound too important in terms of Rosie's care. The doorbell relieved me of that effort. While Doc saved me the hobble to the door, I set the table for lunch.

Lily swept down the hall as if she didn't really need that cane of hers. She was shooting out a bunch of whispered questions and Doc was answering as fast as he could. She stopped at Rosie's door, took a deep breath, and gave the door a few taps. As Doc and Lily slipped into Rosie's room, I went back to work on lunch. Baby Girl soon tired of her highchair, so I let her perch on my hip while I worked. She was still there when Lily came into the kitchen. "Do you think that is the safest place for a baby to be while you're working on a lit stove?" she asked.

The tone of her voice told me she wasn't so much asking me a question as she was scolding me for bad judgment. The churning inside of me let me know that I didn't take to that kind of criticism much better than I did to Daddy's way of correcting me. Just the same, I put Georgia back in her highchair. I learned real young to waste no time fixing my ways so the method of advising didn't get ugly quick. I had no way of knowing how things might progress with Lily. When her hand reached out toward me, I flinched. My reaction took her back some. She stepped closer and said real gently, "I'm sorry, Becky. I don't mean to criticize. I'm just worried about Rosie, and I'm afraid I took it out on you."

Now those were words I would have never heard from Daddy, so I stumbled over my own tongue trying to tell her everything was fine. Lily smiled and said, "My goodness, that soup smells delicious. Is there anything I can do to help you out here? It's been a long time since I cooked, but I take directions well."

I had a hard time believing anyone tried to give Lily directions. She was more the kind of woman whose words everyone else followed. I thought her offer was kind, though, and said as much. "Thank you, but everything is just about ready. Besides," I smiled, "Rosie would not take kindly to me putting our guests to work."

Lily patted my arm. "You need to stop thinking of me in terms of being a guest," she said, before she glided back to Rosie's room.

I went back to work. After sliding the biscuits into the oven, I picked up Baby Girl again and went down to Rosie's room. The conversation in the room ended as soon as I passed through her door. "Lunch is just about ready," I said. "Would you like me to bring you in a tray now or a little later?"

"I don't want you to do any such thing," Rosie answered. "I'll be joining all of you in the dining room."

Doc and Lily passed a look between them before nodding in my direction. I limped on out and got to work setting the dining room table with the good china dishes. I tied a little red bow on the stem of each glass and placed a few Christmas decorations in the center of the table. It sure didn't look like a spread in one of those magazines Rosie was always referring to, but it was the best I could do working with one foot, one hand, and a baby grabbing at everything. I hurried as best as I could back to the kitchen, cleared the clean dishes off the kitchen table, and got the soup and biscuits ready for serving. When the food was on the table, Doc and Lily brought Rosie to the dining room.

"Didn't I tell you she was an artist?" Rosie said. "This girl can make anything look like it belongs in a museum."

I looked at the slipshod job I did on the table and wished I had put a little more effort into making it look festive. I started serving up the soup as soon as everyone settled into their seats.

"Do you plan to study art in college, Becky?" Lily asked as she passed the biscuits to Doc. "You're ready to take your high school tests now."

"I don't have any college plans," I answered. I stood up so fast I almost tipped my chair over. "I forgot Georgia's lunch," I said, and hobbled out to the kitchen.

When I came back, everyone was talking about what a good choice soup was on such a damp and chilly day. "It smells and feels like a storm's heading our way," Doc said. "There was no word of one on the news, but what do those fools know? My bones do a better job predicting the weather than all of their fancy instruments and computers." Rosie and Lily laughed, but nodded their heads in agreement.

My backside had barely met the seat when Lily said, "Maybe we should move you and your belongings up to my house right after lunch, Rosie. You shouldn't be out in a storm."

I tried to focus my attention on Baby Girl's lunch, but my brain wasn't having any of that. I kept my eyes fixed on Baby Girl and my ears perked for Rosie's answer. "Now don't you go putting the cart before the horse," Rosie said. "I told you both I have to talk this over with Becky first. This affects all three of us in a bushel of ways."

"You haven't had a bite of your soup, Becky," Doc said. "Let me take over for a little while." He took Baby Girl's spoon from my hand without waiting for my reply.

I twisted back around in my seat and picked up my own spoon. Lily leaned into the table and said, "Rosie needs someone to keep her company all of the time. That's too much for a young girl with a baby to look after. I have a big house and very competent staff. Rosie will have everything she needs there.

Of course, she is worried about you and Georgia. I tried to tell her you would never want to stand between Rosie and the proper care she needs. Rosie needs to hear that from you, too, of course."

Lily stopped talking, and I understood that I was supposed to do as I was told and encourage Rosie to move into Lily's house. I admit my selfish feelings were keeping those words from rolling off my tongue. What would happen to Baby Girl and me? Where would we live? Could I still work at the store? I did a quick accounting of how much money I had saved over the past months. I had been able to sock away more after I finished paying off the barn. Still, it wouldn't last long if my job came to an end.

"Becky," Lily said. There was a real sharpness to her voice.

"Of course you should go live with Lily," I said. "She will be able to take much better care of you than I can. How long will she need to stay there?" I asked Doc.

Lily answered me instead of Doc. "We are talking about a permanent move," she said. "It is time for Rosie to retire and enjoy being pampered for a change. Why, once she is back on her feet, we may even do a little traveling."

"Will you still be wanting me to work at the store?" I asked.

Rosie looked at me with tears in her eyes. "Like Lily said, you should be thinking about college. Between school and Georgia, there will be no time for the store. I'm afraid we will have to close it." Rosie took a deep breath and smiled. "I don't know what everyone in this town will do without those creations of yours, though."

I nodded my head, wishing for the right words. I stared into my soup for a while before asking, "Would it be all right if Georgia and I stayed here for a couple of days more? I promise I'll take care of everything and make sure the house is closed up tight when we leave."

"Like I told Lily before," Rosie started. "We are a package deal—where I go, you and Georgia go—so if I move up to Lily's, so do the two of you. If you want to spend Christmas in our house, then here is where we will be. There is plenty of time for moving. Besides, we don't want to spend our Christmas Eve trying to pack up all our belongings."

"As Doc said, there likely is a storm coming, and I can send some people down to pack up your things," Lily said.

"There are some things people like to do for themselves," Rosie argued.

"You aren't strong enough yet to be packing," Lily answered.

"Maybe not, but I have Becky here, and I would rather have family going through my things than your hired help," Rosie shot back.

It was clear neither of these ladies was about to back down. I was worrying about what all this arguing was doing to Rosie's health. "On the other hand, it might be nice having Christmas morning at Lily's. I can get whatever you need for this week packed up this afternoon, and come back during the week to get whatever else you need," I offered.

"How are you going to get three people packed up by yourself while you're limping around like that? I thought you were going to fix her up?" Rosie pointed at Doc.

I had never seen Rosie with a hankering to pick a fight before. "My foot is already feeling much better," I said.

Doc patted my arm. "I think you've had enough excitement for one day, Rosie. Let's get you back into bed. Moving can wait a couple of days. Becky, you get together a list of groceries you need for the next couple of days and call your order into Haystack's Market. I'll pick it up and drop it by on my way home."

"We can't take up your whole day," I said.

"No one comes to see the doctor on Christmas Eve," Doc answered. "And you can do me a favor in return. Follow the care instructions I gave you regarding your foot. Rosie will never forgive me if you are not back in perfect shape soon."

"I will," I answered.

CHAPTER 29

I settled onto the sofa in the front parlor and rested my foot on a pillow. I had the television set turned low, so as not to wake Rosie or Georgia. I had been thinking about doing just this from the moment our company left. By the time I finished cleaning up, I was worried there would be no time for a rest before everyone else woke up from their naps. My body was feeling very thankful that my head had been worrying about nothing.

I needed a nap, but it wasn't meant to be. As I rested my eyes, a million worries filled my head. Could Baby Girl and I really move to Lily's house? Lily wasn't the kind of woman who left questions unasked or unanswered. Both Lily and Rosie talked about me going to college. I hadn't told either of them, but I wasn't going to be taking those high school graduation exams. They had both worked hard to get me ready for the exam, but when I went to fill out the application it said I needed a birth certificate or driver's license to take the test. I didn't have a driver's license, and wasn't about to go back home looking for my birth certificate. Rosie had done so much for me over the past six months—so much for both Baby Girl and me. I felt guilty just thinking about leaving her when she needed us the most, but then again, would she really need us after she moved to Lily's home?

The doorbell rang, ending my thinking session. I opened the door and I found John with an armful of Christmas gifts. He looked over the top of the carton and said, "There's more in my truck."

He made six trips between his truck and the parlor before saying, "Merry Christmas!"

"Who is all this from?" I asked.

"Just about everybody in town sent something," John answered. "They wanted to bring their gifts themselves, but Miss Lily would not hear of it. She said Rosie needs her rest more than she needs visitors." John looked at my foot. "Would you like me to help you unpack all of this and get it under the tree?"

Just then Baby Girl started to cry. I detoured into the bedroom, soothed her tears, and gave her a clean dry bottom. By the time we got to the parlor, John had all of the gifts arranged under the tree. The sight brought me back to the gift drive at school. It was the only place I'd ever seen so many gifts under a tree. I used to love looking at that gift tree at school, until I got old enough to realize that some of those gifts were going to end up in our house. Knowing that made me a little sad to think Mama and Daddy never thought buying us gifts was worth the money. Daddy had plenty of money for the things that were important to him, like tools and whiskey, so I was sure it wasn't an actual lack of funds that was stopping them.

"Becky, is everything okay?" John asked.

"I'm sorry, I got lost in my thoughts," I said. "Everything looks beautiful."

"Becky," Rosie called from the bedroom. "Who's out there?"

John walked back to her room and tapped on the door. "It's John," he said. "I was on my way out when I heard you calling Becky. Can I help you out of bed?"

John helped Rosie to her chair. "Will you look at that," Rosie said. "It looks like Santa came a little early this year."

"A lot of people in this town love you, Rosie," John said, pulling his coat tighter around him. "I'm heading home for the night. It feels like we might have a white Christmas, but don't hesitate to call me if you need anything."

"I have everything I need right here," Rosie answered, nodding in my direction. "You go home and enjoy the holiday," she said to John. "You should make a stop by your brother's house. You'll want to get there before he has to get over to the church."

"Yes, ma'am," John said. He sounded like a boy who was just sent to clean his room. I didn't think leaving me was the reason for this turn in his outlook. I was trying to put the pieces of the puzzle together in my head, and once again lost track of what my body was doing, which apparently was staring at John. "My last name is Thompson," John said.

That's all it took to start the puzzle pieces tumbling together. I remembered thinking I knew those eyes the first time I talked with the reverend. Now I could see even more of a resemblance.

I walked our guest to the door and wished him a merry Christmas. John reminded me one last time to call him if I needed any help. I settled Baby Girl in her bouncy seat and went back to my room to gather my gifts for her and Rosie. I had hidden them in the back of my closet. I know that makes me sound silly; Rosie was too old to be hunting for a peek at her gifts, and Baby Girl was too young for such activity. Still, it seemed like the Christmassy thing to do, so I had spent some time finding just the right hiding place.

"What is all that?" Rosie asked, as I walked into the parlor with my armload of gifts.

I put the gifts under the tree, or more like near the tree, as everyone else's gifts prevented me from getting any closer. I bent over and picked up the afghan that had slipped off of Rosie's legs, and tucked it around her again. "Those are my gifts for you and Georgia," I said. "There's something there for Lily, too, to thank her for all of her help with my lessons. I forgot to get it out when she was here earlier."

"It's just like you to think of everyone else when you've been driving yourself into exhaustion trying to take care of us and the store without any help from me. You shouldn't have bothered with anything for me. I already have everything I need."

"It's not much," I said. "Just a few things I made."

Rosie perked up at my words. "Homemade gifts are the best kind," she said. "Of course, I don't have your gift for making things. I hope you'll keep that in mind when you open my gifts. I needed a little help from some mail-order companies. Can you bring them out here for me? I hid them in the back of my bedroom closet."

I laughed out loud at Rosie's secret hiding place. "We think alike," I said. "I hid my gifts in the back of my closet, too."

Rosie was still chuckling when I returned with her gifts. I had just settled on the couch when Baby Girl started fussing. I picked her up, and discovered she was a little warm. I took a good look at her, and wondered if her droopy eyes and drippy nose meant a cold was brewing inside of her. Doc had just given her a once over while he was here. If anything worse was happening, surely he would have caught it and told me about it, but then again, he never mentioned a cold, either. As selfish as this was, and Christmas is no time to be selfish, I was thinking less about Baby Girl's discomfort than about how much I needed a good night's sleep. Or more specifically, how I was never going to get that good night's sleep if Baby Girl had a cold.

A few minutes later, I was feeling mighty guilty about those selfish thoughts. Baby Girl had sunk into the crook of my arm, her feet resting on my other arm, and was sighing as I stroked her silky red curls. I could almost picture her sprouting angel wings as she lay there, content just to be in my arms. Rosie always seemed to have a sixth sense when it came to Baby Girl. Sensing her current need for calm, Rosie spoke in a whisper. "I hope you're not too upset about me closing the store. I know you could do it on your own, but a girl your age has more important things to do with her time. You deserve a chance for an education; you have a real future with those talents of yours. I know you've been worrying about those tests, but there's no need for that. I'm sure you will pass all of them with flying colors."

I guess when it came to feelings, Rosie had a sixth sense about me, too. "I know you want to help me," I said. "And Lily has been so good about tutoring me so I can do well on the tests. But the truth is I don't have the money for college anyway, so all those efforts were for nothing."

"Don't you be worrying about money," Rosie said. "I have enough of that, and I can't imagine a better way to invest it than in your education. I never told you this, but I had a baby when I was your age. My good for nothing first husband up and ran off when my baby girl wasn't any older than Georgia Rose. I know how hard it is to raise up a child when you're still one yourself. You're not alone in this, Becky. Let me help you. Let Lily help you. I know you want to be a good mama to that baby, but you never have a moment without her. I think moving in with Lily will be good for all of us. You won't need to be tending to me so much, and there will be help with the baby, so you can go to school and study, and not have to worry about Georgia Rose. That little one is going to be mighty proud when you graduate from college."

We sat in silence for a minute or two. I was staring at Baby Girl's toes, trying to come up with the right words to say. When I looked up, Rosie was sleeping. I think all that talking just wore her out. I sat there, watching her breathe, until the ammonia smell drifted up from Baby Girl's diaper. She was overdue for a change. I don't know how that got away from me, but I got up and took care of the problem right away.

Later, after I had warmed up some leftover soup for our dinner, Rosie suggested we follow an old family tradition of hers. Each of us was to open one gift before retiring for the night. Rosie pointed at a stack and asked, "Who are those from?"

I read the tags and was surprised to see there were gifts for Baby Girl and me, too. "These gifts are from Dottie and Ray."

Rosie nodded her approval, so I toted the packages over to her. They weren't the most neatly wrapped gifts I'd ever seen, but they sure were the most colorful. Dottie's take on the traditional red and green went to the shades of hot pink and glow-in-the-dark green. A giant sparkling silver and gold bow sat in the middle of the colorful stage. I insisted Rosie open hers first. She put up no argument and tore into the paper as soon as I put the gift on her lap. "A tin of homemade muffins! I'm glad I opened this one tonight. Now we can enjoy these for our Christmas breakfast. Open yours."

I unwrapped the package and found a home manicure set inside. I had never owned anything like that before. Mama and Daddy would have made me throw that right out. I wondered how Dottie had found nail polish in the same shades as the wrapping paper and bows. In the bottom of the box there was a package of writing cards, with brightly colored fingernails across the front of them. I handed Baby Girl's gift to Rosie to open. "Can you do it for her?" I asked. "I don't think she can do it, and if you unwrap I can hold her so she can see it."

Rosie tore through the paper. Inside was a hot pink sweater. Dottie's gifts had a real theme to them. "You won't lose sight of Georgia if she is wearing this," Rosie laughed.

I put the sweater on Baby Girl. "I think it looks pretty on her," I said.

Rosie took a good look at Baby Girl and smiled. "Everything looks pretty on her."

We watched an old black-and-white Christmas movie on television, another one of Rosie's traditions, before going to bed. After I settled Rosie into bed for the night, I dug out the Christmas book I had brought home from the store. I read it to Baby Girl, just like I used to read it to my brothers and sisters at home.

I had read that poem so many times, I practically didn't need the pages to recite Clement C. Moore's words. When I finished, I wiped Baby Girl's nose one more time and rubbed her back until she fell asleep. Then I hurried down the hall as fast as my bad foot would let me go, and stepped into the shower. The warm water seemed to wash away all my worries of the day. When I finished, I climbed into bed with my hair soaking wet, and fell fast asleep.

My hair hadn't had a chance to dry before Baby Girl woke me with her tears. I spent most of the night on my feet bobbing and swaying with Baby Girl in my arms. Nothing seemed to soothe her, as her little nose got stuffier and her cough became more regular. Finally, when the sun rose, she fell asleep. I knew it wouldn't last long, so as soon her head touched the sheets, I crawled into my bed.

I had not even pulled the blankets over me, when I heard Rosie calling my name. I dragged myself out of bed and hobbled over to her room. After I helped her to the bathroom, Rosie looked me over from head to toe and said, "That's a good idea. Why don't we stay in our sleep clothes all day. We can't get out to church, so there is no reason for us to dress up."

I should have offered to help Rosie into a clean nightgown, but I barely had the energy to dress myself. Instead, I just nodded in agreement. I settled her in her kitchen chair and I put the kettle on to boil. Rosie reminded me about Dottie's gift, and I limped off to the parlor. As I came back from fetching the muffins, the phone was ringing. When I lifted the phone off the hook, I looked out the window for the first time that day. Tiny crystals of ice coated the stairs, grass, and tree limbs. The ice was still falling from the sky. The bits of ice pinged as they hit the window.

Lily was calling to make sure we were all right. I brought the phone over to Rosie and let her deal with Lily's concerns. I wanted to get breakfast out of the way before Baby Girl started demanding my attention. When I set Rosie's teacup before her, she quickly said her goodbyes and handed me the phone to put away. "Where's Georgia this morning?" she asked. "Did all the Christmas Eve excitement wear her out?"

I sat down across from Rosie. "Georgia was up most of the night with a cold. She's catching up with some of her sleep needs now."

"Christmas or not," Rosie said, "if you need the doctor, you call him now. Does she have a fever? Is she drinking?"

"She was a little warm last night, but she seems normal now. She has a stuffy nose and a cough. She has a hard time drinking her bottle with her nose so stuffed up, but she is getting plenty to drink, even if it takes a long time. I don't think we need to call Doc out in an ice storm."

"Okay, well, her cold explains why you are moving around here like a robot in one of those old space alien movies. If she didn't get any shuteye last night, I'm sure you didn't either. Why don't you go lay down now?" Rosie said.

I wanted to jump at her suggestion, but I was worried about leaving her awake and unattended. I didn't have time to talk myself into it before Baby Girl started crying out for me. When I returned to the table with Baby Girl in my arms, Rosie had another plan to offer. "Why don't I go back to bed, and you can put Georgia in there with me? I can keep an eye on her while you take a nap."

Another tempting offer, but it only took a few seconds of contemplating this one for me to picture Baby Girl rolling off the bed and Rosie tumbling after her. "I'll take a nap later, when she dozes off again. Let's go open the gifts. I can't wait for you to see what I made for you."

Hours later, I was knee-deep in wrapping paper, and Rosie had replaced the old afghan with the new lap quilt I had made for her. I cleared some space for Baby Girl's new quilt and laid her down with one of her new toys. I gathered the paper and bows, moved everything back under the tree, and dropped onto the couch. Baby Girl was happy rolling back and forth on her quilt and chewing on the toy keys. I decided to leave her be, and take a moment to breathe. I don't know if it was the fact that I had gone two days with nothing more than a couple of cat naps or if it was all the twinkling colored lights, but I looked at the tree and burst into tears. "What's wrong?" Rosie asked.

I wanted to stop the flood of salty tears washing down my face, but I couldn't. "You come on over here," Rosie ordered.

I did as I was told and sat on the floor by Rosie's feet. I was sobbing so hard, I couldn't catch my breath. I was missing Mama, and my sisters and brothers, something fierce right now. Worse than that, I was filled with shame over all the lies I'd been telling since arriving in Watson's Grove. Every gift I'd opened today, every act of kindness, came from someone I had lied to, someone who deserved more respect than I had paid them. Rosie reached over and swept the hair from my face. "You're missing your family today, aren't you? I know they must be missing you, too. You go out there in the kitchen and you call them up right now. I don't need to know who they are, or why you left. You don't need to explain anything, and I don't need to know anything. You go ahead now."

Rosie was wrong. Rosie, who gave me a job, was wrong. Rosie, who gave us a home, a family, and a community, was wrong. She did need to know, and I did need to tell her. I rested my head on her knees and tried to stop my sobbing. Rosie stroked my hair, and for a few minutes the sound of my heaving breaths filled the room. Then the words started pouring out of my mouth like the tears from my eyes. I told her about Mama, Daddy, and my brothers and sisters. I told her about the barn and the boxcar. Then I told her about Baby Girl. When I was done, Rosie whispered, "I'm sorry, Becky. I shouldn't have made you hold this all inside for so long. It's going to be all right. Everything is going to be all right. I promise."

I sat there praying her words would come true. I felt something touch my leg, and my head jerked up. It was Baby Girl. It took a minute to set in my head. She had never moved anywhere on her own before. But here she was. She had rolled onto her belly and crept the couple of feet over to me. She grabbed onto my leg with one hand and pitched forward. Before I could pick her up, she had picked herself up and was balancing on her arms and belly. She gave us a big smile, and Rosie and I both said, "Look, she's crawling on all fours, and she has her first tooth!" It was barely there, but sure enough, a little white pearl was peeking above her gums.

Rosie bent over and hugged my shoulders. "This surely is a day of milestones for our family."

CHAPTER 30

The next few days were filled with sorting and packing. Neither Rosie nor I spoke of the secrets I had shared. Baby Girl's new freedom of movement meant she had to reside on my hip as I readied our things for the move. She was getting big, and my hip and back would ache some by the end of the day, but it was the safest place for her to be. I kept waiting for Rosie to experience a change of heart; I thought seeing her life get packed into old grocery cartons would make her want to stay in her own home. The change never came. Rosie seemed resigned to the move. I collapsed onto my bed each night, exhausted from the day's labor, but sleep usually escaped me. Instead, I lay in my bed, stared at the ceiling, and replayed my Christmas confession to Rosie.

When moving day arrived, John pulled up in front of the house. A big moving truck pulled up to the curb right behind him. Four men got out of the truck and rolled up its back door. John led them into the house, and they wasted no time before lugging the boxes out to the truck. "Well, ladies, are you ready to go?" John asked. "Your chariot awaits you."

Rosie frowned. "I don't know if I can get up into your truck, John."

"I already thought of that. I have the car today," he said, grinning.

"I should have known you would have thought of everything, John," Rosie said, patting his arm. "Let's go, Becky."

"Why don't I stay behind until they get everything in the truck?" I offered. "We don't want them to miss anything."

Rosie shook her head. "These men know their job, I'm sure. I don't want you hanging about, getting sad about moving. It's best we keep moving forward, and not look back."

I nodded and dressed Baby Girl in her winter jacket, hat, and mittens. I grabbed her diaper bag and flung it over my free shoulder. I followed John and Rosie out the door, all the while rubbing my cheek against Baby Girl's forehead. Feeling the softness of her skin against mine gave me the courage to follow Rosie's advice, and not look back.

Rosie and I sat in the back seat of the car with Georgia buckled into her car seat between us. As John drove past the Second Hand Rose, my eyes welled up with tears and I had to turn away to keep Rosie from knowing. Rosie started humming "Sweet Georgia Brown" and helped Baby Girl clap her hands to the beat. I turned back to watch and saw Baby Girl's whole self smiling. By the time John pulled into Lily's long driveway, Rosie was belting out the chorus and swinging to the beat in her seat, and Baby Girl was laughing out loud. Despite my concerns, I found myself laughing and singing along.

When the car came to a stop, I was surprised to see Lily waiting at the door for us. I had never seen her open her own door before. Something else was different, too. It took me a few steps for it to click into my brain. Lily wasn't carrying her cane. As we passed through the doorway, Lily smiled and said, "Welcome home! Mrs. Harper will organize the moving men when they get here. Why don't we go into the parlor and rest a bit before lunch?"

I knew that was another one of those questions not looking for an answer, so I followed Rosie and Lily into the parlor. Watching Lily sweep across the room with Rosie under her wing reminded me of my favorite picture in the hymnbook at church. In the picture, a dove with both wings opened wide is sweeping down from the heavens. I was a different story though. My big toe was still giving me trouble, and with Baby Girl on one hip and her diaper bag on the other I looked more like a pack mule making my way through a canyon. There was nothing peaceful or graceful in the way I was moving. There was nothing making me look like I belonged in that house.

The heavy drapes in the parlor had been pushed open to allow the sunshine to pour into the room. Lily and Rosie set to talking right away. I couldn't concentrate on their conversation, so I just kept nodding my head, every so often pausing to hope I hadn't agreed to anything I shouldn't have. The excitement of the car ride had tuckered Baby Girl out, so she passed the time napping in my arms. When she woke up, I knew it was time for me to rejoin the world, too. "Excuse me, Lily, but I need to be getting Georgia her lunch. May I use your kitchen to fix her something?" I asked.

Lily shook her head. "I want you to start thinking of this place as home, Becky. It isn't my kitchen, it's our kitchen, and you don't need permission to roam around your own home." She looked at her watch and added, "Actually, I think all of our lunches should be ready now."

The words had no sooner passed her lips than Mrs. Harper came into the parlor to announce as much. When we settled in the dining room, I was surprised to find my work done for me. Not only was there lunch for the three of us, but the cook had prepared a special meal for Baby Girl. I must have been half asleep before, because I hadn't heard a peep of noise from the movers, but Baby Girl's highchair was set up in the dining room. I looked down at the flowered rug under my feet and started worrying about Baby Girl's dining etiquette. We would wear out our welcome quickly if she spit her sweet potatoes all over that rug. When I went around the table, I was relieved to see a cloth spread out under her chair. Mrs. Harper must have raised some babies of her own.

I fed Baby Girl before turning to my own plate. I had barely gotten a bite in when Lily decided to turn the subject of conversation to me. "I looked into the art classes at the college John attends," she began. "You can take up to two courses this coming semester and then apply to be a full-time student for the summer sessions. You can take the GED next week, and your scores should be in quickly enough for you to be allowed to take the college classes. I know it is short notice, but I talked to someone and received permission for your late registration, and I'm certain you are ready for the test. We can do some review work to boost your confidence. You can drive the car John picked you up in today to get to school. I know it is a little stuffy-looking for a young girl, but it will do until we get you something more suitable."

Rosie interrupted. "We haven't even settled into our rooms yet. Talk about tests and college courses can wait."

"Well," Lily said, "my point is it can't wait. Becky needs to get her paperwork in now, so she can take classes at the end of January."

Rosie was never one to lose a battle of wills. "We will talk about this later, after we have settled in," she said.

The conversation had killed my appetite, so I offered to clean up from lunch. Lily seemed surprised by my suggestion and explained it was someone else's job to clean up after meals. "Why don't I show you to your rooms," Lily said. "You can get settled in today, and tomorrow we can sit down and get Becky's paperwork finished."

Rosie's room was on the first floor, tucked into a corner of the house I had never seen before. It was about four times the size of her room at home, and had a sitting area with a television. There were big closets on one wall, and a door leading to her very own bathroom. Back home, four of my brothers shared a room half the size of this one. I offered to do her unpacking, but Mrs.

Harper had beaten me to it. Rosie's clothes were hanging in the closets and her photos, knickknacks, and medicine bottles were lined up on her dressers and tables. Rosie settled into a chair in front of the television and sent us on our way.

I followed Lily back into the hallway. "Your room is upstairs," she explained. As I followed her up the staircase, two things came to mind. First, I didn't like the idea of being so far from Rosie. What if I couldn't hear her calling for help in the night? Second, I wondered if Mrs. Harper was the snooping kind. If she had gone through all of Rosie's things, had she gone through mine too? I ran my hand through Baby Girl's diaper bag and felt my notebook buried in the middle of her things. I was grateful I'd thought to do that before we left Rosie's house. Lily stopped in front of an open door. "Here you are," she said with a sweep of her arm.

The room was even bigger than Rosie's room downstairs. At one end was a big bed dressed in a yellow and white striped comforter. Nightstands with tall crystal lamps stood guard at both sides of the bed. I could see a huge tub through an open door near the corner of the room. At the other end of the room stood a sofa, a chair, some small tables, and a television. A small nook contained a desk and a pair of bookcases. It was beautiful, but what was missing was more important to me than all of those pretty things. "Where is Georgia's crib?" I asked.

Lily looked surprised by my question. "Her crib is in her room," she answered. "It's right this way."

I tightened my grip on Baby Girl as I followed Lily. A door just beyond the nook connected my room to a nursery. It was decorated in pink and white, with dolls and stuffed animals lined up on shelves. A rocking chair was placed next to her crib. The room looked like a picture in a magazine, but all I could think about was how far the crib was from my bed. I think I could have run from the Second Hand Rose to the Super Suds faster than I could make it from my bed to hers.

I didn't want to seem ungrateful, so I kept my concerns to myself and decided to find my own solution to this problem. One glance at Lily and I knew it was the right decision. Her eyes clouded with tears as she looked around the room. I had been so worried about myself that I hadn't stopped to think about how difficult it was for Lily to have a different baby moving into the room that must have been intended for her own. "Thank you for everything," I said. "I'm going to change Georgia's diaper and put her down for her afternoon nap."

"You must be exhausted from all of the packing," Lily said. "And your foot is still bothering you. I'll change Georgia and rock her to sleep, so you can get some rest."

"I can take care of her myself," I said.

We stood staring into each other's faces in silence for a minute or so. "I know you can," Lily answered. "I'll go check on Rosie."

I watched Lily leave the room. Her shoulders drooped and her stride lacked the lightness and energy I had seen earlier in the day. I changed Baby Girl's diaper and laid her in her crib. I only needed to rub her back for a few minutes before she fell asleep. I stood by the crib watching her back rise and fall for a few minutes before tiptoeing off to my room. I explored the drawers and closets before collapsing onto the sofa. I propped my foot up on a pillow and turned on the television. I rested for a bit, turning the television's volume lower and lower until finally I turned off the set. I was worried I wouldn't hear Baby Girl if she cried. I kept telling myself the sofa wasn't much further from the crib than the front room of Rosie's house was from our bedroom. Knowing I was being silly for worrying didn't make the worrying go away, so I moved to the rocking chair in Baby Girl's room.

That night at dinner, Lily was as quiet as she had been the first time I'd met her. I wondered what was wrong, but held my questions inside. When the table was cleared, Lily suggested we go to the parlor. "Rosie and I had a long talk this afternoon," she said.

"I want to hear your story straight from your mouth." I could hear the anger in her voice.

I stared at Rosie. Had she told all of my secrets to Lily? My answer was in Rosie's eyes.

I stood up and lifted Baby Girl onto my hip. "We'll clear out of here in the morning," I said.

"You'll do no such thing," Rosie said. "I only told her because I knew she could help. You two aren't going anywhere without me."

I walked out of the room before some angry words slipped out of me.

I spent that night sleeping on the floor beside Baby Girl's crib. I didn't think Lily would mind my leaving, but I wasn't sure about how she would feel about me taking Baby Girl with me.

CHAPTER 31

I woke up the next morning and discovered the little piece of floor I had slept on had become a stage. I had an audience of two—Mrs. Harper and Lily, who was standing with her hands on her hips. I was taken aback by the sight and let out a little yelp. The noise woke Baby Girl. I stumbled to my feet, so I could be the first one to her. Lily cleared her throat. "Mrs. Harper came up to see if you would be having breakfast downstairs or in your room. When she saw your bed hadn't been slept in, she came and got me."

"I was worried Georgia might be afraid sleeping on her own. She's never been this far from me before," I said. This may have not been the whole truth, but it was a part of it. The look on Lily's face though told me she heard what I wasn't saying just as loud and clear as the words I spoke. I turned away from her and focused my attention on Mrs. Harper. There was a real softness, a kindness in her eyes.

"I brought a bottle for the baby," Mrs. Harper said. "It might not be warm enough anymore, though."

I reached out and took the bottle. "Thank you," I said. "I'll feed it to her right after I change her diaper. We'll come downstairs after we're dressed. I don't want you waiting on us. Save your energy for Rosie."

I placed the bottle on the table next to the rocking chair and walked around the ladies to the changing table. When I started changing Baby Girl's diaper, my audience must have decided the show was over, because they left.

After the changing and feeding came the bathing and dressing. When I had Baby Girl looking and smelling as fresh as a daisy, I decided it was time to get to work on me. I settled her into her little seat and carried it into the bathroom with me. The bathroom was big enough to hold a class in, so it was easy enough to find a safe place for her seat. I picked a spot where she couldn't touch or grab anything, gave her one of her little toys to play with, and stepped into the shower.

By the time I was showered and dressed, Baby Girl was in need of another diaper changing. I tended to her needs and then carried her downstairs for breakfast. I heard voices in the dining room, so I peeked in there on my way to the kitchen. Rosie and Lily were sipping tea and discussing the weather. I slipped away unnoticed and went to the kitchen. The woman wiping a counter looked startled at first, but a smile quickly spread across her face. She dropped her rag and wiped her hands on her apron before petting Baby Girl's head. She said a few words in a language I didn't know. My lack of understanding must have shown on my face, because she quickly switched to single word communications. "Hungry?" she asked, and without waiting for an answer, "Go!" She pointed me back in the direction I had come from.

I walked down the hall to the dining room and was surprised to see our breakfast had gotten there before us. I mumbled a good morning to Rosie as I settled Baby Girl into her highchair and started feeding her the warm cereal mush and fruit. I slipped bites of my own breakfast into my mouth between Baby Girl's spoonfuls. I was hoping working this way would get us out of that room quicker. I was wiping Baby Girl's face clean when the doorbell rang. Mrs. Harper came and whispered something in Lily's ear. Lily excused herself and walked toward the front hall. "Would you like me to help you back to your room, Rosie?" I asked. I planted Baby Girl on my hip and came around the table

to help Rosie to her feet. She held onto my arm for balance as we shuffled out of the room.

"I only told her, because I know she can help," Rosie repeated her words from the night before. "You can't spend your life running away, Becky. You deserve better than that, and so does Georgia Rose."

Rosie stopped walking when we entered the hallway. I thought she was feeling weak, so I nodded toward the chair against the wall. "Rosie, you had no right to go behind my back like that, no matter what your reason. I've never given you cause to think I would do anything but my best for Georgia."

"Of course you haven't," Rosie said, looking like a wounded bird. "I know how much you love this baby, but growing up is hard enough even without a baby to tend to on your own. Lily can help, if we let her." Rosie brought her finger to her lips. "That doesn't sound like Doc, does it?"

I listened to the voices in the front hall. "No, I don't think that's him," I said. "Do you want me to call him?"

"No, I'm fine," Rosie said. "I'm just being a little nosy." The voices and footsteps faded and then disappeared when a door clicked shut. "Sounds like they went to her study," Rosie said, as she started moving again. It wasn't until we got to her bedroom door that I realized Rosie was already bathed and dressed.

"Did someone help you this morning?" I asked.

"Lily went and hired me a nursemaid," Rosie grunted.

"A nursemaid?"

Rosie shook her head. "She gets me out of bed, gets me bathed and dressed, and makes sure I take my medicines. She told me she was going to plan out my napping and exercising time while I was at breakfast. Another way you and I are alike, Becky, is that neither one of us is good at recognizing the need for, or accepting, help. We both need to get past that." I nodded and opened her door for her. Sure enough, the nurse was

standing there, grinning and holding an open folder when we walked in. "Becky, you'll probably want to go upstairs and find another sock for Georgia Rose now. Nurse and I need to have a little talk."

I looked down at Baby Girl's feet and saw one covered and one naked foot. I figured she must have kicked off her other sock while we were eating or walking to Rosie's room. I watched the floor as we retraced our steps, but found nothing, not even a speck of dust, until we got back to the dining room. The woman from the kitchen was standing beside the highchair and staring out the window. She had Baby Girl's sock in her hand and a look of worry on her face. Baby Girl let out a sound, causing the woman to turn toward us and force a smile on her face. I waved Baby Girl's bare foot at her and thanked her as she handed me the sock. She hurried through a sliding panel to what I guessed was the kitchen. I slipped over to the window. I wanted a peek at whatever was worrying her. A chill ran up my spine when I saw the black and white car in the driveway. The man Lily was talking to in her office was a police officer.

I hurried upstairs and grabbed my backpack and Baby Girl's diaper bag. I started stuffing in anything that seemed very necessary. I wished I knew where the movers had put the stroller. I could move a lot faster pushing Baby Girl in the carriage than carrying her in my arms. I had just grabbed Baby Girl's coat when Lily tapped twice on the door and walked in. I looked in the hall behind her but did not see a policeman. "Are the police with you?" I asked, swallowing hard.

"He left, but that's what I want to talk to you about," Lily said. "This morning someone noticed one of the front windows of the Second Hand Rose is broken. The officer came looking for Rosie. I don't want her bothered with this. John is going down now to board up the window. Can you go with him later today to see if anything important is missing? Maybe you can pack up

any personal items the two of you have there, and any of her financial records. It was probably just the windstorm last night, but it would be best to start clearing things out of the store." I nodded my head.

Lily looked at our packed bags. "My lawyer is on his way here. I've told him a little bit about your situation. He wants to talk to you himself. He needs a little more information in order for him to get your birth records and such. Since you are seventeen, you don't need parental permission to get the papers. My lawyer will be able to do it quietly, so no one even knows you needed them. He'll be here shortly. I will appreciate it if you could join us in my study in about fifteen minutes." I nodded my head once more. Lily stared at our bags again. "Rosie needs you in her life, Becky. I hope you'll remember that."

The smell coming from Baby Girl's diaper took over the conversation. "I need to change her diaper," I said. This time it was Lily's turn to nod her head.

"I bet a year ago you would never have pictured yourself doing that so many times a day," Lily smiled. "Raising a baby is a lot of work," she said, walking out the door.

CHAPTER 32

With Lily gone and Baby Girl with a clean bottom, I sat down in the rocking chair. I got to thinking about Lily's words. They seemed odd coming from a woman who didn't cook her own food, do her own laundry, or even open her own door. I changed a baby diaper for the first time when I was seven years old, and from that day on it was my job at home. Mama did it when I was at school, but once I got home it was one of my duties. Looking back, school was a real break for me from wiping bottoms, filling bottles, and looking out for my little brothers and sisters. I didn't see it that way back then, but then again, I didn't give a whole lot of thought to all my chores, either. It was just the way it was, and Mama and my brother Joseph didn't have it much better than me.

The biggest difference between Mama, Joseph, and me was that for the past year I'd known my life would be different someday. I don't believe Mama or Joseph ever held that idea in their heads. I'm sure if Mama saw me here rocking a sleeping baby in my arms, she would laugh at the idea that I had escaped my old life. In some ways, she would be right. I still wasn't seeing the world, or having adventures with friends. My days were mainly spent taking care of others. But some things had changed. The people around me wanted to help me; they wanted better for me. I needed to keep reminding myself of that.

A tap at the door pulled me out of my head. I laid Baby Girl down in her crib and went to the door. "Miss Lily would like you to come to her study now," Mrs. Harper said. I looked back toward the crib. "I brought you a baby monitor," Mrs. Harper said. "You put this piece near the crib and carry this piece with you. Then you'll be able to hear the baby from any room in the house."

I thanked her and set up the monitor on the table next to the rocking chair. I was surprised to see Mrs. Harper still in my doorway when I turned around. I guess she had orders to make sure I showed up in the study. I was nervous about the meeting, so as usual I started babbling on about anything. "Those baby monitors are a real clever idea," I said. "Now I need someone to invent a Rosie monitor. Her room is about a mile away from mine. I don't like the feeling she can't talk to me if she needs me. I know she has that nurse, but still . . ."

"The house has an intercom system." Mrs. Harper patted my arm. "Later, I'll show you how to use it. You can call her room, and she can call yours."

I was trembling by the time I walked into Lily's office. Lily introduced me to her lawyer, but I was so nervous I didn't hear the name and was too embarrassed to tell them I missed it. After shaking my hand, he nodded in the direction of a chair and said, "Please, be seated." I did as I was told, balancing my behind on the edge of the chair. "I need you to write down some basic information for me," the lawyer said. "I need your full name, date and place of birth, parents' names, and your mother's maiden name. List the schools you've attended, and the year you stopped attending." He handed me a pad of paper and a pen.

"I don't know my mother's maiden name," I whispered.

"Just do the best you can," he said.

When I finished, I handed the pad back to him. He looked it over for a minute and said, "Very good. Now comes the hard part. I need you to tell me everything you can remember about finding the baby. Where and when did you find her? What was she wearing? Did you find anything else in the vicinity of the baby? Did you notice anyone else hanging around?"

I took a deep breath and looked at Lily. She crossed the room and sat in a chair next to me. She held my hands in hers. "If my being here helps you tell your story, then I'll stay. If it would be easier for you without me here, then I'll leave. You decide."

I didn't believe there was anything that could make telling my story easy. "You can stay," I said. I was surprised to hear those words come out of my mouth, but the truth was Lily was trying to help me, despite learning about my lies. No matter what her words were saying, I knew she wanted to stay, and I owed her that much. I rubbed my finger back and forth across my half of the baby monitor before speaking again. Then I started my story and I didn't stop for as much as a deep breath until I got it all out.

"So you have no idea who the baby's birth mother is?" the lawyer asked.

"No, sir," I answered.

"None whatsoever?"

"No, sir," I repeated.

The lawyer rubbed his chin with one hand and tapped the desktop with the other. "How old was the baby when you found her?"

"Maybe a few hours. Maybe a few days," I shrugged. "She couldn't have been older than that. She still had her belly button stump, and she still had the new baby sleepiness."

"And you saw no references to a missing baby in any of the papers you checked?"

I shook my head. "No, sir."

The lawyer turned his attention to Lily. "As I told you before, getting Becky's documentation should not prove difficult. Straightening out the situation with the baby is another matter. Give me a day or two to see what I can come up with, and we can proceed from there." He stood up and looked at me again. "Are you sure you don't want to go home to your family? Do you want someone to let them know you are safe and well? We wouldn't have to disclose your location."

When I told my story, I had left out the part about Daddy telling me he didn't need to hear from me anymore. I had an ache inside of me from wanting to see Mama and the kids. Daddy had made up his mind, though, and reaching out to any of them would just stir Daddy's anger. They didn't need me bringing more trouble down on them. I looked at the lawyer. "No, sir. No one needs to hear from me."

While Lily accompanied her lawyer to the door, I made my way down to Rosie's room. Rosie's eyes lit up when I came in. "I was hoping you would come by for a visit," she said. "This house is so big it hardly feels like we're living together. Where's Georgia Rose?"

"She's napping," I said. I showed her the baby monitor and told her what Mrs. Harper had said about the intercom system.

"Well, I like that idea," she said. "But I prefer sitting face to face with you over talking to you through the walls. What have you been up to this morning? I hope you're getting some rest. You've been carrying too heavy a load for months now. You deserve a little time to catch your breath."

I told Rosie about my meeting with Lily and her lawyer. She wanted an instant replay of the meeting, and I did my best to accommodate her. When I had finished, she asked, "That's it? He didn't say anything else?"

"I don't think so," I answered. "I was real nervous, so I hope I didn't miss anything important."

Rosie reached over and patted my hands. "Of course, you were nervous," she said. "From now on, I want to be there when you meet with that lawyer. I have a few questions of my own for him, and two sets of ears are always better than one."

I looked at Rosie for a moment before shifting my glance to the floor. Rosie wanted things between us to be business as usual, but I couldn't help but feel like a wall had been built between us. No matter how many times she explained her actions, it all came back to the fact she'd betrayed my trust. Who knew what other promises would be broken?

Baby Girl's voice came through the monitor and stopped the conversation. She had woken up from her nap like a lamb, and was cooing and making all kinds of happy sounds. "I need to get upstairs," I said.

Rosie pulled herself up out of the chair and wrapped her arms around me. "I know I've hurt you, and I'm truly sorry. I've told you why I had to tell Lily, but there's no excuse for not trusting you enough to talk it over with you before I shared your secrets. You should have been a part of the decision-making process. We can't undo what's done, but I hope you can find it in your heart to forgive me."

Tears welled in my eyes. Rosie was right, but I knew it might take some time for forgiveness to take hold of my heart.

CHAPTER 33

We split the next couple of days between Lily's house and the Second Hand Rose. I collected the cash and important papers Rosie needed from the store, and boxed the remaining merchandise to donate to the church. Mornings I spent tending to Baby Girl and Rosie, and after lunch Baby Girl and I rode into town with John. I packed up boxes, and John hauled them over to the church.

On the first day, Baby Girl seemed as happy as I was to be back in the store. By the second day, I was spending most of my time packing with one hand and holding her on my hip with the other. By late afternoon, I was questioning the wisdom of my bringing her with me. Lily and Rosie had offered to keep watch over her at home, but I had refused their help. Rosie wasn't up to changing and carrying a baby around, and I couldn't picture Lily knowing how. I figured the work would fall on the shoulders of Mrs. Harper, and she had enough to do without adding diaper duty to her chore list. I knew I might have been thinking unfairly of Lily. After all, she had been planning on becoming a mama. But the truth is the *idea* of taking care of a baby is real different from actually taking care of one, and I didn't think Lily knew that yet.

We were finishing up for the day when Dottie came through the door. "Ray said I should leave you be so you can get your work done, but I needed to see how everybody is doing. How is Rosie? Is she getting stronger? You girls moving out to Lily's house must be a real blessing for Lily. How is she doing? I don't need to ask how this little one is doing. Georgia looks as happy as a hound on the trail of a jackrabbit. How about you? You look a little tired. Do you need some help with all this packing up? I guess the rumor's true, then. The Second Hand Rose really is closing down. The reverend's looking for volunteers to figure out what goes to families, what goes to the rummage sale, and what goes to the church nursery. You know, that's a real nice cash register. I can't imagine the church will have any use for that. You know who would, though? Pete Garcia, that's who. I don't think he has anything in that bike shop but an old tin box to keep his money and receipts in." Dottie paused to catch her breath.

I took advantage of the moment. "We're all fine," I said. "We were just finishing up for the day. I appreciate your idea about the register. I think Rosie would want Pete to have it. I'll let Rosie and Lily know you were asking after them. I don't want to keep you; I know you must be getting ready for the dinner crowd." I started walking toward the door. As I reached for the handle, Dottie stopped me in my tracks.

"Lily's lawyer stopped in the diner for coffee the other day. He was asking about you."

"How do you know Lily's lawyer?" I asked.

"I don't, really," Dottie said. "When he started asking questions about you, I asked him who he was and what business you were of his. He told me he was Lily's lawyer and that he had just met you. He said he was just wondering how a young girl like you got along in this town. I told him you have lots of friends here, and he won't find a single soul in town with a bad word to say about you. He seemed happy to hear that."

I looked at Dottie. Here I was wishing she hadn't noticed me in the store, and there she was defending me to a stranger. I moved over and hugged her with my free arm. "I noticed the same fellow's car driving straight through town a few minutes before I came over here," Dottie said. "You make sure Rosie knows if she needs help with anything, Ray and I will do everything we can for her. Do you need a ride out to the house?"

"No," I said. "John will be back from the church in a minute or two. Thank you anyway." I watched Dottie walk back across the street before I bundled up Baby Girl and walked to the bike shop. Pete greeted me like a long-lost relative. He hugged me so tight, I was afraid Baby Girl might get squashed between us. He was grateful for the offer of the cash register and wasted no time finding a wagon to load it into. A little wooden fence surrounded the back half of the wagon. Pete spread a blanket across the bottom and said, "Why don't we give Georgia a ride back to the Second Hand Rose? It will be fun for her, and it will give you a little break. She looks like she is glued to your hip."

Pete pulled the wagon and I walked alongside Baby Girl. The fence would keep her safe, but I felt better knowing I could grab hold of her if need be. When we got to the store, I lifted Baby Girl out of the wagon and Pete followed us into the store. He looked at the mostly empty shelves and said, "This town's going to miss this shop." Pete carried the cash register down to the wagon and wrapped it with the same care he had shown for Baby Girl. When he stood up, he turned to me and said, "We all have trouble in our past if you dig deep enough. We just have to keep people from digging." I didn't respond. Pete lowered his voice. "Dottie told me about that man asking about you. If Georgia's father or anybody else is trying to cause you trouble, don't you worry. Folks around here won't help them with their digging. We'll just keep breaking their shovels."

John's truck pulled up to the curb and John jumped out. He came over and shook Pete's hand, and the two men got to talking. I slipped away and went into the store to gather Baby Girl's belongings and turn off the lights. I was struggling down the steps when John caught sight of me. "Careful," he warned, grabbing most of the things from my arms. He turned back to Pete.

"Good luck with the register," he said. John stowed our gear while I settled Baby Girl into her car seat. John climbed in the truck and started the engine. "Are you okay, Becky? You looked like you had seen a ghost when I pulled up."

I forced a smile on my face. "I'm fine," I said.

John stared at me for a few seconds and then looked away. "People in small towns talk, Becky. It's their way. I think you'll be happier living out with Lily than here in town. You won't always have someone looking over your shoulder wondering what you're doing, why you're doing it, and who you're doing it with."

I didn't want to lie to John by agreeing with him. Living out of town might work for him, but I didn't believe geography was my problem or my solution. I held on to the door as John made a U-turn on Main Street. I saw Pete admiring the cash register on his counter as we passed by the bike shop. I wished Rosie could see the look on his face.

I looked at Baby Girl in her car seat. The smooth, steady movement of the truck had already lulled her to sleep. I knew taking a nap so late in the afternoon would cause serious problems with her bedtime, but I was so grateful for a few minutes of peace and quiet, I let her sleep.

I had found Sarah's book in the drawer under the counter at the store. I had intended to return it to her on many occasions, but life had gotten in the way of my follow-through. I wrote a note apologizing for my bad behavior and put it inside the book. I asked John if we could stop by her house so I could slip it into her mailbox. When we pulled up in front of her house, I hopped down from the truck and opened her box. As I did, I heard Sarah call my name. She was jogging up the road. I wanted to jump into the truck and ask John to drive away before she could reach me, but I knew Sarah hadn't done anything to earn her such treatment.

When she reached me, she bent over panting and put her fingers on my arm as if she thought they could hold me there till she had her say. She stood almost upright, holding her middle with her free arm. "Sorry about that! My mother decided jogging together would be another great stop on our togetherness trail. Yesterday, I went with her. Do you have any idea how embarrassing it is to discover your mother is faster and in better shape than you? Now I feel like I have to run every day, so I can keep up with her the next time we go together. Anyway, what brings you here? I've seen you around town several times, but you always look away when I wave. I know why you would be mad at Mickey, but why are you mad at me? I didn't do anything to hurt you, did I?"

"No, you didn't, and I'm not mad at you. I probably just didn't see you. I've had so much going on these past few months, which is why I haven't gotten this back to you sooner. I hope you weren't thinking of me as a book thief. I don't keep things that don't belong to me. I just had it longer than I should have."

Sarah laughed. "I didn't think you'd taken off for some deserted island with my book. There was no rush to get it back. I had already read it. I'm sorry things have been so crazy for you, though. I don't have my cell on me. Do you?"

I shook my head. I didn't tell her that I didn't own one.

"Do you have a pen and paper? I'll give you my cell number and you can call me when things get easier."

John reached across the front seat to hand me a pen and a slip of paper. I hadn't realized he had been listening. Sarah wrote down her number and gave it to me. I climbed back into the truck. Before I closed the door, Sarah said, "Talk to you soon!" and jogged up her driveway.

John seemed to sense my need for peace, because he kept quiet for the rest of the ride. The heater in the truck was blasting and the warmth washed over me. I felt my eyelids getting heavy and shut them for a minute. I sat in the quiet, resting my eyes and thinking about all I heard that day. I knew people were talking about me when I first arrived, but was shaken by the fact they still were. I tried hard to push the worries from my head. I started concentrating on the warm air blowing out at me. The next thing I felt was my head clunking against the window. I forced my eyes open and rubbed the sore spot on my head. It took me a few seconds to realize I had fallen asleep, too. We were already rolling up Lily's bumpy stone driveway. I twisted around quickly to check on Baby Girl. "She's fine," John said. "She slept the whole way home."

"I'm sorry for falling asleep," I said, hoping I hadn't drooled all over John's seat.

"You sure are prone to apologies," John said, putting the truck into park. I unbuckled my seatbelt, but before I could open my door John reached over and took my hand. "Try not to worry so much, Becky. Everything is going to turn out all right. You need to believe that, and trust Rosie and Lily. They are looking out for you." He gave my hand a squeeze. "I'm looking out for you, too," he said. "I know you are dealing with more things than it's fair to ask of a person. I want to help you and make things easier if I can. I'm sure you know how I feel about you, and I hope someday we can be more than friends . . ."

I pulled my hand away.

"Let me finish," he said. "I hope someday we can be more than friends, but I can tell you're not ready for that now. I'm going to give you as much time and space as you need. Just know that I'm willing to wait until you decide you're ready. In the meantime, I hope you'll see me as a good friend who you can lean on whenever the need arises."

My voice shook when I answered. "John, there's just so many truths about me you don't know."

"Maybe someday you'll be ready and able to tell me those. But if that day doesn't come, I'm okay with it. I know who you are today; the past is the past."

He reached over and held my hand again for a moment before getting out of the truck. I was still staring at that hand when John reached my car door and swung it open. I slid down off the seat, avoiding eye contact with him. Truth be told, this was not easy for me because I was aching to stare into those eyes of his and see that every word he had spoken was the truth. But I was afraid if I did, he would see into my soul, too. He'd see all the ugliness my lies had created in there since leaving Daddy's farm. I didn't think I could bear John knowing all my secrets yet.

Mrs. Harper met me in the hallway when we got inside. "Miss Lily is waiting for you in her study," she said.

I understood that to mean I shouldn't let any dust settle on me before getting myself in there. I peeled Baby Girl's coat off as I walked down the hall. I paused when I heard the voices on the other side of the study door. I wasn't trying to eavesdrop; I was just in need of a shot of courage. I could hear the lawyer's voice issuing a warning to Lily. "Have you really thought this through? You barely know this girl. From what my men could find out, she had a good reason to leave home. Her father has quite a reputation around town. But how do you know her story about the baby is true? This situation could bring you more trouble than you're prepared to handle."

Rosie's voice rippled through the door. "Her name is Becky, and she deserves to be shown the respect of being called that. I trust her completely. If she says she found Georgia Rose in a train car, then she found her in a train car."

"Lily," the lawyer said.

"Rosie is right," Lily said. "She lied because she was trying to protect herself and Georgia. I believe her story, too, and I want you to do everything possible to help her."

I looked up quickly when I heard Mrs. Harper's shoes clacking along the wooden floor, bypassing the carpet completely. I knocked on the door and started turning the doorknob before

I received a welcoming. I slipped inside the room and all the talking stopped. We all stared at each other for a minute or two before Rosie said, "This gentleman has come bearing good news for us, Becky."

Now those were words I wasn't prepared to hear. I sat on the only empty seat in the room. Lily passed me a brown envelope and signaled for me to open it. Inside was my birth certificate. I shifted my attention to Rosie and then Lily. They both were staring at that piece of paper like it was the winning ticket in the lottery. Lily must have realized I didn't see the document the same way they did. "Becky," she began, "that piece of paper means you can get a driving permit. It means you can take your graduation exams and go to college. It means you can move forward with your life."

I looked in the envelope again. It was empty. "What about Georgia?" I asked. "Doesn't she need one of these, too?"

The lawyer stood up and cleared his throat. "I told you it would be more difficult to straighten things out with the baby. We have to follow the law. My office has had a notice published in the newspaper. If after thirty days no one claims the child, we can go forward in the adoption process. If what you say is true, it is unlikely anyone will come forward."

I spent that night right where I'd spent every night since coming to Lily's house: on the floor next to Baby Girl's crib. I tried counting the slats on the side of the crib so as to push those words "if what you say is true" out of my head. If he still didn't believe my story, how hard would he work to make things right? When my eyes finally closed and my mind was partway between awake and asleep, the lawyer's words left me and were replaced by John's words. I could still feel the warmth of his hand over mine, and I believed what he said. Everything was going to be all right.

CHAPTER 34

My first class in my first year of high school had been a science class. The teacher, Mr. Mayfield, had a huge contraption set up on the table in the front of the class. He dropped a marble into a plastic chute made by cutting a giant straw in half. The marble rolled down the chute and set off a series of actions as it rolled and looped its way around. At the end, the marble fell into a small cup and set off a bell. Mr. Mayfield broke us into teams and handed each team a box of parts. He told us we would use those parts to build a mechanical maze of our own at least four times that year, and that he was certain by the end of the year, every team would have constructed a piece allowing the marble to travel the entire distance of the chute, setting off each action along the way. I thought that class was going to be the most fun I had ever had in school. I was wrong, but then again, so was Mr. Mayfield. My group never did get that bell to ring.

My birth certificate was a lot like that marble. Possessing it set off all kinds of actions. In no time at all, I had a driving permit and an appointment to take my high school equivalency exams. Practicing driving proved to be a sharp curve in the chute, and threatened to cause the marble to jump off the path. John was to set some time aside every day for taking me out in Lily's car and teaching me how to drive it. The problem was Baby Girl. I didn't want to risk her getting hurt with me behind the wheel, but I didn't want to leave her alone with Lily, either. After a whole lot of pushing and tugging from Lily, Rosie, and John, I agreed to practice while Baby Girl took her afternoon nap.

I must say I took to driving like a duckling to a pond. It seemed like the most natural thing, and John couldn't help but mention how impressed he was with my progress, too. I was getting quite a swelled head about it, until I started practicing parallel parking. It was then that John suggested I practice during Baby Girl's morning nap, too. I needed that time for showering, tidying up myself and our space, and studying for my upcoming tests. I was just going to have to conquer parking during my afternoon driving sessions.

My driving lessons also gave me a chance to know John was true to his word. It hadn't taken but a bit of thought to realize he had been right about me needing time and space. I had to focus on Georgia, Rosie, and Lily right now. Having a boyfriend would have given me one more relationship to have to figure out for the first time. I already felt like I was drowning most days. So instead of asking anything of me, John spent this time figuring out what I needed most to hear and providing it. Sometimes it was an encouraging story; sometimes it was a funny one. It felt good to laugh and forgot about my troubles for a moment or two.

One afternoon after my lesson, I came upstairs to find Baby Girl nestled in Lily's arms. Lily was humming a tune while she rocked back and forth. "I'm sorry, Lily," I said. "My lessons shouldn't mean my responsibilities with Georgia fall on your shoulders. I'll tell John we need to stop for a few days, until I see what Georgia's sleeping pattern has become."

"Nonsense," Lily said. "I enjoyed having a little time alone with her. I'll let you know if it becomes a problem."

Her words didn't soothe my mind, and neither did knowing this scene would likely repeat itself several more times. "I don't want to take art classes," I blurted.

Jumping tracks like that in the middle of a conversation threw Lily off. "I'm more than happy to pay for the classes," she said, "and Georgia will be fine here with us while you're at class."

My spine stiffened and I said, “Money doesn’t make everything right, you know, and I’m aware that Georgia is safe here. I don’t want to study art. I never wanted to study art. I want to be a writer someday.”

For a while neither of us spoke. Then Lily said, “Then you should take writing classes. I’ll get you the course catalogues to look through. And Becky, I know money doesn’t solve all of life’s problems.”

Weeks passed before I saw the lawyer’s car parked in front of Lily’s house again. I had finished a driving session and was hurrying into the house. As I passed the lawyer’s car, I brushed up against it. I could feel the warmth of the engine through the hood and knew the man must have just arrived. I rushed up the stairs two at a time, and when I reached Baby Girl’s bedroom the door was wide open. Lily was sitting in the rocking chair holding Baby Girl and chatting away to her. Mrs. Harper was standing over her like a guard at Buckingham Palace. Lily smiled at me. “Slow down, Becky, everything’s fine. Georgia and I have been having a delightful visit.” To prove her point, she kissed Baby Girl’s forehead.

I swallowed hard and said, “I saw your lawyer’s car outside.”

“Oh dear,” Lily said. “I forgot all about him. I’m sure Rosie has asked him a thousand questions by now.” She stood up and passed Baby Girl back to me. “Georgia has a clean diaper and a full tummy.” She pointed to the empty bottle on the table.

Seeing Lily holding and playing with Baby Girl always made me feel a little dizzy, but hearing how she had tended to her needs really made my head swim. I never seemed to give Lily the credit she rightly deserved. “Thank you for looking out for Georgia,” I said. “I appreciate your help.”

“I hope someday you won’t see our situation in that way. I enjoy spending time with Georgia. I don’t feel like you are burdening me. I see us more as a team working together to make sure each of us has what we need," Lily said. She gave me a quick hug. "We help each other."

I should have found Lily's words about us being a team reassuring, but I couldn't help picturing that marble careening off the chute, hitting Mr. Mayfield's tooth and cracking it in half.

CHAPTER 35

I sat by the window with Baby Girl on my lap. Everything outside was shades of gray and brown, but Baby Girl didn't seem to take notice. She was too busy playing peek-a-boo with a bird that kept flying back and forth to a branch by the window. This game went on for some time before I started wondering why I hadn't been called to Lily's office.

I lifted Baby Girl onto my hip. "You are getting big," I said to her, kissing her on her nose. I headed downstairs and toward the office. I knocked on the door and let myself in. The first thing that caught my eye was the envelope sitting on the desk. It looked like the one that held my birth certificate. A smile spread across my face. Then I took notice of the looks on Rosie's and Lily's faces.

"Explain everything again so Becky can hear it with her own ears," Rosie demanded.

Rosie's tone was not wasted on Lily's lawyer. He cleared his throat and said, "There was no response to the notice we put in the newspaper."

That sounded like a good thing. Why were Rosie and Lily so on edge?

"It's possible the parents did not see the notice. It's also possible they are afraid to come forward. There is no guarantee they won't come looking for her sometime down the road. We've met the legal requirements, but I suggested perhaps the best thing to do would be to turn the baby over to Child Protective Services," he began. I held Baby Girl tighter. "Rosie and Lily both feel that is an unacceptable option. They both believe the baby should stay with the three of you. I do have some acquaintances who can arrange for a private adoption."

I exhaled and closed my eyes. I was going to be able to adopt Baby Girl. I wanted to hug that man. Then he spoke again. "My colleagues are experts in private adoptions and particularly in keeping matters private. They can take care of this matter; however, there is a problem." He glanced at Lily. "You can't be the adoptive mother, Becky."

I stared at him. What did he mean? He said they were experts. He said they could take care of everything, and now he was saying they couldn't.

"The state does not allow an unmarried minor to adopt a child," he said. "You are seventeen years old. There is a solution, though. Georgia can be adopted by Lily. She can provide everything a child needs."

"You want to take Georgia from me?" I glared at Lily. Had this been their plan all along? Had they brought me here just so they could take Baby Girl away from me? "I'm the only mother she knows," I said.

"It's not like that," Lily protested. "I know how important you are in Georgia's life and I know what it's like to lose a child—no matter how little time you've spent together."

The lawyer stood up. "Lily says she won't sign anything without your permission. I'm leaving the papers here. You need to think about what's best for Georgia." He put the envelope back on the desk, nodded to Lily and Rosie, and walked out the door.

Lily and Rosie both began speaking at once. I heard voices, but not words. I stood up and carried Baby Girl out of the room. I don't even remember walking up the stairs, but when Baby Girl's room grew dark, I realized I had been sitting in the rocking chair for quite some time. Baby Girl was in my lap, gazing up at me. Now, I know she couldn't have had any idea about what was going on, but I would swear she had a worried look on her face. The smell of ammonia floated up from her bottom and reminded me that I wasn't doing my duty for her. I got up and changed her diaper, and discovered she needed a whole new outfit. She had peed so much it had soaked her clothes, and my clothes, too.

Once Baby Girl was clean and smelling pretty, I changed my clothes. I knew Baby Girl was in need of her dinner, but I didn't want to come face to face with Rosie or Lily. I tried to think of a way to achieve both of those things, but found myself short of ideas. Baby Girl's howling cut my thinking session short. She needed dinner, plain and simple, and she needed me to get it for her.

I couldn't get to the kitchen without passing the dining room. As I did, Rosie turned around and said, "We were waiting on you for dinner. I'm glad you came down."

As if they were listening by the door, the kitchen ladies appeared with dishes filled with pasta tossed with chicken and vegetables. The sight of it made me aware of how hungry I was, too. I settled Baby Girl into her highchair and fed her before turning my attention back to my own plate. I tried to avoid eye contact with either of my adult dining companions, but Lily wasn't having any of that. "I'm not going to pressure you to make a decision," she began. "But I want you to know that if you do want me to adopt Georgia, you will always be a part of her family. I promise I won't come between the two of you. I know how important your relationship is for both of you. I will give you time to think about it. You know you can come to Rosie or me with any questions you have. I'm going to give the papers to you. You can tear them up, or give them back to me to sign. The choice is yours."

I nodded my head and looked at Rosie. She looked as if she was feeling the same pain I was. As empty as my stomach was, I spent more time rearranging the food on my plate than eating it. Rosie asked me to help her to her room after the table had been cleared. As we were walking, I reminded myself neither Rosie nor Lily were responsible for putting me in my current corner. I could have gone to the police as soon as I found Baby Girl. I could have faced my punishment and gone back home to Mama and Daddy. I could have, but I didn't. Instead, I'd pulled Rosie into my net of lies. Despite it all, here was Rosie, still walking beside me, still trying to help.

When we were sitting opposite each other in her room, I asked Rosie a direct question. "What would you do if you were me? What do you think is best for Georgia Rose?"

Rosie's eyes filled with tears. "You have been the kind of mama Georgia needed. Without you, this little girl wouldn't be here today. I know you love her with all your heart. But letting Lily adopt Georgia would not be giving her up; it would be letting someone else carry a bigger part of the load. You will still be in her life, but you'll have a lot fewer worries. This little girl is going to grow up and have all kinds of questions and problems. Have you thought about how she can get an education without a birth certificate? What if she meets a Prince Charming and wants to get married when she's grown?"

I wondered if Rosie would understand if she knew all I had been thinking about since I left home had been the here and now. When nothing seems certain in life, even thinking ahead to the next week seems a little unwise.

Rosie reached out and stroked my arm. "This isn't just about her, you know. If you let Lily take a bigger part in raising this child, you will have a chance to go to school and do so many of the things you have missed out on."

"Thinking about my own wants and needs is what got me into this spot in the first place. If I had just done what was expected of me at home, I never would have met any of you, and all of your lives would be better," I said.

"Nonsense," Rosie said. "You gave a real sense of purpose to my life and to Lily's, and I don't even want to think about what would have happened to Georgia if not for you. Whatever you decide, I will always stand by you, Becky. You and Georgia Rose will have a home with me for as long as I'm on this earth."

I hugged Rosie before going upstairs to put Baby Girl to bed. A few minutes later, I stood by the crib watching her sleep. I had to do right by her. I knew Lily could give her all the things money could buy, but could she love her as much as I did? On the other hand, what kind of future would Baby Girl have with me as a mama? As usual, I found myself with more questions than answers.

CHAPTER 36

The next morning I decided I needed to clear my head before I self-combusted. This would only be possible if I could manage to get away from the house for a few hours. I called Jeanie, and despite not having heard from me in a long while, she quickly agreed to get together. We decided to meet at the park in town. I still didn't have a driver's license, so I had to ask John to bring me. When I shared my plans at breakfast, Lily paled, but Rosie said, "That sounds wonderful. You and Jeanie can catch up, while the babies enjoy each other's company."

The buds were bulging on the trees that lined the path through the park. I was glad the thick canopy of the trees hadn't filled in yet. The gaps allowed the warm sunshine to pour down on us as we pushed the girls' strollers along. When we reached the swings, we strapped the girls into neighboring seats. Chloe needed a lot of coaxing to get her to stay in the swing. Baby Girl, though, took to it immediately. A steady stream of giggles spilled out of her as she sailed back and forth.

"That child was born with a sense of adventure," Jeanie said.

We sat at a picnic table and enjoyed the lunch Jeanie had packed for all of us. We compared notes on how Chloe and Baby Girl were growing and changing, and then Jeanie shared news of a new project of her own. One of Jeanie's old college friends was editing a book on small towns in America and had hired Jeanie to photograph our town for the book. When she talked about the different shots she wanted to include, Jeanie looked more alive than I had ever seen her. I couldn't help but get caught up in her joy.

When we were ready to leave, Jeanie handed me her phone to call John. I stared at it for a minute or so, and then I fumbled through my pockets. I didn't want to find John's number too quickly. I hoped I could figure out the phone on my own without having to embarrass myself in front of Jeanie. When she saw me jabbing my free hand in all of my pockets like an angry hen searching for feed, she said, "Let me take the phone back while you look for the number."

When I pulled the slip from my pocket, she asked, "What's the number?" and dialed it before handing the phone back to me.

We walked down the path to the park entrance. As we sat on the bench, waiting for John to arrive, Jeanie asked, "How is Lily adjusting to a full house? Are you and Rosie planning to stay there for good?"

"She wants to adopt Georgia," I whispered.

"What?" Jeanie asked.

"She wants to adopt Georgia," I said again.

Jeanie nodded slowly. "Did you ask her to do it, or was this her idea?"

"It was her idea. I'm only seventeen," I said. "I don't have an education; I don't have a job; and I can't provide the kinds of things a girl should have growing up."

I could hear Jeanie breathing. Finally, she reached down and swept a curl from Baby Girl's forehead. "I wonder if you know what a lucky little girl you are," she said.

Her words stung. "Lucky, because Lily wants to adopt her?"

"No, lucky because you love her enough to consider this possibility. Lucky because Lily is a part of your lives. Losing her baby must have cut Lily to the core, yet she is willing to open herself to such pain again for the good of you and this baby. Making that offer when she knows fully well you could say no and pack up your things and leave takes a lot of courage, a lot of willingness to be hurt again. She has to really love you both to be willing to chance having her insides ripped out of her again."

Telling Jeanie even part of the story hadn't been in my plans for the day. She didn't even bat an eye when I told her, and I felt a whole lot of anger churning inside of me because of that. I tried telling myself she was just thinking about what was best for Baby Girl, but that just led me back to thinking she didn't believe I was what was best for Georgia. I was starting to feel betrayed by everyone I knew.

As if she could read my mind, Jeanie wrapped her arms around me. "This is the most difficult decision you'll ever have to make," she whispered. "But I know you'll make the right choice."

We sat in silence until John arrived. On the way back to the house, John asked, "Is everything okay?"

I just stared out the window, not knowing what okay might feel like. I wondered how Jeanie could sound so sure I was capable of doing the right thing when I didn't even know what the right thing was. It seemed like everyone was giving me credit for wisdom I didn't possess. When I got inside, I settled Baby Girl down for a nap and went in search of Lily. I was glad to find her alone; this conversation needed to be just between the two of us. "Why do you want to adopt Georgia?" I asked.

Lily put down her book and studied me for a few minutes. "Becky, my lawyer explained why I would have to be the mother of record instead of you."

"That's not what I asked; I want to know why you *want* to do it."

"I've wanted to be a mother for as long as I can remember," Lily answered.

"That's not what I mean," I said. "Why Georgia? Why not another baby?"

Lily studied her hands for a minute. "Do you mean why would I want to adopt a baby who will never truly be only mine? A baby who already has someone to love her?"

I nodded.

"I love her. I want her to have everything she needs in life, and what she needs is to be surrounded by the people who love her most—you, Rosie, and me. By adopting her I can make that happen. I can give her a stable, secure life," Lily said.

I stood up and started toward the door. Lily said, "I want that for you, too, Becky. I want you to have all of the opportunities life holds for a young woman. You have so much to think about, but maybe knowing this will help you make your decisions. Becky, I would also like to adopt you. That way you'll have a legal connection to us, too. My lawyer isn't sure there is a way to do this without your birth parents' involvement, though. He is looking into it for us."

My insides were moving every which way. Now she wanted to adopt me, too? I opened my mouth, but no words spilled out.

Lily stepped toward me and put her hand on my arm. "I know this is your decision to make, not mine. If you decide to take Georgia and leave, I won't call the authorities and I'll give you money to get a start in life. But I hope you stay. I hope we can be a family."

I spent the next few days thinking, making lists, and holding Baby Girl. On more than one occasion I came close to talking to John about it. I held back, though. The words Rosie, Lily, Jeanie, and the lawyer had spoken were already swirling around in my head. It was hard to hear my own thoughts with so many other voices in my brain. Each day wore away at me more than a whole week of working in Daddy's fields could.

On Monday morning, I walked downstairs and turned toward Lily's study. I handed her that brown envelope and a pen. In the end, I knew I had to let go. Baby Girl was never really mine to keep or give away. As for me, I will always be glad Lily offered to adopt me. I wouldn't take her up on it, though. Baby Girl and I already had a bond that couldn't be broken. I didn't need a piece of paper to prove that. As for Lily and me, we were still in the seed-sprouting stage. Time and nurturing were the only things that could get us from seedlings to flowers; no piece of paper could make it go faster. Besides, if Rosie could be a part of this family without any help from a lawyer, then so could I.

Lily put the envelope down, wrapped her arms around Baby Girl and me, and asked, "Are you sure?"

I shifted Baby Girl from my hip to Lily's. Then I reached down and picked up that college catalogue Lily had been pushing me to read. I knew someday Georgia would be big enough to hear the story about how we all became a family. I wanted to be sure when that day came, I would have the right words to tell it.

ABOUT THE AUTHOR

Lisa Colozza Cocca grew up in upstate New York. After college, she moved to New Jersey and still lives there today. Always an avid reader, Lisa shared her love of the printed word with her own children at home and her students at school. Like her main character, Lisa loves new adventures and looks forward to having many more in the future. For more than a decade, she has worked full-time as a freelance writer of educational materials and school and library books. *Providence* is her debut novel.

AUTHOR'S NOTE

Sadly, babies are sometimes abandoned under unsafe conditions in the real world, too. The Safe Haven Laws in the United States provide a way for mothers to relinquish their parental rights in a way that protects both the infant and the mother. Each state has designated centers, such as hospitals, where mothers can safely leave their infants. For more information on the Safe Haven Laws in your state, visit the Child Welfare Information Gateway website at *www.childwelfare.gov/systemwide/laws_policies/statutes/safehaven.cfm*.